Matt Howard's firs e
Wakefield Press) w .
The film adaptation .
Matt Howard lives ir

# TAKING OFF

## Matt Howard

ARENA
ALLEN&UNWIN

First published in 2008

Arena, an imprint of
Allen & Unwin
83 Alexander Street
Crows Nest NSW 2065
Australia
Phone:     (61 2) 8425 0100
Fax:       (61 2) 9906 2218
Email:     info@allenandunwin.com
Web:       www.allenandunwin.com

National Library of Australia
Cataloguing-in-Publication entry:

Howard, Matt, 1963–

Taking off/Matt Howard.

ISBN 978 1 74175 605 0 (pbk.)

A823.4

Internal design by Midland Typesetters, Australia
Set in 12/15 pt Fairfield by Midland Typesetters, Australia
Printed in Australia by McPherson's Printing Group

10 9 8 7 6 5 4 3 2 1

For

*Simon Proud*
*Matt Wakeham*
*Maya Donevska*
*Ana Kingi*

# PART 1

## HOLDING PATTERN

# 1

The sound of planes taking off has always been my alarm clock. My bedroom window provides a perfect view of the daily airborne additions and subtractions to Perth's population – and when you can see the jets so easily you have no problem hearing them.

When I was younger I allowed myself the luxury of staying in bed until the third takeoff before finally launching my scrawny being into my own little world. Nowadays, having been stirred awake by Singapore Airlines, I'm propelled into motion by the takeoff of the next plane – a Qantas jumbo. You won't catch me lingering about in bed waiting to hear the United get off the ground. Not anymore.

Ironically, for someone who's never actually flown, I catch the airport-city shuttle bus into town each day, sitting right behind the driver, Ian, like the biggest dork you can imagine. While this free service is intended for travellers rather than locals, Ian – heavily-tanned right arm and sympathetic smile – has never once made a fuss. He still calls me young Ash and by doing so sort of lets me off the hook for drifting through the same routine year on year, implying I've got a whole life ahead of me yet.

Ian is Canadian and told me once that he had lived on four continents. He said the world was his lobster.

Unlike me, everyone else on the bus is always heavily laden with bags containing dirty clothes or fresh, gifts received or to be given, and before or after expressions. Some faces are foreign and some look familiar, but their voices sound of elsewhere. Others are local – though none so local as me.

The ride west, along the Great Eastern, is broken by a massive roundabout – the turn-off point for all sorts of places, including the local casino. I always automatically close my eyes until the listing of the bus is over. Not that I have a problem going around in circles normally – it's just this particular one that gets me down.

My iPod's shuffle mode provides some sort of randomness ahead of workdays that play out the same tunes – Water Cooler Conversation, Allocations, Lunch Cafeteria, Allocations (extended mix) and Polite Farewell – in the identical order every day.

My workplace in the city is about a sixteen-track walk-bus-walk from my house, which I've lived in since time began. During the last leg of my morning journey I mostly think about what I need to do at work that day. Quite often it's Second Life. I need to seriously get into it.

I work at Integrated Distribution Services, which we lovingly refer to as IDS. As I've been reminded regularly since starting there, IDS is one of the nation's top three distributors of magazines. Redefined, this actually means we're number three and haven't improved that position in the near on ten years I've worked there since leaving school.

On behalf of a lot of big magazine publishers, who prefer to conduct the editorial and advertising sides of their business in Sydney or Melbourne, we perform the less exciting job of allocating the quantities and organising the delivery of every new issue of their magazines to every single newsagent, petrol station or supermarket around the country which takes them. I'm not changing the world – maybe I need to locate it first I suppose.

I take care of *InStyle*, or should I say I *am* InStyle – we often refer to each other by our magazine names, perhaps because it saves having to remember two pieces of information about any single person – their magazine AND their name. I've been *InStyle* for just about my whole time at IDS. Originally I was also Big Trucks Monthly, but that name has long since been handed over to someone who cares.

As he drops me off this morning at the shuttle bus terminal just a short walk from the IDS office, Ian gives me a wink and a 'See ya, young Ash' and I leave the bus ahead of the baggage-laden passengers. A while back I tipped Ian, but he laughed so loud I wanted to grab it back.

As always I keep the music loud to drown out the traffic. Today a guy in a 4WD hits his horn, rousing me from my daydream that I'm the lead singer of Black Rebel Motorcycle Club. I look up to see he's swerved while talking on his mobile. Who the fuck are all these people on their mobiles talking to? Each other, I guess.

I mute the sound and order my coffee at the same Starbucks that wakes most of the people headed to work in the buildings throwing shadows over our city centre. As I wait my turn, somebody from a table of friends by the window calls out 'Hey Harvey, over here' several times, before finally coming over and tapping me on the shoulder. When I turn around he realises I'm not Harvey and says, 'Sorry mate'.

He and his group continue to enjoy themselves without Harvey, relaxing effortlessly into conversation. Without knowing them, I presume their friendship is solid and real. My few school friends seem to have disappeared into the ether over the years. Silently I wish I *were* Harvey.

Further daydreaming is placed on hold as I carry my coffee through the foyer of the small tower where IDS occupies the tenth and top floors. There's no-one in the mirrored lift – but I gave up ruffling my hair a while back.

'Good morning, Ash,' says the temp receptionist, miraculously remembering my name.

I wonder what trick she's used. Maybe relating the word 'Ash' to 'fire' and then to how hot I am. Joke. Said receptionist has been introduced around the office, as they always are, but I must have been caught up with exactly how many copies of the upcoming May issue of *InStyle* to ship off to the Newslink stores in New South Wales to have done her the return favour of remembering her name. Or more likely I was trying to think of some way of making that day's blog entry even vaguely interesting.

'Hey,' I respond, and head to my desk.

Evan – Men's Health – is entertaining Amelia – Inside Sport – and assorted others in the kitchen, so I join them on the pretence of grabbing some water but in actuality to avoid listening to my computer fire up. These two are the only colleagues I know by both their magazine and real names: Evan because I knew his before he was a magazine and Amelia because she demands it.

The purpose of morning conversation is mostly about avoiding the inevitable, and it's generally brought to an abrupt halt when our 'group leader', Cynthia, makes her way in to grab a yoghurt. The fact that this is a ploy to make us hurry off to our computers – Cynthia's assistant apparently returning the yoghurt later – is borne out by the use-by date showing it to have long since expired.

Cynthia duly breaks up the party today, feigning embarrassment at interrupting our conversation with a limp 'Excuse me' as she offers a fake smile around the group and proceeds to grab her aged yoghurt from the refrigerator. We scatter like so many office mice and I set about getting into my Second Life.

# 2

Evan is the person I hang out with most at IDS. We started here at much the same time and we have the easy familiarity born of years watching people come and go. I'm aware, though, that our friendship is not very *Friends*, and I curse television for making so many things seem inadequate.

I vaguely remember Evan from high school – he was a year ahead of me – and from what I recall was one of the cool kids. For his part he has no recollection of me from back then.

Evan moved out of his parents' place a while back and now lives in a city studio that's just big enough to be not completely depressing. His olds' house, in Belmont – the nice part – is actually twenty-nine times larger than his unit. He calculated this recently during a particularly long work afternoon. However, as Evan explains, the downside of all that space is that it contains his mum and dad and their cherished Lewis, his younger brother. This is where television doesn't set the benchmark too high – Evan's family are very

*Arrested Development.* Evan swears that more than once his mum has referred to him as 'Lewis's brother'. Lewis goes to university and Evan works at IDS and lives in a box.

His family issues aside, Evan can be a jerk. But at least he has a family, I suppose. Mine's not much to talk about – just my sister Denise and her husband Jake since my parents died. Denise is quite a bit older than me but has done the extra years with little impact on her looks. Her skin is paler than mine, though she's got our mother's dark eyes. Her shoulder-length hair, being almost Asian-black, contrasts to her complexion. She has a strong, stern expression most times. Her voice is also quite ordered, and sometimes I catch her having to explain that it's *her* answering the phone, not the machine.

In this she is the complete opposite of warm, welcoming Jake. Stuck in a wheelchair with only one of his four limbs working – the result of a car accident – you'd think he'd have cause to complain, but he doesn't. It's Jake's smile that makes our house a home.

And my parents? Well, every once in a while during my morning flight ritual I'm reminded of that day back when I was sixteen.

On that morning I actually stirred a lot earlier as my mum stood at the bedroom door asking if I was awake until I was. It really was a big deal that they were heading off to New Zealand, given they'd never left Perth, let alone the country. From the doorway my Mum reminded me yet again that Denise and Jake, who were living in their own flat at the time, would check in on me. I was asleep again before Mum and Dad's taxi arrived to take them the short distance to the airport that we'd never previously used for anything other than timekeeping.

The rarely heard or observed Lufthansa departure suddenly woke me later that morning, meaning my routine was all gone to shit.

I arrived late to school that day. Tuesdays kicked off with Home Ec, however, so nothing much was lost and I was pretty well caught up with the rest of the class when the elusive school counsellor slipped into the room.

'Is Ash Lynch in this class?' she called over the rustle and chop of food preparation, and I remember thinking this was a bit over the top for being barely ten minutes late.

'Can you come with me, Ash?' the counsellor asked softly.

As we walked to her office in silence, I briefly debated with myself what reason I would give for my late arrival. As it was the counsellor, I was leaning towards family disharmony or a dead pet.

When we reached her office I was presented with my sister and Jake. For only the briefest of moments, that which occurs between thunder and lightning, did I think this was still about my tardiness. Then I saw Denise's expression.

It was Jake who held me as the counsellor told me my parents' plane hadn't managed to get far off the ground before nosediving back into the runway. All aboard were now gone. Forever.

After the blur of the funeral and scattering of ashes had played out, I kept the school counsellor busy for a while as the sad faces around me slowly retreated. Meanwhile, Denise and Jake moved themselves and their things back into the only home I'd ever known. With two more years left at school for me to manoeuvre, they decided to save me any more disruption. They were probably glad to be rid of their rented flat as well.

Back then Denise spun a wheel five nights a week at Burswood Casino, same as now, while Jake maintained a tidy desk at the local sub-branch office of United Airlines. Though he hated flying himself, he'd sorted out my parents' tickets using some of the normally ignored frequent flyer points he'd accumulated as part of his recompense for turning up year after year. For this he felt partway responsible for our parents' untimely demise, though we always assured him this wasn't the case. So for the best part of two years Denise and Jake brought the money in to sustain us as I scraped my way to eighteen.

# 3

Some mornings Denise makes me pancakes if she hasn't been able to get to sleep after a long night at the casino. Cooking was something Denise never quite got the hang of when Mum was around, but she's since come into her own. Today I'm lucky, and the smell is enough to get me out of bed even before Singapore is due to take off. My appetite has improved since my school days, though mostly I stick with what I know.

Despite Denise moving back after my parents died, I can't say we immediately became much closer. It wasn't until Jake's accident a couple of years later that I got the sense she valued me.

The easiest way to describe someone is by way of comparison to a celebrity, and for Jake it's *our very own* Heath Ledger, as he's referred to in *our very own* ridiculously parochial media. Jake is not really 'one of us' – being originally from Adelaide – though marrying a local did count for something with the stay-putters. When Heath sadly passed away, Jake being his doppelganger made it all feel somehow more personal.

Jake's accident happened one January night only a couple of years after my parents died and just as I'd started to classify that disaster as a one-off. In the blur that followed his accident, someone told me he'd been driving out to the casino to surprise Denise with a ride home. I was probably lying on my bed at the time thinking about up and leaving Perth and going to uni in Sydney, Melbourne or anywhere other than here, though I doubt I would have had the guts.

It was television that first told me that a car had run-jumped prematurely onto the huge new round-about. Though the television showed the mangled wreck, dwarfed by a huge and unscathed sign reminding us to enjoy Coca-Cola, I didn't recognise Jake's car in the driving rain. Then the telephone told me that Jake was in hospital in a critical condition, and I was there, even before Denise. At the time, the news that Jake wouldn't walk again and that one arm was also totally fucked seemed secondary to the joy I felt that he wasn't leaving us entirely.

Denise stayed in the hospital that first night but I decided to cab it home so as to get things back to normal as soon as possible. Outside my window it was hours before the planes were due to start their familiar sequence of departures, but I didn't miss a single one – thinking about my parents, and about how Denise and Jake had moved back to look after my sixteen-year-old self without hesitation. Two years on I wanted to pay back that favour. I still do.

Of course, it took Jake a while to come to terms with his situation. He gave up his desk job at United, though he probably needn't have, traded his gym membership for Cable, and made us laugh by swearing that he 'Didn't want to look like any of the guys at the gym anyways.'

As the muscles in his legs disintegrated, those in my arms started getting some use at long last. Jake and his new mate, Cable, became my two best friends. Later, Broadband would complete our gang.

In fact I couldn't remember being any happier with my folks than I was with the ever-stoic Jake, who suddenly needed me as much as I needed him. The government provided a cheerful physio called Lucy who kept us entertained while she tried to bend, massage and knead some life into Jake's three dead limbs.

When I told Jake I might give the whole university thing a miss, he made me swear it was not on account of him, and I did. I'm pretty sure Denise was relieved at my decision – her job at the casino didn't pay very well, and my parents had never managed to pay off the house in their short lifetimes, so it was going to be hard without two wages. Denise and Jake had kept us going after my parents had gone, and I couldn't think of a better reason to stick it out now.

Some of Denise's shifts would finish early enough in the evening that she'd get the chance to talk to us both about our days, but normally she'd slip in well after I'd dropped Jake into his downstairs bed and head upstairs to fall asleep before the 'red-eye' set off for the east coast.

A few months after establishing this routine, which continues still, I woke one morning to find Jake on the front porch catching the early sun on his face while sitting in a regular chair like anyone might.

'How'd you get out here?' I asked, not awake enough to be certain I wasn't dreaming.

'Denise helped me out here last night,' he replied as if it were the most normal thing in the world.

'Are you in the doghouse?' I asked.

'No, Ash, I'm on the porch,' he said, laughing.

'So why are you still out here?'

'I wanted to break the routine a little.'

'So is it broke?'

'For now.'

'Did you sleep any?' I asked Jake, who seemed to be enjoying my confusion.

'I was planning to. It was certainly a warm enough evening, but just as I started to get tired of watching the darkness, that first Singapore flight took off,' he said.

'Do you want me to bring you inside before I head?'

'Nah, I'll see you off from here and then I might give Lucy the same surprise I've given you, though she'll take it more in her stride, I reckon,' he said mischievously.

Every summer since, Jake repeats his porch all-nighter at least once, though now he mostly allows me to wrangle him outside so he can surprise Denise when she gets in late. I always worry that it's going to rain on him, but it never has.

When I get out of the shower, the television is already on in the living room and Jake's smile makes the morning more tolerable. I shift him to the sofa while he gives me the morning news: Iraq, Afghanistan, and the rest. Today I sit for a while so that it won't seem like I'm just doing my chores, and it occurs to me that it might be time to brighten up the living room, given Jake has to stare at this space for a clockload of hours every single day.

Denise and I have made little change to the decor of our house. Apart from rearranging some stuff to accommodate Jake, it's all pretty well how Mum liked it. I once asked Denise if she wanted to make any changes, to make things more to our taste, and she said keeping things as they were *was* to her taste. I couldn't criticise her on this score, I guess, given my own distinct lack of mixing it up.

After grabbing a couple of extra pancakes to go, I head out the gate just as Lucy arrives to really get Jake's day going. Lucy is a morning person and squeezes as much chat into our passing of each other as she can.

Our tree-lined street links directly to the road into the airport. Even though I've lived in this street my whole twenty-seven years, it still amazes me how similar all the houses are with their three cement steps descending from the centre of an uncovered porch that introduces a two-level house of time-resistant painted brick. Thankfully we also have vast gum trees, one for each front yard, no two of which contort in exactly the same fashion.

Several of our meaner neighbours place their caged budgies onto their verandas each morning so they have to endure another day of seeing what they're missing. 'Leave us inside' they chirp.

# 4

Picking the dried fruit out of his bowl of muesli, Evan greets me as I wander into the kitchen, and he warns me that this morning's discussion is all about celebrities. Amelia – who refuses to be known as Inside Sport – and a couple of other girls, Modern Bride and Practical Parenting, share the belief that Lindsay Lohan is somebody. The more notable thing about Amelia, though, is that she's been on *Australian Survivor*. She was second kicked off – theory is she would have been first off if she'd been in the other tribe. Her opening line – 'I rollerblade every day and I think it shows' – didn't endear her to her fellow cast-mates, apparently. So they doused her torch. Less famous is Modern Bride, who tried out for *Idol*. She was shown crying for help in the 'What were they thinking?' montage.

My fellow water cooler dawdlers ask me who I think is the most stalk-worthy actress of the moment. When I reply 'Renee Silverspoon' they're aghast. Only Evan laughs, thinking I'd intended to fuck her name up. So I go with that and the three girls soon join him, applauding my wit as I struggle to think what I was meaning to say.

'Is it Tuesday or Wednesday?' Evan calls out as he heads idly towards his desk, which is just next to mine.

'You don't even know what day it is?!' I say, desperately trying to work it out myself, 'I'm fucking counting the minutes.'

'Till what?'

And I have no answer.

The May issue of *InStyle* is proving complicated enough. Borders stores are offering a free back-issue exclusive to their customers, but if you buy your copy in a petrol station you get a complimentary lipstick (colour – slut red). The variations and permutations are so numerous that preparing instructions for the distribution centres around the country is fucking with my head. Instead of devoting my day to sorting it out, I have instead channelled my energy into ranting about it in my blog on MySpace, though not a single one of my e-friends has seen fit to respond. It's boring the shit out of me too, so I can't blame their lack of interest.

Evan and Denise both occasionally annoy me with disparaging comments about my blog friends, like 'What's their name in real life?' and 'What do they do for a job in real life?' Of course I go off when they suggest that friends on the internet are not real, then they bide some time before saying it again. I did in fact meet one of my e-friends once, though to be honest it wasn't the same.

After I sort out the increase in sales that petrol stations will make with the free lipstick and stuff, I move closer to determining the final print run. Announcing this magic number, once a month, is the triumphant part of my job and is when the guys in Sydney seem the keenest to hear from me. Once done, it's all go for the next issue. Same old circle.

Lunch in the cafeteria today involves a choice between watching Evan pick peas out of his fried rice or trying to look the other way as Practical Parenting snuggles with her boyfriend, Fortune Magazine. Theirs is not the only inter-office romance – most people here don't seem to go far in their search. Amelia agonises over meeting a guy called Josh as she already knows a Josh and likes the clean look of only having first names in her mobile. Clearly a major crisis.

Cynthia makes a point of joining us with five minutes of the official lunch hour to go to remind the group that some of the heads from 'creative' (editorial and marketing) will be flying over next week to talk at us, which is part of an exercise to help us feel more part of their teams. This is enough to bring today's break to an end – as was the purpose.

Normally I leave work right on five so as to get home and be with Jake before Denise leaves for the casino. Tonight, however, there are drinks for Modern Bride's birthday at a bar near work that we go to for birthdays and farewells. On learning of this event when answering a call for me from Evan last night, Lucy had insisted that she could spend a few extra hours with Jake till my return. Fact is, I'd prefer to just head home, but Lucy seemed so keen it was pointless arguing.

At these events I generally coast alongside Evan, but the fact that I rarely have a real one-on-one conversation with anyone besides Evan in the group means awkwardness is always imminent. Also likely is the type of polite conversation that's built on awareness that apart from work we have nothing to talk about. Worst scenario of all is that we'll sit there, beyond conversation, both sides giving up the pretence of any chance of sparkling repartee entirely. Like those married couples in restaurants.

From what I can ascertain, Evan and I are both quite okay looking. He had unruly long black hair and permanent stubble when he started at IDS but is now a lot more corporate looking. His aim is to rise to the giddy heights of the *Who Weekly* magazine account. I'm fairer and a bit taller, with blue eyes and absolutely no desire to push the work part of my life any harder.

Typically, we're both without anyone to bring along to the drinks tonight. Amelia is bringing Josh Number 2, Practical Parenting and Fortune are tied at the spines, Modern Bride has made a fuss of mentioning she's invited a friend, and then there'll be Evan and me, stuck in Planet Couples.

On arrival I head to the neon-lit bar to get the first round, Evan reminding me to grab a bowl of Bombay Mix (that he can pick the sultanas out of). The barman is new and so cool looking – tall and lean with close-shaved dark hair and tattoos down one arm – that I'm surprised he's friendly. He introduces himself as Miller, and I wonder if he's looking to get a tip as he strikes up a bit of a chat.

I turn just in time to see Modern Bride's friend arrive at our table, nearly dropping the tray of drinks at the sight of her.

Zoe is an explosion in every way – not just looks but personality too. Despite she and Josh 2 being the only ones who don't work at IDS, she soon becomes the centre of the group. Her soft blonde hair sits gently on bare shoulders, and her eyes, where green meets blue, seem to work their way around the table, ensuring she doesn't miss anyone. *Reese Witherspoon, that's who I meant*, I nearly say out loud.

'I needed that!' Zoe says to just me as she polishes off the beer Modern Bride ordered for her. She's glugged it down as fast as any guy could.

*I need you!* Please may that have been only in my head as well.

'Do you want another?' I ask, hoping it doesn't sound like I'm trying to get her drunk.

'Better not. That one will still be busy catching up with me,' she says with a smile. 'I should get you one.'

I say I'm fine, which I am – sitting beside her. There's no way I'm letting Zoe anywhere near that hot-looking barman.

Having had the great fortune, no pun intended, to be sat next to Zoe, I lean forward to block off any chance Evan will sidle in on our conversation.

'So, how long have you worked at IDS?' Zoe asks, and suddenly I feel like George Costanza having to explain how he still lives with his folks in Queens.

'About ten years,' I say, deciding to be up front. If she likes me after finding out how unadventurous I am, then this will really have been a great night.

'Wow. A decade,' Zoe says, making it sound doubly bad.

'They must really like you there,' she continues, and suddenly it nearly sounds like a good thing. This girl could paint anything positive. She should do spin for the tobacco industry.

I stay a lot longer than originally planned, surprising Modern Bride at how into celebrating her birthday I've become. Thankfully Evan doesn't seem to be as overwhelmed by Zoe as me and makes sure I'm in beer without me having to leave my prized position. Even Fortune and Josh 2 don't appear to be stealing looks at her.

I check the bar occasionally, and Miller's either watching the television or caught up with working his next tip. Are they all blind?

At one point Zoe catches me analysing her face and asks if I'm drunk.

I say something charming like, 'Nah, just thinking.'

This is true. I'd been thinking that she seems so perfect I bet she could eat a bowl of corn cobs sprinkled with tabouli and not get anything caught between her teeth. I calculate the possibility that she likes me at 34 per cent, ambivalence 49 per cent, complete disregard 17 per cent. This is, in fact, quite optimistic for me.

'You don't speak much, do you?' Zoe says at some point.

It seems useless to try and make myself out to be more exciting than I am, so I just reply, 'I don't want to say stuff just for the sake of it,' hoping that doesn't sound too wet.

Zoe looks around at some of the less verbally lazy members of our table and turns back to me with a knowing wink. I'm now utterly and completely gone – beer or no beer. If she was just simply gorgeous but on some other wavelength then I'd easily survive never getting any closer to her, but now it's either winner takes all or loser gets totally fucked up.

'So what do you do?' I ask Zoe, hoping she'll get that I think it worthwhile finding out more about her.

'After uni I got a crap job I could have gotten four years earlier. But now I'm doing a photography course at night, so hopefully I can make some money from it one day.'

'What sort of photography?' All the women's magazines that Denise leaves lying about suggest that it's very important to show an interest in what the man does. I'm sure it works on the flipside as well, and in any case I'm more interested in Zoe right now than any other topic you could name.

'Wildlife is my dream but I'm practising on pets at the moment,' she says, then laughs at herself, which is not such a common practice among the crowd at IDS.

'I've just about mastered catching Snowball feeding at dusk down by the old Go-Cat bowl!' Zoe continues, mocking her first steps on the very long journey to where she'd rather be.

Running with the theme, we brainstorm other mock-safari shoots she could do among the genteel wildlife of our town. The rest of the table keep trying to rope us back into the group with tit-bits of celebrity gossip or workplace bitching, but we're both oblivious.

While the going's good I make my farewells, remembering to look Zoe in the eye as you're meant to, and hoping she sees something in mine. Other than beer. Maybe I should stay longer, listening as the remaining drinkers assess the character of each person after they leave, to ensure I'm not maligned in front of Zoe. Worse still would be Zoe being hijacked by Evan, Miller or any guy with a brain. Lucy wouldn't mind me being late, but I don't want to push my luck with Zoe and I'm actually looking forward to the long walk home, contemplating the possibility of Zoe and me before I do anything to fuck things up. At least I can get Zoe's details from Modern Bride tomorrow if courage allows, and just maybe she'll ask The Bride about me.

Normally after these social things I think about how I seem destined not to have many close friends, let alone a relationship. But tonight I couldn't care less about that stuff – the fact is, the bigger the group the more replaceable and forgettable you are. I'd be happy with fewer friends so long as they value friendship with me. I'd be happier with Zoe.

# 5

My name is Ash and I'm a Zoe-a-holic. I've thought about little else since meeting Modern Bride's wing-chick last Friday, and have woken each day, before any takeoffs, smiling and with a hard-on impossible to ignore.

My calculation of the chance she'll like me has dropped to around 17 per cent – about equal to the possibility Harrison Ford will take on a challenging role at some point in his never-ending career. Television has told me that the average guy can get the better-than-average girl, but TV can be a little overly optimistic at times.

Modern Bride hasn't said anything to me about Zoe at work this week, but on the upside she hasn't said anything to Evan either. I thought about placing a veto on her but was not entirely sure I should even indicate my interest to Evan, who hasn't earned the nickname The Lawnmower for nothing. He has never cut my grass, but I've tended to fuck up my few relationships well before I've had a chance to introduce any of the women involved to my work friends.

I've gotten into the habit of calling into Hungry Jack's as I commence the long walk home from work. Their consistent standards always exceed what Lucy prepares for Jake. Last night she presented baked potatoes covered with the contents of a jar of Chicken Tonight. Despite Denise's superior cooking skills, Jake still puts on a show of eating whatever Lucy feeds him, and offers all sorts of supportive compliments, no doubt inspiring her to continue her recipe experimentations. Unbeknownst to Lucy, I've stocked up the top shelf of the pantry and the back of the freezer with a stash of meal substitutes and snack packs with ironic names like 'Up & Go', and 'On the Run' for Jake to have once Lucy has headed home. With his right arm nearly as useless as his legs, I peel, pop or cut open the securely sealed portions for Jake. And Lucy is none the wiser.

I always order my Hungry Jack's meal deal 'to go' so as to be spared the ignominy of sitting by myself in the well-lit family restaurant contemplating the shared lives around me. A while ago I misheard the attendant up-selling the fries as 'Would you like a life with that?', and it's now stuck in my head every time I come here. The tree's worth of packaging is ditched well before I get anywhere near our place, where, high on sugar, I leap the three steps onto our porch and go inside.

'Hey Ash,' Lucy calls from the kitchen. 'I'm about to order pizza. You want some?'

Just my luck, I think. Oh well, you take a gamble.

'No, I'm fine. Thanks.'

I seek out Jake, who's lying on the sofa watching Cable. He smiles at me – 'Takeaway pizza, buddy!' – and makes a victory fist with his only functioning limb.

'Yeah, great,' I reply unconvincingly, my stomach bursting, as Lucy explains her order to the no-doubt-bewildered pizza pusher: 'A large Vegorama with extra ham and a large Hawaiian without pineapple thanks.' Jake and Lucy are both big ham lovers. They can each swallow more ham than you'd find in a movie starring Robin Williams AND Jim Carrey.

Lucy is petite and has the sort of light-brown hair that's called blonde by the kind and mouse-brown by the not-so-kind. I'm not sure if she's still officially Jake's physio or just a friend. Presumably the normal period of physiotherapy is well over, and I've no idea if she's paid for her visits or not. Not by us, certainly. Her visits are no longer timetabled and have increased, rather than decreased, over the years since she was first appointed to Jake after his accident. Jake is able to be left alone but this rarely happens, and for someone who's lost so much he actually seems pretty happy, and I suppose a lot of this is due to Lucy. For though she can't cook, she can laugh, she can clean, she can talk, she can wash and she gives a good massage.

I often think how I know so little about Lucy. I've never seen where she lives or met any of her friends, for example. But then I know her favourite number – not 7 or 10 like most people, but 91. Favourite colour? Forget blue or red or pink. Yellow. I mean, whose favourite colour is yellow? Her family sound even more bizarre than Evan's but in an entirely different way. She gets nostalgic about the ding of a microwave or the knock of a pizza delivery. This explains a lot.

As laid-back as Lucy is, I've never seen her in any clothes you'd class as 'comfortable' or what she'd refer to as 'defeatist'. Her style is best described as 'thematic'. From Swiss goat-herder to street whore, Woodstock attendee and beyond – the list is endless. That said, it's been a long time since she's come dressed in any of the gear you'd expect to see wrapped around a nurse or physiotherapist. She takes her coffee with chocolate milk, listens to Bollywood music on her iPod, has a morbid fear of birds, and makes Jake laugh. I don't know where she comes from but I guess Jake does.

Whenever there's a knock on the front door, Lucy likes to look at Jake and Jake comes up with something along the lines of, 'Can you get that, I'm a bit stuck on the sofa' or a hundred variations on the theme. They never get sick of laughing at it.

'Okay, Mister Lazy Bones,' Lucy replies this time and fetches the pizzas from the voice on the porch.

'Could you at least get the plates?' Lucy asks Jake.

'Would you mind?' Jake replies. 'I'm sort of tied up for the minute.'

'I have to do everything,' Lucy says in the cheeriest way that sentence has ever been uttered.

'Is this as good as my home-made pizza?' Lucy asks Jake.

I shudder as I recall the beetroot, mango and bacon 'gourmet' pizza that Lucy made a few weeks back.

'It's less colourful,' Jake replies.

Lucy accepts this as a 100 per cent compliment. 'It's nice to be appreciated,' she says, smiling at me.

That she is, I think.

After pigging out on the pig pizzas and unloading the washing machine, Lucy has gone into the night leaving Jake and me to Cable without her running commentary, which annoys me but entertains Jake. He runs his left hand through the permanent week's growth on his face, due entirely to my laziness, and seems to want to say something about Lucy, as you do when someone leaves, but stops himself short. I want to talk to Jake about Zoe but decide to wait till there's more to say. So when all the stations collude to present crap simultaneously, we just talk about nothing of real consequence.

'Earlier on, during the news, they showed what it's like for people living in Iraq,' says Jake, raising the level of our chat. 'Basic foods are priced like they're luxury items and you never know when the next bomb is going to go off.'

'Did that guy next door end up enlisting?' I ask. One of our neighbours has been trying to get into the army for months.

'Nah. He reckons he's stuck here. Colour blind, apparently.'

'Maybe just as well,' I say.

'Yeah. We have it pretty good here,' says the guy with one functioning limb, making me want to cry.

Once I've lifted Jake onto the bed I've set up in the small alcove in the living room, I log onto the net and decide to Google Zoe. Apart from graduation details and some sporting achievements at uni, there's nothing. No mention of her burning desire for me. I wonder if she has a blog and consider asking Modern Bride to send me the link, but of course I won't.

I'm still fucking around on the net when Denise is dropped home by one of her co-workers. She makes do with some leftover pizza and sits on the sofa without turning the TV on. It seems odd that she shows no interest in where the pizza came from and has never seemed at all bothered by the close friendship between Lucy and Jake. I obviously got all the jealousy genes that were meant to be split between us. As for Jake and Lucy, if my sister questioned their relationship then maybe I would as well. But she doesn't seem to, so I let it go. And since I don't understand how she thinks, the thought of explaining to Denise that I want to have someone in my life who is all mine seems pointless. I really don't know where she and Jake are at either. During the week I never even see them together.

'How was the casino?' I ask, not expecting to elicit anything new about the job Denise has had since she left school.

'It was quiet tonight. Anything much happening with you?' she asks, picking the ham off an all-ham slice. I want to talk to Denise about Zoe but decide again to wait till there's more to say.

# 6

'So, Evan and Zoe, huh?'

Amelia has decided to arrive at work early for once, and this is my reward. Inside I am immediately breaking, but to her I go for an Academy award in appearing oblivious.

'Zoe. You know, Katrina's friend,' says Amelia, enunciating the words clearly and loudly in the way some people speak at those who struggle with English.

I maintain an appearance of confusion, which is easier given I've long since forgotten that Modern Bride's parents had actually named her Katrina.

Amelia continues to spell it out for me. 'I saw her and Evan meet up after work yesterday. Looked pretty tight. Katrina didn't even know.' Amelia is pleased she's been able to break the news to Modern Bride as well. I'm sure Modern Bride doesn't care in quite the same way as me.

Yes, I am a slow mover. First to admit it. But so is Evan. It must have been Zoe who got her skates on first. And she chose Evan!

When Modern Bride walks past our stretch of office she gives me a look that I know I'll attempt to decipher for at least the next year of my life. Does she know how I feel about Zoe? Is she suggesting I had already known via Evan? Or is she implying that I should have moved a little faster than a drunken tortoise?

Evan's not even at work and yet I am in pain.

I cannot contemplate doing anything until he arrives. Not MySpace, not YouTube, not eBay or iTunes. And as for work – it isn't even on the table for consideration at this point.

In the movie Evan would arrive, walking on air, burning with self-satisfaction, ruffled dark hair atop a happy though tired face. As it turns out, he looks nothing like that as he sits at his desk, ignoring Amelia's wink entirely.

I hold out for an agonisingly long three seconds so as not to give myself away before launching with 'Hey'.

'Hey,' Evan says.

'Amelia tells me you've hooked up with the friend of The Bride.' I can't drag this out any longer and it was never going to be smooth.

'Yeah, she called me up yesterday at work and suggested a drink. She's pretty cool actually. You'd like her, I think.' Evan speaks as if I wasn't even at the drinks last week, but more bizarrely he seems totally laid-back about all of this.

'So are you guys together?' At last, Amelia's intrusiveness works in my favour, saving me from having to ask.

'Guess so,' Evan responds as his computer fires up and the distribution wunderkind of *Men's Health* is in the house. I don't know if it's Evan's recent obsession with climbing our rickety corporate ladder all the way to *Who Weekly* or a genuine nonchalance about Zoe that's making him seem so not into this sudden new relationship.

I can't really recall how I spend the rest of the day, but it isn't on work – that I know.

Not long before we're due to head home, Amelia sends an email around saying she's just discovered that it's Pet Problems' birthday today and she thinks we should make an effort and do the drinks thing. Maybe Amelia is an alcoholic and she's calendarising all staff birthdays to ensure as many drinks nights as possible. All I know about Pet Problems is that she's much the same age as the bulk of our group, barely speaks to any of us, wears the makeup of a Russian prostitute, and her magazine has always been a real dog. Evan has long discounted the Petster as an obstruction to his career rise way back on account of her poor circulation. Oh, and she's married, has only recently returned from a stint of maternity leave, and lives in a cul-de-sac.

Completely against form, I surprise even myself by agreeing to attend. Lucy has nowhere else to be and, though it feels like a big mistake, I want to see Zoe again, even if she has latched onto Evan.

Pet Problems seems pleased that we've made the effort to have drinks for her at such short notice. She's even dragged her husband along to meet her work friends.

He is blue – blue shirt, blue eyes, foul mouth. We arrive as a posse from the office and await Zoe and Amelia's Josh 2 to complete our picture. Practical Parenting and Fortune are still in the early stages of their relationship, so make Pet Problems and her husband look a little lacklustre. By rights, Evan and Zoe should blow us away but when Zoe arrives, immediately sucking the breath out of me with her smile, Evan is as relaxed as I used to be.

Evan definitely has no idea how I feel, inviting me and Modern Bride to play pool against him and Zoe. It's a relief to leave the more established couples discussing home renovations, reality television and, on account of Pet Problems, babies.

Zoe seems a little unsure about how to connect with me, and I worry that she knows I'm into her. Not looking into her eyes when speaking is a desperate measure to control mine from dilating out of their sockets and giving the game away. As the game progresses I try to concentrate on anything other than Zoe. Watching her lean to take her shots is causing all sorts of problems for me, and I have to take my time getting up to follow her each time. I should have got Modern Bride to follow on after Zoe.

The game moves so slowly, as a result of my stalling tactics after Zoe's shots, that we leave it at just one and rejoin the group. Evan immediately picks his way through the bowl of nuts and I remind myself that the actual chance of Zoe liking me now is about 0 per cent.

The couples are now discussing who they can set up with Josh 2's older brother, who has, horrifically, found himself single. Fortune points at me and says, 'Ash, what about your sister?'

'Dude, she's married!' I respond.

'Oh yeah, that casino guy,' says Amelia.

'No, my sister works at the casino, Jake used to work at United Airlines,' I say, a little exasperated.

'Pilot?' Now it's Practical Parenting's turn to fuck up.

'Admin,' I say, in the low voice of a deflated Lisa Simpson. Maybe I should elaborate to prevent further proof that my work colleagues never listen to me. 'But he hasn't worked there since his accident years ago.'

Blank stares.

At last Evan explains, 'He's a quadriplegic.'

'Well paraplegic actually.'

'What about the arm?' says Evan, actually questioning my ability to get the story right.

'That's a separate thing.'

'So I guess he's midway between?' Amelia adds helpfully.

'Yep. OK,' I say.

As the white noise of the group moves on to other subjects, I sit there unsure if I'm fuming or waking up. Suddenly I feel alienated, like one of those kids at school desperate to be in the cool group. Watching the others, I notice that at any given moment the number of people speaking, or preparing to, outweighs those actually listening. I suppose I've always been the least likely to speak, but have I listened any better than they do? Sure, I know a bit about Evan's family, but as for the others there's little I've taken in. I think seriously about what I know about Amelia, about Modern Bride – at least I now remember her real name – and about Practical Parenting and Fortune. Virtually nothing, and what I do know is pretty well more about their magazines than their families or dreams or anything real. I've worked with some of these guys for close to ten years – that's like at least seventy birthday drinks. But hypocrisy be damned, it still stings that they've pretty well buried my stuff with their long-expired fears about Y2K.

The current choice is to sit here and contemplate my fragile work friendships or to watch Zoe with Evan. Instead I decide to grab another beer.

The barman, Miller, remembering that we met the previous week, signals over to our group and says, 'You guys regulars here, huh?'

'Taureans,' I explain. 'Seems to be a lot of them in our office.'

'So Lucy's looking out for Jake again tonight?' asks Miller.

Barmen and hairdressers are meant to listen to their clientele, remembering small details about their lives so as to prove that somehow you've made an impact on them. The irony that this barman, with whom I have had only one passing conversation, seems to know more about my family than most of my work friends is so obvious that even the most humourless would trip over it.

I drink my latest beer and wait around with my deaf friends a little longer so that I can maybe catch Miller on a break and prove to myself that he's just another person caught up with himself.

'How long you plan to work here?' I ask as I see him making his way towards the pool table.

'As long as it takes to get enough money to fix my car,' he answers, not at all surprised that I've ditched my group to make smalltalk with him. Apparently he was on a bit of a road trip around Australia and, just as he decided there was nothing much to see in Perth and there was no reason to stop long, his car decided suddenly to go high maintenance. Without enough cash for the cost of a new engine, Miller found work at our birthday bar and is saving up the required money while itching for time to pass.

Another person stuck here.

We talk about nothing as he easily beats me at pool, but I glean from our conversation that he's a few years older than me and – like me – hasn't done time at university.

He notices me looking over at Zoe a few times and seems to get it – strange that Evan still seems so clueless.

While Miller says little, I guess him to be the sort of person who takes solace in us all being mere specks in the universe, one of a trillion stars, one grain of sand.

# 7

Even though most of the others at work are freaking out about tomorrow's visitors from Sydney, I've been pretty well doing nothing other than thinking of Zoe. I've got to the point where I can leave it an hour before bringing her into conversation with Evan, in passing of course.

He is unconcerned by my interest – as he should be. I would never do anything while he's with her – just as I most likely wouldn't if she were still single.

As it's five minutes until I can safely mention Zoe to Evan again, I decide to earn my wage for a bit and prepare the short presentation on my future plans for growing the circulation of *InStyle* through ingenious tweaks to the standard distribution algorithm. We all have to talk for ten minutes, which for Evan and Amelia is proving restrictive, whereas I'll need more padding than Eddie Murphy used in *The Klumps*.

'So I guess Zoe isn't happy that you'll be working late tonight?' I faux-casually ask Evan, having agonised over the phrasing of this hour's question much longer than tomorrow's presentation.

'Not sure I mentioned it,' Evan answers vaguely, engrossed in what looks like some sort of PowerPoint slide he's incorporating into his presentation extravaganza. Maybe I should do a handout. Nah, fuck it. I'm not attempting to wrestle *Who Weekly* off the schmuck who currently allocates its stupidly high print runs.

Evan continues to fuck me off with his attitude to his fledgling relationship with Zoe – he has her and I'm the one who's stuck. You're meant to be stuck *in* relationships, not out of them. I wonder if it's the same for Lucy. Tonight I'll be late again and Lucy is going to stay till Denise gets home. Am I driving her and Jake together? My own sister's husband. Denise seems just as unconcerned about Lucy as Evan is about Zoe.

I make a point of having lunch with Evan so that I can increase the number of Zoe-enquiries. While I realise that it's doing me no good, just mentioning her name to someone else – even her supposed boyfriend – seems to be becoming addictive. While Evan picks out the capsicum from his salad roll, he talks about his plans to wow the Sydney crew. Meanwhile, I muse about how long after a mate's break-up one should wait before making a move. I do learn that Evan's family shows little interest in Zoe – which proves Evan is probably not adopted, ambivalence being genetic and all. And, he informs me nonchalantly, she refuses to blow him without a condom. My princess!

The presentation I've prepared underwhelms even me, but by ten at night, or 'dark ten' as Lucy calls it, I give up staring at the lame speech and say goodnight to my overwrought colleagues. I'm pretty hungry, but after spending my longest day ever in the IDS office, all the cash I had on me this morning now rests in our cafeteria's vending machines.

As I walk past our birthday bar, Miller is leaving and I say 'Hey' in a manner that would be appropriate whether he remembers me or not. He says hello and shakes my hand, and we continue our conversation from the other night as if the desk calendar had not flipped any pages since.

'So nobody's special day today?' he asks.

'Definitely not mine,' I say gloomily.

'Still pining after your mate's girlfriend, huh?'

'How'd you know that?' I ask, surprised. How has he picked it up, given Evan himself still has no idea?

'I can relate is all – but for me it's an old girlfriend who dumped me and ended up with a friend of mine. It was a while ago now but I still hate having sex without her there.'

'Why'd she dump you?' I ask.

'She had it in her head that I wasn't someone who'd stick around long, and she was ready to settle. Some people believe they have you pegged, and you can't convince them otherwise.'

'So where are you living while your car's being fixed?' I ask, wanting to show Miller that I had the ability to listen as well.

'Some short-term share place a ways out of town. Gonna grab a pizza and head home for some beers if you wanna come along.'

'No money,' I say, signalling empty pockets and hoping that will suffice as a valid excuse. As much as I'd like this cool guy to think I'm not the boring, rut-bound person I actually am, maybe I want to remain that boring, rut-bound person.

'No worries. I only have enough for a pizza or a cab, so we might have to get ourselves home-delivered.'

Suddenly I'm being diverted, like a flight avoiding its fog-laden destination.

After ordering a large Hawaiian without removing any of the core ingredients like Lucy would have, we wait in the car park until the guy who's going to deliver it makes his way to the smallest car you've ever seen. Miller steps forward and asks if we can hitch a ride. So we escort our pizza to Miller's place and Miller tips the driver a smile.

The flat is above a mechanic's workshop and I realise that this is where Miller's car is being fixed. The place is a dump and the living area is filled with clothes, broken furniture, empty food containers, and people.

Miller looks at the assembled people as if he's not sure who may be here. He seems relieved when he's established who is and, it appears, who's not.

'How's my baby?' Miller asks, and I can't imagine who of this motley bunch he can be referring to.

On the unlevel dining table, among the piles of discarded takeaway containers and dope-smoking apparatus, is a shoebox without a lid and inside is a cowering blue budgie. Miller gently scoops the bird out of its box and brings it to his chest – right about heart level. The bird looks tiny in his big hand, and gets calmer and calmer as Miller softly strokes its head.

'I found him yesterday. I reckon he's been stunned by a car but not so bad as to have broken anything. He just needs time to get his confidence back,' he says, then slides the budgie back into the box.

Miller asks my name but then doesn't bother introducing me to the others when he intuits from my expression that I'd prefer the least amount of attention be drawn to me as possible.

There's a couple sitting inside a huge bright-red beanbag about a metre from a TV screen screaming with news of a live police pursuit of some guy trying to flee the city after ripping a cash machine out of the side of a bank. The network's helicopter shows the police car nudge the villain's car off the highway and into a ditch just before he gets the opportunity to escape town. The beanbag couple seem pleased, and simultaneously scoop from a bowl of chips in celebration.

Sitting on a crate behind the couple is a guy with a shaved head, skinny and pale as a vegan. He doesn't even have enough energy to acknowledge us, and that's fine by me. Somehow he does find it in himself to hoist a bong to his mouth and draw in a lungful of fun. I dread the prospect of the bong being passed around, given I've never tried dope in my life. Luckily, Vegan doesn't look like he'll be giving it up for anyone else. Ever.

Miller makes space for us on the only sofa, ditching all sorts of crap onto the floor in the process. Once I'm seated he goes and grabs some beers from the adjoining kitchen. I can sense someone else is in the kitchen, but Miller doesn't seem to say anything to whoever it is and throws me a beer as he opens the pizza box at our feet. I've forgotten how hungry I was and pretty well Bogart the pizza in much the same way Vegan does with the bong.

Though there are at least four other people in the flat, and likely at least that many rodents, I feel like no-one is really listening to Miller and me. Sort of like a work drinks thing. So I ask him some more about how he ended up here on the other side of the country from where he usually lives. By the time the pizza is gone, along with the first few rounds of beers, I've established that Miller has no real idea where he's headed after the car repairs get paid for – but most likely north somewhere. Seems he alternates between bar work, roadie work with various bands, and no work.

'So mostly you've been working in Sydney?' I say to keep the conversation going.

'Yeah, there and Melbourne – it's where the gigs are,' Miller replies flatly.

'Which do you prefer?'

'Sydney is full of flashy wankers and Melbourne loves itself to death. So neither really.'

'You must have met some pretty cool people working with bands and going on tour with them,' I say like some star-struck teenager. Or any one of my IDS colleagues.

'You're just there to make them sound good. Mostly they care about the crew, whose job it is to make them *look* good.'

Vegan passes out sometime during the evening, the beanbag stops moving, and whoever's in the kitchen seems content to stay there, so Miller and I talk as if in an empty library. Once we get past our fifth beer Miller talks mostly about his mother, who he tells me left him when he was five. I ask him if he knows where she is now and he says he doesn't, pre-empting my next question by adding that he's not looking for her.

'So do you remember much about her?' I ask as Miller pours us some clear spirit into plastic cups, the beer having run out.

'Just small stuff – like her getting me to eat as we walked around the supermarket. Probably so she had more money for booze and fags. I remember the day she left as well. I think I knew it before she did. She didn't take her stuff with her, and as the day wore on I sensed that she was somewhere tossing a coin in her head. She ended up calling a neighbour to come fetch me, and I haven't seen or heard from her since.'

Miller tells the story so matter-of-factly that I don't feel as sad for him as I might have. He seems resilient, but maybe that has come with time and wasn't the same back then. After hearing his story I feel a bit lame for bitching to him about my work friends and how little they seem to listen to me.

When I'd complained to him, Miller had suggested that maybe I'd never really told them very much as I instinctively knew there was no point, and I've since decided this might actually be true.

Just as I'm forgetting there are other people in the apartment, a girl with hard-matted hair and an unfortunate nose comes out of the kitchen holding a huge carton of chocolate milk. She shakes Vegan awake and then kicks the beanbag, gaining the couple's attention. Once she has her audience's full attention, she spits into the milk carton, glares at each of us in turn and says curtly, 'No-one drink my milk, okay', then returns the carton to the fridge.

Miller laughs at my face and I'm drunk enough to enjoy the stupidity of it all.

'Is she who you were scoping for when we arrived?' I ask.

'Nah, I was just checking to see if Last Night was still here,' Miller replies, looking embarrassed.

'I'm guessing her name wasn't actually Last Night, unless of course she was some New Age type or something,' I joke. I'd recently learnt that one of the more alternative people from my year at school had changed her name to Winter's Dove.

'Hopefully her name was Linda as that's what I was calling her, as far as I can recall,' Miller says with the sort of smile that would charm most anyone.

The others have all taken the milk spitting performance as their cue to retire. Yawning, Miller asks if I'm cool to sleep on the sofa. I say yeah and, without even bothering to take off my shoes or think of Zoe, am done with awake.

# 8

Without any aeroplanes taking off, Miller has to wake me – shaking me out of the place where Zoe and I are together. My head aching, I make my way to the bathroom and am surprised when I see myself in the mirror. Without familiar things around me, my daily routine is fucked immediately. I eat a squeeze of someone's toothpaste, hoping Milk Girl hasn't somehow spat into the tube. Unable to shave or change into fresh clothes, I decide to get to work on time at the expense of all else. The plan is to find a cash machine, grab a cab into town, and then shape myself as best I can in the IDS men's room. Normally there's no need for a plan.

I linger in the living room, making enough noise to prompt Miller to come out and farewell me so I can get a chance to thank him for the pizza, beer, and night on the sofa. I won't thank him for providing an utterly new experience from my normal routine for fear he'll realise how dull my life is. The box on the table cheeps, so I check on the small bird, which is looking eight hours better. With time to better survey the dumping ground that is the table-top, I notice a random collection of scraps of paper, each with a phone number – some with a girl's name or a smiley face or a love heart. Several say 'thank you' as well. All, I assume, have been left for Miller.

Miller clearly passed out immediately after reaching his bedroom last night as he's still wearing his bar clothes – jeans and a T-shirt. He decides to update to daywear by swapping his black T-shirt for a white one, which he does in front of me and whoever it is I can hear lost in the beanbag. I notice the tattoos that run the length of Miller's left arm continue down the entire left side of his chest and back and into his jeans.

'How you feeling, buddy?' Miller asks me as his body tattoos disappear under the fresh shirt.

'Fine,' I lie.

'Feel like some breakfast? There's more than just chocolate milk.'

'Don't think I could hold it down. I'll just grab a coffee near work. Thanks for the pizza and beer and sofa, though.'

Miller sets about opening the windows and front door and immediately I ask, 'What about the budgie – isn't he a flight risk?'

'I hope so,' Miller replies.

I'm silent, not sure what to make of this.

'Hope work is not too hideous, dude,' he says, slapping me on the back before I descend the stairs that dump me out onto the street.

'Maybe Zoe will like the rough look!' he calls out at me from the top of the stairs.

The first bank I come to has a hole in the side of it where its cash machine used to be, so I continue on and find one that has survived the night. The cab gets me to the city, where the town hall's clock tells me I have about ten minutes to spare before work, so I revert to my usual routine and head for Starbucks. I decide to enjoy some sunshine while drinking my Grande. Sitting on the steps that eventually ease one into the IDS foyer, I watch everyone criss-cross the main drag with far more urgency than I can ever muster. It's years since I've been hung over, and though it feels bad it feels good too.

With my coffee only half empty, my neck must have decided to call it quits on holding my head up. I'm brought back to consciousness a few minutes later by the sound of something splashing into my cup and realise that some suit has read me as a derro and dumped some coins into my pick-me-up. Looking at my watch, I finish off the coffee anyway and pocket the gold quickly before attempting to leap to my feet about as gracefully as a new-born giraffe trying to stand for the first time.

Straight into the bathroom, I first decide to redo the buttons on my shirt so they actually match their corresponding holes. I can't do much about my stubble but drag enough water through my hair that it looks nearly as dark as my sister's. The crinkled shirt is pretty well repair-proof, so I console myself that the visitors are from magazine publishing. And from Sydney to boot. Hopefully they'll be far too fucked up on cocaine to notice me. And maybe grunge is making a return and I'm so far behind that I'm finally in front.

Given Evan barely pays attention to Zoe, I'm not surprised when he ignores the fact I've come in looking like white trash. Amelia, however, is thrown into a complete panic.

'Ash – what are you *doing*? The Easterners are here today!'

It sounds like we're being invaded. Maybe we are.

'I sort of had a big one last night – didn't get home.' Weird thing is I feel kind of proud of myself as I say this, even if for Amelia it's just another reason to consider me a loser. She writes something down. Is she keeping a list?

I find the notes I prepared yesterday and just hope I get to go first, as there's little doubt my ten minutes will be the most pathetic of the lot. Apparently we are to assemble in the boardroom for presentations all round and then there's a big lunch on the rooftop terrace. At least this all means there'll be less time for actual work today.

Since the last time I paid any attention, a new guy – Shaun – has taken over our biggest account, *Who Weekly*. This was the job Evan was itching for, and as a result he seems to have developed an intense dislike for Shaun. It doesn't help that Cynthia had built the new guy up to the status of superhero – gabbling on about his brilliant understanding of statistics, superhuman memory, and talent for remembering details. He is an X-Man surrounded by mere mortals. Amelia is charged with quickly introducing this guy, who is now effectively Cynthia's number two, to all of us before he represents IDS as our most senior account manager.

'Hi, my name is Shaun,' he says and shakes my hand as Amelia charges off to join Cynthia in corralling the rest of the team into the boardroom.

'I'm Ash. I do *InStyle*,' I say, pleased he hasn't baulked at my dishevelled look even though he is impeccably groomed.

Evan leans over with an uncharacteristic Cheshire smile and offers his hand, 'I'm Evan. *Men's Health.*'

I presume my drinking session has fucked my hearing – along with a bunch of other senses – until Shaun responds, 'Good to meet you, Ewen,' and Evan does not correct him.

Evan has long been the fashion leader at IDS, among the males at any rate. He was the first to wear belt-less trousers and the only one confident enough to knot the too-short tie. Today he's made a special effort and is going to challenge Shaun all the way. Me, I certainly provide no opposition most days, but today I'm not even in the same ballpark. By way of comparison I'm back with the IT guys and their polo shirts tucked into way cheap jeans atop spotless runners.

As we assemble in the boardroom, I notice that all the IDS females are wearing scarves. On account of the visitors. When we're all settled around the huge table, Cynthia enters with eight people who seem dressed for a funeral. Aside from one woman's red blouse, it's all pretty well black. Cynthia introduces them each in turn, listing which magazines they have editorial responsibility for. I've already met the guy who publishes *InStyle*, of course, and he gives me a nod. He is as dull as an Olympic swimmer but rarely hassles me about the stagnant circulation numbers, so swim on I say. It occurs to me that one of the visitors might have been the one who ditched the coins in my morning coffee – being as they are from Sydney and all – but none of them gives me a second glance.

Once the interlopers have all sat down at the very far end of the table, Cynthia stands at the top of the table and gives her 'As one of the nation's top three magazine distributors . . .' speech. That over, she introduces Shaun so he can outline his plans for *Who Weekly*. Seems we'll be going by size of publication, so I'll be third, after Evan, worse luck. Pet Problems last.

Shaun is pretty impressive, though Evan, sitting next to me, emits low, sarcastic groans as each of Shaun's PowerPoint slides comes up, which means they must be better than Evan's. It seems Cynthia is right about Shaun's fabled memory and grasp of numbers, because for someone who's just started he's amazingly familiar with sales patterns and issue numbers of *Who Weekly*. Moving right along, he reveals intricate plans for upping numbers of the next 'Most Intriguing People' issue to a mesmerised audience. When he's done wowing everyone – except Evan – he wraps up and introduces the surly one next to me.

'Next, for *Men's Health*, is Ewen.'

'Evan actually,' Evan says curtly, looking directly at the group of publishers, and I begin to think what a jerk my friend is.

Evan does a less impressive job than Shaun, though it will seem absolutely dazzling in hindsight. After my turn, that is.

Evan introduces me using my correct name, and I face the rapidly tiring visitors from Sydney and go through the motions of feigning interest in the ebb and tide of *InStyle*'s circulation numbers and it's better-performing outlets. I choose to focus on the lady with the red blouse, who is the sort of woman who might sometimes be described as 'handsome'. Next to her is the publisher of my magazine, who by rights should be the keenest to hear what I have to say, though apparently he's not. His lolling head reminds me of my own this morning as I slumped over my Starbucks. On the other side of him is the most attractive woman in the group. Not naturally beautiful like my Zoe, *Evan's Zoe actually*, but with such fabulously presented hair and eyes that she's presumably failed to bother building a personality. The other women are pretty well mutton dressed as mutton.

After introducing Amelia, I plan to relax all the way through the rest of the group without actually listening to anything that's said. That is until I get nudged alert by Evan during Fortune's presentation. For some reason Fortune seems to have a graph lighting up the wall showing the rise of *Fortune*'s fortunes against some sad old magazine. Looking more closely I see that the magazine being unfavourably compared to is in fact *InStyle*. Could he not have used another stagnant magazine to highlight his success? Then it occurs to me that he's actually gunning for my account. He wants a bigger magazine and he's going for it in front of everyone.

I fume until Pet Problems, who Evan snippily whispers should be introduced with 'And last, and also least', has finished highlighting what a dire mess she and her magazine are in. Then, when everyone is milling about before heading to the terrace for lunch, I go straight up to Fortune and say 'Thanks, buddy' with all the sarcasm I can vent.

Fortune actually looks perplexed and says something along the lines of how we're meant to compete with each other and it not being personal. He genuinely does not understand why I'm annoyed, and ends with, 'That's what it's all about – you don't care about this stuff anyway, dude.'

'If I don't care about my magazine, why am I here then?' I snap, making my point to Fortune.

'Fucked if I know.'

# 9

Over lunch Evan casts himself in the role of Macho Jerk, Fortune plays the part of Bright Young Thing, and Cynthia stars as Smug Bitch. Pet Problems merely loads carbs – under the guise of feeding two – which I guess remains true even if the kid is out of her now. I study the faces of our lovely eastern visitors to see if they are as dismayed by my colleagues as I'm slowly finding myself to be, but it's hard to glean any signs of life beyond the forced smiles. Their eyes are as dead as zombies' and they offer as much conversation. As for the IDS team, I seem to have landed the more try-hard of the two large tables on our roof-top terrace.

When in such situations it's best just to daydream yourself to where you'd prefer to be, and I find myself contemplating last night hanging with Miller. Suddenly the routine I've devised, avoiding people and accepting the pattern, collecting food and televisioning with Jake, is coming unstuck with the arrival of Miller. For the first time in years I haven't lifted Jake onto his bed at night, and haven't slept in my own. Jake would have happily stayed on the sofa, like I did at Miller's. He probably had to calm Denise down, who in turn is probably preparing to interrogate me when I get home tonight. The second helping of fantastic blueberry shortcake has pretty well rid me of my hangover, and I think about the last time I was really drunk – not long after Jake's accident – when one night he asked me to help him get even more legless.

I can hear Pet Problems droning on about the new homemaker centre which opened recently. Apparently three of the couples in our work group have already been there and two are yet to go. This is the most exciting thing I've learned about my friends in quite a while. Their lives seem to be dedicated to buying coverings for floors and windows, attending open houses on weekends, and treadmill-walking through malls. Leading ordinary lives and having ordinary aspirations. And all up, having more fun than me.

Fortune starts an observation with 'As I was telling my dentist the other day . . .', as if the story being on his high-rotation list somehow adds further worth to it. Most people in our office haven't yet learned that not every thought they have is worth expressing. I turn my hearing down again.

Evan continues to pick at his food, this time removing pretty well everything from his fruit salad, leaving a plate of honeydew, while Red Blouse nearly gags on the blueberry shortcake, declaring it 'tragic' to the entire table who've just observed me stash two huge slices before eyeing a third. I am outside myself now watching myself through other eyes – they look at me and see a loser, feel sorry for me. I clearly don't want what they have, what they strive for, what they rate. Problem is, all I know is what I *don't* want.

As Cynthia explains her theory of organising to meet friends outside cafes at five before twelve or five before one, thereby beating to a table the groups of people who meet at more standard times, I decide to leave our table without a word. Evan signals with his eyes that I should stay put, but I can't take it anymore. I head down to the office feeling like I need to do something to convince myself that I truly do not intend to stay still for ever. Suddenly I find myself opening my CV with the intention of updating it. This might just be a meaningless gesture, like joining a gym, but maybe I should try and go somewhere else.

Updating my CV is embarrassingly easy – nothing has changed since I last looked at it several years ago. All I have to alter is the current date and that about sums things up. Searching on Seek, I use keywords like 'magazine' and 'account manager' to bring up a bunch of jobs in Perth that could just as well be the one I have. At least the building would be different, and the people. Maybe even the morning conversation.

My dull profile flies through the afternoon air towards the velvet ghettoes that are the human resource departments of other large firms seeking my average abilities. Then I decide to give myself the rest of the day off and make up for my recent slackness to Jake.

On the way home I call in at the birthday bar to say 'Hey' to Miller.

'Hey,' I say as Miller is preparing a drink for the sort of guy you'd expect to be in a bar mid-afternoon mid-week. Miller has not shaved today either – he catches me noting this and declares, 'Hey, buddy. Monday is shaving day for me.' Drink delivered, he takes a break and I fill him in on the presentations. He immediately gets my sudden discontent with my job: 'I can't believe you've worked there for so long. You must be a bit distracted to stick at something as dull as that.'

He means this as a compliment, that he sees me as being more like him than my other friends. I wish he had me right, but to date I've stuck to the course like the mangy rabbit at the greyhound track. And though it's hardly radical, I tell Miller that I've applied for some jobs. He congratulates my spontaneity, unaware that the positions are probably identical to the one I've counted time in for nearly a decade.

We talk for a while about Zoe, which is more interesting but no more life-affirming. It feels a bit fraudulent, discussing my friend's girlfriend, knowing she's never going to be mine. I tell Miller how I hear Evan speaking to Zoe on the phone each afternoon, wrapping with an 'I love you too.'

'Yeah, well that's just about the easiest thing in the world to say. In fact it's easier to say than not. What's really tough is to launch the "I love you",' Miller advises me.

'That's nearly worse, though, as she's the one that loves him the more, it seems,' I say, fully aware that either way it is Evan and Zoe, not Ash and Zoe, and even if Evan is phoning it in, he has her number and I don't. And won't.

I ask Miller if, having seen Zoe the other night, he fancied her at all.

'Not now,' he says without hesitation.

Once his break is over I set off to hang with Jake. It'll be cool to surprise him by getting home early, rather than late, and I think I'll even eat Lucy's cooking tonight and it won't be so bad for once.

# 10

*Wanna catch up?*

I barely recognise the sound of an incoming SMS and am pleased to see it's from Miller. Other than being from Zoe, that's about the best result possible.

It being Saturday, I've been lying here with no idea what time it is and no need to know. The flight schedules are different on weekends from during the week and I've always avoided learning their pattern, which would be too pathetic even for me. From the sound of things it's about ten minutes after Denise getting up.

*Sure*, I text Miller back.

*Maybe I should swing by your place and check out your world?*

*Sure*, I reply, not so sure.

Denise has been a bit intrigued by Miller since the night I didn't come home. She didn't try to make me feel slack for leaving Jake to sleep on the sofa, though. I think she feels bad enough herself that she has to work five nights a week, leaving me and Lucy to tag-team looking out for him.

After texting Miller our address, I get up and let Denise know that he may be coming over.

'He can have some lunch with us,' she says coolly, pulling at something wedged in the freezer.

'Don't go to any trouble – we can probably wander down the street for something,' I say, trying not to load my words with sway of any type.

'It's fine, Ash. Honestly.' And she's suddenly calm again.

Having seen where Miller lives, I'm freaking out a bit as to what he will make of us. I doubt he'd even contemplate sitting down at a table for lunch on a Saturday. I know we're not entirely normal. This world is not all I've seen – I've been in other houses and watched TV. Our families couldn't have been more different. From what I've gathered, the couple who took Miller in after his mother left were happy to see him leave, while Denise seems pleased I've never wanted to go anywhere.

I wish I could introduce Miller to the Denise who came home to look after me when our parents tried to fly. It's funny, but Jake is the same as he's always been. Despite most of his body failing him, he's held onto everything that makes him Jake. Denise looks identical to the sister who loved life, Jake and me in equal measure, but somewhere along the line she's given up caring if people win on quiz shows, if Australia triumphs at sport. She rarely even watches a movie through to its end. As the live audiences for shows like Oprah and Dr Phil become more enraptured and excitable year-on-year, my sister has lost her interest in just about everything.

Lifting Jake off his bed and into his chair, I mention that Miller is coming over and he seems pleased. Soon enough, Miller's repaired but unpaid-for car has broken our silence, and Miller knocks on the door harder than anyone before him.

'Hey,' he says as I let him in.

After he shakes Jake's good arm, we make our way into the kitchen to stash his beers in the fridge, catching Denise as she's stirring something good enough to eat.

'Miller, this is my sister Denise,' I say as Denise fails to ignore the colourful arm hanging from Miller's white T-shirt's left sleeve. I know her so well that I know she equates tattoos with 'drug-taking fiend'.

'Do you want a beer, Denise? They're Japanese – got them from the bar I work in,' Miller says politely.

'I'm fine, thanks,' Denise says blankly.

'Jake – feel like a Sapporo?' Miller calls through to the living room.

'Cool,' Jake calls back cheerily, probably unaware what he's getting but up for anything new as usual. I look a bit undecided, so Miller offers me a swig from his bottle so I can make an informed decision. The beer tastes a lot different from Australian ones, but not worse, so I accept a bottle for myself and we head in to join Jake watching cable – no particular station. Hopefully Denise will take the cue and dull the formality by letting us eat in front of the TV. This she does, though she quizzes Miller from first mouthful to last.

From his name, to his job, future plans and relationship status, Denise shows more interest in Miller than anything she has for a long time. However, I suspect she's just drilling for holes.

That said, I learn a bunch of stuff myself, including that Miller is the surname of the family that tolerated him from kindergarten through to Year 10.

In the debate about living for the day versus planning for the future, it's not entirely surprising that my sister and my new friend come as close as the Israelis and Palestinians. However, at one point I sense a moment when, though Denise continues arguing for the negative, her expression makes like envy as Miller talks about hitting the road soon. And the resulting upside that he will not therefore be a permanent part of our lives soon brightens her spirit.

As I will Jake's good arm to finish feeding his mouth so this agony can end and Miller and I can lounge in the backyard, finishing the Japanese beers as far away from Denise's unhappiness as possible, she inquires when exactly Miller will be going.

Jake initially thinks she means leaving our house, not Perth, and needs to be slapped out of choking.

'Once I earn enough to pay off the repairs and my rent. I won't hold my breath, though,' Miller answers.

'No, please do,' Denise says.

Miller assumes she's joking and laughs, with Denise smiling just enough to carry it off.

That's enough for me, so I take the plates to the kitchen while Miller thanks Denise for the food. Then we head into the barren backyard, where the only shade comes from wandering clouds and passing plane underbellies. Miller seems unconcerned by Denise's attitude and says that in comparison to his flatmates my sister has been positively welcoming.

Now that we've both been tourists in each other's worlds, there's heaps more to talk about and the beers play their part as well. Being as we are in my childhood house, Miller asks after my parents and I tell stories that might offer quick insights into how things were.

When I press Miller for more details about his own mother, he tells me his original surname, her surname, which I don't know I'll ever be able to pronounce. He doesn't seem to exactly know its origin, but the jumble of letters seems reminiscent of Eastern Europe. His first name, however, is a big surprise – Jet.

'Jet?' I repeat back to him, incredulous, thinking back to when Kramer became Cosmo.

'Uh-huh.'

Miller has some tomato sauce on his face that I've failed to mention. When he returns from the bathroom it's still there and I ponder how many people as good looking as him go to a bathroom without once looking in a mirror.

'So where do you actually consider your home to be? Like where is your stuff?' I ask, hopefully not sounding too much like I'm speaking to an alien.

'I don't actually live anywhere and the only quote I try and remember is that Ruskin one about every increased possession loading you with new weariness.'

He left school at sixteen and seems to have been incapable of normal things like sticking with a regular job (I could give him a lesson or two there), but I'm beginning to realise he may just be the smartest person I know. I've tried books but they don't do it for me, and most no-one in Redcliffe reads newspapers, whereas Miller seems well-read and confident enough to talk about near anything. On the other hand, I've never tried drugs and I know Denise is assuming Miller is no stranger to stuff stronger than beer, and I guess she's probably right. Drugs and books, brains and beer – he's a combination I have no experience of.

My mates, which is maybe too strong a term – *my friends* – all just seem to have taken up wandering through homemaker centres or thinking about their career trajectories and keeping all their original ideas, if they have any, pretty much to themselves. Later tonight my sister will no doubt tell me how unsuited Miller and I are, and she'll be right. I just hope it doesn't have to be the deal-breaker. Mostly, though, I fear it won't be up to me as to whether I can forge a strong friendship with someone so unlike anyone I've ever known. I've often contemplated whether I'll ever have the type of friendship television reckons everyone has.

'You wanna head into town for some more beers, dude?' Miller asks, and I leap to my feet immediately.

After I lend him a black T-shirt, he's dressed for the evening. In fashion at least, Miller has things as either black or white.

I quietly check that Jake is okay with the possibility of ending up sleeping on the sofa again tonight if I'm late in, and he strikes a single thumbs up.

As we pass down our street, in the direction of the cab-infested highway, Miller comments on the poor birds kept small in their cages on our neighbour's porches.

'We should let them out,' he says.

'Nah – they say that once they've been caged for a while you can't let them out in the world. They won't survive,' I reply, wishing it weren't true.

'Crap. They'd enjoy it all the more I reckon,' says Miller.

# 11

'So Ash, tell us why you're keen to work at UPA?'

*Keen is not a word I'd use.* 'I'm interested in applying the skills I've acquired in the magazine distribution field to something more dynamic, such as home entertainment.'

'Tell us why you want to leave your current position at IDS?'

*The people suck and they are starting to monitor any time we waste internet surfing.* 'I'm very loyal, which is why I've worked so long at IDS, but I think I've achieved all I can there now and would like to broaden my horizons.'

'And what can you offer the UPA DVD distribution team?'

*Poor attitude but regular enough attendance.* 'Fresh eyes and a real desire to increase the reach of your titles into all current and possible future market segments,' I say, trying not to gag on my own crap.

'Do you feel confident you can master the intricacies of our distribution software and programs?'

*How difficult can it be?* 'I look forward to any new challenges.'

'Finally, what are your interests outside work?'

*Television, fast food and sex.* 'I enjoy solitary pursuits like reading, but also like team sports such as soccer. And movies of course!'

Smiles all round.

I'd been a bit perplexed when UPA called me in for this interview in their offices just a few doors down from IDS. All the other applications I'd sent off that fateful afternoon after the Sydney-people presentations were speedily met with formula rejection emails. But somehow my UPA application must have risen to the top of the pile. Maybe they were impressed with the font I used, or they like *InStyle* (someone has to).

Denise, bizarrely, had offered the most encouragement as I prepared my sterile responses to the anticipated interview questions. Jake tried to sound excited, whereas Miller couldn't even fake that. I hadn't bothered telling Evan.

The guy asking the questions had kicked off this lightest of grillings with a description of UPA and the job in question in the same manner as a presenter at an Oscar ceremony who's been forced to read an introduction spiel they wish to distance themselves from. Expressionless and robotic. He is late-thirties with spiky hair, man boobs and an uncomfortable jacket. He sort of looks like a lesbian.

The other man is slightly older and allows Lesbian to run through the job interview shopping list. Since he leans forward the whole while, I assume his hearing must be a bit fucked – though his ears are as big as anyone's grandfather's. He wears a bright, multicoloured shirt, borrowed from Dr Karl, which is presumably intended to indicate his wacky personality.

Denise had warned me that I should not pre-empt all the questions and that there was likely to be at least one where it would be unclear what they wanted me to say. But the entire interview has been one long cliché, with me spitting back the reflex responses like other people do when faced with a 'Do you want seconds?' or a 'Do you love me?' Not that I've often been bombarded with either question.

With the final question ending on a good note, I sit back as Big Ears seems to give Lesbian a nod, and soon I'm standing and shaking hands while murmuring thank you for something I'm no way near being sure I want or even understand. Suddenly it occurs to me that my application was probably the only one. They'd certainly been very flexible regarding setting a time for the interview, and the foyer was devoid of any life other than wilting flowers and a perky desk jockey.

'Ash, we'd really like you to start as soon as you can, and if you have the time now I can take you around the office and introduce you to some of your new colleagues,' Lesbian says with a warm enough smile as Big Ears shakes my hand and disappears.

I certainly have the time – I've taken the entire day off sick.

Maybe this is not the biggest of sea changes, I think, but at the very least I'll meet a whole group of different people to share birthday drinks with.

I'm led to the first desk in the vast office space, which is opposite the room where the interview took place. Here I am introduced to a guy who's intent on making an impression and I want to tell him not to waste his time. He shakes my hand way too long and hard to be not trying to prove something, and I imagine him to be the sort of bloke who needs to drive a big car and proclaim a hate of cats so as to reinforce his manliness. As I'm told his name and role, all I can think is that this is Evan. Next up is a girl who we disturb while she's bitching to a colleague about some other girl who apparently drinks like a fish through a mouth like a sewer. So they have an Amelia as well. On it goes – meeting a cast who are simply reprising their roles from IDS.

In fact I recognise a couple of workers who are actual refugees from IDS, and though I can't remember their magazines let alone names, I'm familiar with their expressions. They seem no happier here among the clones of Evan, Amelia, Modern Bride, Practical Parenting, Fortune and Pet Problems. After meeting with bizarro world's Cynthia, dressed as mutton squeezed into lamb, I'm coming to the conclusion that this leap is barely worth the energy. Out of the pot and back into the same pot. I'll email Lesbian tomorrow with the unfortunate news that my parents have died or my brother-in-law was mangled in a car accident or some such thing and I'll have to pass on this amazing opportunity.

As I make a hasty retreat from the UPA office tower, I turn my mobile back on and a text from Miller greets me —

*What are we doing 2morrow?*

So I text back. *I plan to quit both my jobs.*

Within seconds a smiley face beeps at me. ☺

# 12

At least five times today I've psyched myself up to go into Cynthia's office and tell her I'm leaving IDS, but each time something holds me back. I've prepared myself for all possible responses – her bewilderment that I could walk away from such a stellar career or her pity that I'm destined to struggle to find a better job, or even her disinterest and failure to make any attempt to dissuade me. But it isn't Cynthia's reaction that stalls me. It's Denise's.

Late last night when I told Denise that my interview at UPA had gone badly and there seemed to be a lot of applicants, she gave me a hug and murmured encouraging words about sticking with what I had.

Telling Lesbian from UPA that I won't in fact be taking the job is easy. I email him. No face, no attitude, no guilt. However, after nearly a decade working at IDS, and with her office purposefully within viewing distance of our desks, even I can't get away with emailing my notice to Cynthia. And the thought of weeks or maybe months of interviews constrained by a suit and conventional answers makes me want to puke.

So I resign myself to not resigning and holding on here until something else comes my way. Hopefully that will happen before Y3K.

Heading to the cafeteria with Evan and not announcing my resignation like I'd planned makes this particular lunch feel somewhat anticlimactic. Like pretty well all the others, really. That is until I ask, as I always do, after Zoe.

'We had a nice old deep and meaningful last night, actually,' says Evan, and I force a neutral expression.

'Cool,' I say frostily.

'She explained about you,' says Evan, 'I owe you one, dude.'

I am so oblivious to what he's talking about that it hurts, and trying to read his face is pretty well telling me zilch.

'What do you mean?'

'You know, how the morning after we met her that first time, she went over to your place and left you her number,' Evan says as I prepare for the shout of 'April fool'.

This being May and all, he looks at me to follow up and I have nothing.

'I didn't see Zoe the next day,' I finally state.

'Yeah, she told me she dropped by, talked to your sister, and gave her a post-it note for you. Thanks for not calling her, buddy – I didn't even know that you knew I liked her. I mean, I can appear pretty laid-back about this stuff.'

My head is racing and I'm trying to control my left knee, which has decided to dance. So all this time Zoe has been thinking that I dissed her, and now Evan is thanking me. I now recall Modern Bride's look just after Amelia told me about Evan and Zoe hooking up, and my stomach joins my left knee for the cha-cha.

'So you guys are okay?' I ask, trying not to sound invested in the outcome of their chat.

'Sure are. Thanks again, dude,' Evan says, with more sincerity than I've ever seen from him, before chucking all the things he's picked out of today's lunch into the rubbish and heading back to his desk.

I contemplate calling Denise but she's likely to be sleeping, so I just have to suck it up until I see her later tonight. More time on pause.

The second my computer clicks over to exactly five, I kill it and am entering Miller's bar within minutes. Seems now I come here every night *except* those that are IDS birthday drinks nights.

Miller does a good job of making me look like a customer and not just a friend distracting him from work as I tell him about my lunchtime conversation with Evan. Miller says I can ask Denise about it directly as he's driving over to the casino straight after his shift to ask about getting some extra work. So I hang at the bar for a few hours trying not to think about Zoe, and failing miserably.

Miller's car sure goes well enough now and a part of me is surprised he hasn't just kept going, even with the debt holding him here. As we approach the roundabout, larger than any Iowa crop circle, it entices us with many options, including the casino, north, and even Adelaide. This is normally where I automatically close my eyes but tonight I point out the spot where Jake's car had baulked at going any further all those years ago. As we sit at the same spot Jake had inexplicably sailed through, apparently without checking for oncoming dodgem cars, Miller surveys the position where Jake's car and the huge sign it ended up trying to take a bite out of met.

'I thought you said Jake was going to collect Denise from work when he crashed?' says Miller, scanning the layout of the exits.

'He was,' I reply.

'But if he ended up there, going in that direction, then he must have been *coming* from the casino,' says Miller, pointing towards the casino exit for effect.

'Well, Denise wasn't with him, so I guess he'd vagued out so much he did an extra bit of the loop before getting shoved off the thing,' I reply. 'He's always said his head was in another place when it happened and that's why he fucked up his entry in the first place.'

'Fair enough,' says Miller unconvincingly.

As Miller heads off to the casino's human resources office to charm some hours out of the night-duty supervisor, I make to the tables Denise has worked five nights a week since I can remember. I cannot see Denise spinning any of the wheels, so I tell the least busy of the croupiers I'm Denise's brother and ask where she is. He looks at me strangely and says she never works Thursday nights.

'Denise Lynch,' I state, adding the surname she has kept using despite her marriage to Jake.

'I know who you mean. She works Monday to Wednesday. Always has for as long as I can remember,' the croupier says with such certainty that even I start to doubt the fact he must be an idiot.

I track down Miller and watch as he eats the bulk out of the twenty-dollar buffet. There's no work available, apparently, though I suspect the guy who turned Miller away decided his patterned left arm clashes with the green felt and colourful décor. When I tell Miller that the croupier I spoke to swore Denise only works three nights a week, he immediately smells a rat.

'Dude, sorry but your sister's a bitch.'

'There'll be some explanation,' I say, jumping to Denise's defence. 'And she can't be that bad. I mean she looked after me when I was still at school and she's stuck by Jake.'

'Okay, she's only 77 per cent bitch – but bitch is still the majority shareholder in her psyche.'

I avoid his eyes.

'What night was Jake's accident?' Miller asks – the same question I'd quickly considered just moments ago.

'Thursday. Same as tonight,' I say flatly.

'So what if Jake came to collect her, as a surprise, and found out what you just did. That might have helped him vague out, huh?' Miller's questions are catching up to my fears.

'If that did happen they've obviously sorted it out. I mean, they've stayed together,' I say.

'Sure, but she's still pretending to work five nights and has done for years. And for most of that time you and Lucy have been stuck looking after Jake.' Miller is now ahead of me in putting this together, but I decide to wait and ask Denise. I've got two big questions for her now.

'I'm not going to know what she does on Thursday and Friday nights until I ask her, and we can't even be sure Jake has a clue.'

'Well, be sure and ask her what happened to the post-it Zoe left with her to give you while you're at it,' he says.

I know Miller is looking out for me, and I appreciate it, but I'm not quite ready to write Denise off. And so I continue to defend her to him, just as I'd recently been defending Miller to Denise.

The rest of the trip back to my place, Miller leaves it alone, probably aware that I'm silently making my own share of deductions.

We sit on the steps awhile and listen to Jake listen to Lucy. I don't want to face him until I've worked out what he already knows, and that means waiting for Denise to come home from wherever she is.

Lucy leaves before Denise gets home and is surprised to find me and Miller sitting in silence.

'How long have you guys been here?'

'A while,' I say in a hushed tone, but Jake has heard us and calls out to me.

'Just having a talk with Miller,' I call, trying to imply that Miller needs some personal time with me.

For his part, Miller carries off me scapegoating him real well with a quickly contrived sad face in Lucy's direction.

Lucy skips off with a caring look for Miller and whatever problem she imagines him to be wrestling with, and for once I'm glad that Jake is unable to get out onto the porch himself.

We stay outside for a long time and I feel guilty for letting Jake fall asleep on the sofa. Finally, when most of our neighbours' houses are already in darkness, I see a car stop at the very beginning of our street and make out someone alighting from the passenger side and walking in our direction.

For the second time today I'm shaking, and Miller puts a hand on my shoulder.

As Denise coolly walks up to us acting none-too-surprised to have a welcoming committee, Miller says, 'Speak of the devil,' adding, 'literally.'

Denise doesn't retaliate so I know she knows something's doing.

'Talk to you tomorrow,' Miller says to me, then ups and goes without acknowledging Denise.

'Sit down,' I say to my sister, barely constraining my fury, and I suppose it's because she's so shocked by my tone that she does exactly so without hesitating.

I look at her in the dull light and decide to just ask the questions I need answered, without any fucking about.

'Where've you been tonight?'

She knows by the mere fact I'm questioning her that I know where she has not been, and she decides not to waste time pretending.

'Why are you asking?'

'Miller and I went to the casino and you weren't there. They say you only work three days a week.' At least we're getting to the point and not dragging this out over four snail-speed episodes like *The Bold and the Beautiful* would.

'I was with a friend,' she says, and I actually think she may be misting up. The night, and her eyes, are so dark that it's hard to tell for sure.

'Where's Jake?' she asks.

'He's asleep,' I say, remembering to continue to speak softly. 'Are you with the same friend two nights every week?'

I wonder if I have the right to ask these questions.

'Yes.'

'And back then, when Jake went to collect you, were you with him then?' I decide to cut to the chase and refer to the friend as a man.

'Yes.'

I get up and go inside. Suddenly, asking about what happened to the note Zoe left with Denise to give me seems so insignificant. Jake is fast asleep so there's no point waking him just to carry him over to his bed.

As I lie awake during all the hours that no planes take off or land, I try to understand why both Denise and Jake are still here. Is it for me? Is Denise just here out of guilt about Jake's accident? Is Jake here because he still loves Denise or because he needs to be looked after? Though it's Denise that is my blood, it's Jake my tears are for.

# 13

This morning I needed no planes to bring me round – in fact the only time I dozed at all was once they'd started their familiar migrations.

I can hear Denise in the kitchen and wish that I could somehow avoid her, but know that's impossible.

Checking in first on Jake, who's waiting for me to help him get sorted, I realise that, other than Miller, I would most like to talk with him about yesterday but can't. As I manoeuvre Jake onto the sofa I realise Denise is making pancakes – small compensation – but now I'm so sick of what she's been feeding me that when I head into the kitchen and she offers them I say, 'No thanks.'

Denise looks more hurt than when I left her alone on the porch last night.

'Ash, we need to talk. I want you to understand how difficult this all is for me as well. I don't want you to hate me.'

My head is in the refrigerator, where I've briefly mistaken a stranded Kraft cheese single for the missing post-it note from Zoe. Good to see I'm thinking about myself again. Must be a family trait.

'I don't hate you. Never will. It's just that now I don't understand why we're all here together. Who is here for who and why?'

'We're all here because so much binds us together and the thing is that Jake and I are okay with how things work.'

I look at Denise surprised: 'Does Jake know you're still seeing the guy you were seeing the night he came to pick you up?'

Denise hugs me and I surprise myself by falling into it. 'Ash, you should speak to Jake about this. Talk to him tonight,' she says.

I decide that's a good idea, but of course refuse to acknowledge it.

'You know I'm here for Jake,' I say, and Denise is aware of what I mean. But she also probably knows, and banks on the fact, that I need Jake as much as he needs me. Where would I be if I didn't have to be here?

After helping Jake eat my pancakes, and talking about nothing, I punch him on his only good limb and make out to be as happy to go to work as I ever am.

The trip to work is even longer today if you measure the ground covered in my head. First I consider Miller. Where will I be when he drives out of Perth? If anyone can break through the city limits without being struck down, it will be Miller. He seems to be the least needy of all those important to me, but for me needy is good – I don't want to be forever destined to having just peripheral friends like Evan and my other work colleagues. Could Miller really be happy alone?

There won't be another opportunity with Zoe – in my mind she will remain Evan's even if they don't last. You can't move in on a friend's ex, can you? The fact that back when I considered the chance she liked me to have plummeted to single digits it had actually been 100 per cent keeps taunting me, but the moment has passed.

Denise wants nothing to change, just like my parents used to until they got it into their heads to shake things up.

I can't leave Jake. He would never leave me. And that's what it's about. And even if he were to roll off into the horizon with Lucy, what would I do then?

Methodically visiting every website in my favourites, I ingeniously avoid spending even one minute thinking about the reason I'm paid to ride this ergonomic chair. The only time I even contemplate anything work-like is imagining the walk to Cynthia's door – a stroll that is my Everest for reasons that are less clear now than ever.

At lunch Evan continues to revere me for stepping aside and allowing the rightful pairing of him and Zoe to blossom. I still struggle to work out his initial blasé attitude, which completely put me off my guard as to how he felt about her. Maybe he just wanted to play her down to me. Evan's competition with Shaun, who is masterfully increasing *Who Weekly*'s market share to a point comparable with the iPod, is completely fucking with Evan's head. He even mentioned Shaun and Saddam Hussein in the same sentence today.

If Evan obsessed about Zoe as much as he does about Shaun forcing him into the shadows at work, I'd be a bit more comfortable with walking away. I wake up each morning with Evan's girlfriend on my mind, while Evan is waking up with Shaun filling his thoughts and competitive bile rising in his throat.

Shaun had a day off earlier in the week, and when he told us the next day that he'd been experiencing stabbing pains in his arm the previous night I'm sure I wasn't the only one who immediately pictured Evan in his studio-box furiously whacking some pins into a well-dressed voodoo doll.

Automatically, I call by to see Miller on my way home to briefly update him about my discussion with Denise this morning, to get some perspective before I head home to talk to Jake. I have to wait until a cute blonde girl ordering a colourful drink has finished flirting with him. It's not the first time I've noticed Miller simply not responding to flirting at all. He's even impervious to most praise. When I've commented on his street smarts or how cool his tattoos are he doesn't agree or feign modesty. Maybe he's heard it too much. Denise thinks it means he's just full of himself, but when you think about it the natural reaction of deflecting a compliment usually results in it being repeated.

Across the room I see Pet Problems and her husband sitting with Practical Parenting and Fortune, sharing a drink and couple smugness. I can't turn my head back to the bar fast enough before Fortune calls me over. Despite my need to resolve things with Jake, my reaction is to take even this lame opportunity to delay the necessary discussion. After telling Miller that I'm going to have to make nice with my office friends for a bit, he tells me he'll be on a break shortly and will come save me with a couple of beers.

'Have you met my husband?' Pet Problems purrs.

'Yes,' her husband and I respond simultaneously.

That's enough smalltalk before Pet Problems drives conversation back to the brilliance of baby making. I sit and smile as I think about one of the wittier things Evan said recently. As we were wasting company time by the water cooler the other day, waiting for Cynthia to collect her tub of dead yoghurt, Modern Bride had predicted that Pet Problems would probably drop out of socialising entirely now that she'd had her kid, as most couples do. Practical Parenting had assured us all that it was perfectly normal for a new parent to become totally immersed in all things baby, and Evan had said, 'Yeah, the kid had her at vomit.'

Miller comes over, quite meekly for him, and I allow everyone to introduce themselves so I don't have to admit I have no idea what their real names are. He sits down and passes me a beer before Pet Problems is right back into it, trilling 'You know, I just can't believe that we' – quick hugging acknowledgement of husband – 'created a little person.'

'Well, you had sex. Even bugs can do that,' says Miller, and I don't know whether to laugh or cry.

Pet Problems does her best to ignore him and continues to laud her talent for people-making.

'I mean, it's what life is all about, isn't it?' The question is now assuredly targeted to Practical Parenting but Miller answers anyway.

'No, it's not.'

Suddenly I've forgotten to be anxious about Jake as now I have Miller to freak me out.

'Excuse me. What would you know?' Pet Problems replies, incensed. Mister Pet Problems is silent, either on account of Miller's tattoos or the fact that he could do with a break from her ranting about babies himself.

'What would *you* know?' Miller says back and then adds, 'You're like one of those people who scream that Perth is the best place in the world but have never been anywhere else.'

'So how many countries have you been to, smartass?' says Pet Problems, taking the maternity gloves off.

'I ain't the one declaring what's what,' says Miller barely raising a sweat, let alone his voice. I'm getting the impression he considers this just a normal conversation, only one step beyond polite.

Miller may not have travelled that far yet, though you just know he's seen a bunch more than anyone else at the table and there's little doubt he isn't done with looking. But this group conversation is done with and soon I make farewells and Miller, bizarrely, shakes each and everyone's hand before we head back to the bar.

'I hope I didn't offend them,' he says.

I assume that normally he wouldn't make such a concession except that he might have caused some problems for me with my work friends.

'I hope she didn't offend you,' I reply, knowing there was no chance she could.

'Nah, she's just spewing what she's been fed. Carrot chunks and all.'

So now my work colleagues who've met Miller are, like Denise, totally unimpressed by him. And not so long ago I probably would've agreed with them, but suddenly I also want to be the sort of person who's dismissed by the sort of person I've been.

It's time to head home and take on a much bigger challenge than matching wits with Pet Problems and her kind.


'Hey Lucy, you can take the rest of the night off,' I say cheerfully, masking my apprehension about the upcoming talk with Jake. We're in the kitchen, where she's ruining something on the stove top. From the kitchen window I can see Jake sitting in his wheelchair, looking out at nothing much.

'I'm happy to hang around,' she says, meaning it.

'Actually I sort of wanted to hang with Jake by myself if that's okay' I say, not wanting to hurt her feelings – though, as with Miller, it's virtually impossible to offend Lucy.

'Jake will like that,' she says with a real smile. 'I'll leave his dinner to simmer a while more.'

'Can't hurt,' I reply, to make myself smile.

Lucy kisses Jake goodnight, and once I hear her car leave I turn off the stove so whatever she's been stirring can congeal even more before I toss it. I'm not hungry but

I grab some indestructible food from the private stash, then take it out to Jake and sit on the grass facing him.

'What are you looking at?' I ask Jake, who seems somehow aware that things are not fine, like a dog headed for the vet.

'Been watching the planes', he says. 'For some reason, every time I've seen one today I've thought about how long I worked at United and how long ago that seems.'

'You probably stayed there as long as I've been at IDS,' I say, and that makes me sad, though I'm not sure why entirely.

'You know that as part of our package they gave us a load of frequent flyer points every year we worked? The only time I used any of them was buying those tickets for your mum and dad,' Jake says.

'I'd forgotten about those. What happened to the rest of the points?' I ask.

'They're still there. I get a statement occasionally,' Jake tells me.

'Really? I've never seen one,' I say.

'Denise ditches them pretty quickly,' he replies.

'Why?' I ask, but Jake doesn't respond and it's probably for the same reason Denise kept the Zoe post-it note from me.

'Is Denise allergic to change?' I ask, well aware that my life to date pretty well mirrors my sister's so far as the adventure level goes.

'Let's face it, none of us have gotten out of our chairs that often,' Jake replies, and we both laugh at ourselves.

Night begins to push down on us as the number of planes coming home to roost increases, like the restless birds I can hear fussing around the gum tree in our front yard.

'I didn't go to collect Denise from the casino that night,' Jake says without looking at me directly, but still facing south.

'Where were you going?' I say, clueless.

'I was leaving her. I was going home.' Jake's eyes have welled up.

'Adelaide?'

'I must have done three laps of that roundabout. Thinking about Denise. And nothing stopped me going around in circles until that damn sign jumped out in front of me while my head was elsewhere,' says Jake, then laughs so as not to cry.

'Did you know she wasn't at the casino anyhow?'

'No. She told me that today.'

Part of me wants to say it's okay, but I'm already pissed off that it was not just Denise he was leaving that night, but me as well. Until this city pummelled him.

I think Jake can see how I feel, and he tells me, 'It was over between me and Denise even before we moved in here. I wanted to stay while you finished school because your parents couldn't. And now it's you who's kept here by me and I hate that, buddy. That's fucked up.'

'But you stayed while I needed you, and I want to do the same,' I say.

'Seeing you waste your life doesn't make me feel the least bit better,' says Jake and then asks me to help him inside.

It's totally dark now and something stupid on the television calls for our attention.

# 14

It's as if Miller has been saving it up all weekend. He allows me to rant about my meaningless job and collapsing family as we hang at his place and then head out on a pub crawl through every bar in Perth he doesn't work in. Not once does he point out that his lot is hardly better. And as I continually wring the heart I wear permanently attached to my sleeve, he, as usual, keeps his well buried in his chest.

'I've been meaning to tell you, I'm heading off next week,' he says in a break between my whining.

I can feel my face make like the horror you see on a cabbie's face when you try for change from a fifty dollar note.

'You should come with me,' he adds casually. 'I'd be happy to wait a bit longer if you want to.'

I immediately know that I will. With Jake and Denise no longer being Jake *and* Denise, and Zoe well gone, my excuses for turning up to this life are fast drying up.

'What do you have to stay for?' he asks, reading my mind.

'Where'll we go?'

'Continue north I reckon, then east. Find some work. Have some fun.'

'You sure you want me along?' I ask.

'I wouldn't have asked you otherwise. You know I'm not about being polite for the sake of it,' he says with a smile.

'So long as you realise I'm not necessarily the most worldly of travelling companions,' I say.

'If I wanted to hang with some self-assured person who knows all there is to know, then you'd be right in thinking you'd be way down the list,' says Miller. 'But I don't, so you're not.'

'Thanks, I think,' I say.

'Most everyone I meet seems so certain that what they've got is pretty well it, and I can't relate to that feeling and you sure don't seem to either,' he goes on, knowing I'm in need of a bunch of reassurance about how we two misfits actually connect.

'It's gonna be weird leaving this place,' I say. 'Weird but good.'

'Just because you're stuck here doesn't mean you fit,' says Miller, clinching it.

For the first time I can remember, I'm actually itching to tell Denise something she's sure to have a problem with. A big problem. Miller, on the other hand, though he'd never admit it, appears mightily pleased and surprised that I've agreed to head off with him so easily. Inside, my guts are in freefall, but all the beer I've drunk is softening their landing. I can make out some splashing but.

I decide to walk home from Miller's place, or at least as far as I can before hailing a cab. The inevitable doubts have started already and I wonder if I'm avoiding catching Denise before she goes to bed. Or maybe the idea of walking all this way is so I end up sober and back where I was.

Everything I see on the walk home and everything it makes me think of relates back to my decision to hit the road. As a biker stands up on his back wheel just ahead of me, I think about how he must have come to do that the first time. Life is a series of firsts and finals, the rest is nothing.

A regular day of IDS and television is comfortable enough, but multiplied into thousands it's become numbing. Miller has come from somewhere else and seeks what he doesn't have securely fastened into his experience. I have no idea whether he'll be there as each day commences, and maybe that's the point. Transporting myself back to me as a kid and what I wanted for my future life, other than being able to stay up as late as possible and having chocolate available around the clock, it never included pretty well anything I currently have or do.

Now that I'm virtually convinced of the merits of leaving, it's time for irrational fear to flex its muscles in the debate. The irony of Perth being a city seemingly devoted to the car, yet no-one going anywhere, nips at my resolve. No-one leaves Perth, ever. Or so it seems in my family at least. If Jake couldn't make it back to Adelaide or my parents to New Zealand, what are the odds I won't be swatted for attempting to make free?

The lights are still on, and Denise and Jake are actually sharing the sofa. I decide to inform Denise by telling Jake.

'Miller is continuing his road trip around Australia next week and I'm going north with him,' I say matter-of-factly to the face that is least likely to explode.

'How long for?' Jake asks.

'There's no plan. Indefinite,' I say trying to sound assured and relaxed while all the while the heart that I thought was on my sleeve is making a big fuss in my core.

'What about your job?' says Denise, keeping a lid on it. For now.

'I'm gonna quit tomorrow.'

'How about this place? How am I supposed to keep this going?'

By this she means Jake, and he hates her for saying it. For trying to hold me with that.

'Well, maybe if you work five nights a week it'll be fine.' As soon as I say it I wish I hadn't.

'Are you sure you're not in love with Miller?' Denise snaps back sarcastically. I deserve her swipe so choose to suck it up.

'Denise, I want to do something different. I know you're mad at me, but things are changing already and this is part of it. Lucy will help with Jake, and if he's cool with this then you should be too.'

Denise looks at Jake but he's giving her nothing. She ups and goes to bed without another word.

'Buddy, I am going to sleep real well tonight,' Jake says to me as I try and hold back my Richter-scale-worthy shaking. I sit down beside him and hug him for letting me go.

'Ash, have you thought of up-sizing your trip?' Jake asks, and for a second it sounds like he's trying to sell me some drugs.

'What do you mean?'

'I told you I have all those frequent flyer points. Why don't you and Miller take them and land yourselves in America. Or Europe. Wherever you like.'

'Are you *serious*?'

'Well, I'm not going to use them. And the thing is, the world is not only bigger than Perth, it's bigger than Australia.'

Not for a second do I think Miller will not take up Jake's offer, and so it's up to me, I suppose. As I lie in my bed, thinking about catching a plane even larger than the one that took my parents it occurs to me that their ashes have flown even further than their Ash has, and maybe this ground has held on to me long enough. Without clipped wings will this chicken be able to fly?

I look out the window towards a departing flight and try to see me on it. Behind the windows there may be someone else who's never had a serious relationship, never left this town before or been to the beach or taken drugs or done much of anything. At least they got on the plane, though.

Quitting your job on a Monday seems way more spontaneous than on a Friday, and as I sneak through the house, before Denise is out of bed, thoughts of informing Cynthia, and Evan, fill my already overloaded brain. I've decided to tell Cynthia last thing this afternoon, and hope this is not a further stalling manoeuvre on my part.

Much of the morning is spent consoling Evan about the fact that his office nemesis, Shaun, has been invited to fly to Sydney by the *Who Weekly* editorial team. Nobody at our level has ever, to my knowledge, been treated so royally, and Evan is aghast. Naturally, he avoids the notion that Shaun is more successful than the rest of us and vents his disbelief to anyone dumb enough to pass by his desk.

It sure seems like a good time to leave IDS, but I can't tell Miller about Jake's frequent flyer points offer until I'm completely confident that I'll actually quit. And that won't be until I've done it.

Evan's continued petulance helps stoke the fires of uprising throughout the afternoon, and I busy myself observing my colleagues and my general work environment in the hope of finding more fuel to propel me.

Evan and Amelia have organised for all magazines, except Who Weekly, to have lunch outside of the work cafeteria today so they can bitch more easily about Shaun. I'm keen to go along as I expect watching Evan disassemble another meal and Amelia and the others writing my opinions off as of no consequence might just be all I need to finally shove me into Cynthia's office.

Our waitress can tell we're likely to be no-tippers so takes her time before interrupting Evan's bleating to fetch our order. When presented with a menu that's not as instantly recognisable as the one we face every other day, our group is thrown into complete chaos. The choices are so plentiful that I automatically look for the simplest option. Evan selects a Greek salad but without olives. Seems he can't even be bothered picking them out himself now. Amelia says she'll have his olives but Evan insists he doesn't even want them touching his salad. The waitress has heard all of this before, it seems, and awaits further stupid orders patiently.

'I'll have the Mediterranean foccacia but with extra Spanish onion,' Amelia says without once looking at the order taker.

'Turkish with salami.' Fortune also avoids the use of any superfluous words. Like please.

'Hungarian or Danish salami?' the waitress asks.

'Hungarian.'

Like he knows the difference.

'Cheese?' Our waitress up-sells.

'Swiss,' says Fortune, taking the bait.

And so it goes until my turn. 'Can I have a beef and mushroom pie and chips please?'

Modern Bride looks at me and says, 'That's very unadventurous, Ash. It's exactly what you have in the office.' The group all look at me with some sort of pity.

'Maybe you'd like to try our famous Parisian-style baguette?' says the waitress.

I deliberate briefly then say, 'Okay. Thanks.' My mind's made up.

# 15

Waking up to Jake calling us to check out Sky News and seeing our modest city swarming with international television crews is a once-in-a-lifetime event. As is having a meteorite crash into your house. Which is exactly what has apparently happened to one of Perth's residents.

Only when I get to work for my final day at IDS do I discover that it's Shaun's bedroom that now has a mini skylight and a five kilo boulder steaming atop the suitcase he'd packed for his trip to Sydney.

Cynthia gathers us into the boardroom to reassure us that Shaun is fine – apparently his bed was at least a metre from where the boulder came to land. He was peppered with ceiling debris, though, which caused him to think the sky was falling in for the briefest of moments.

We're all genuinely pleased he's okay – even Evan, who somehow interprets this to be a sign that he was lucky not to have been the one invited to visit Sydney as it might then have been him the meteorite came after.

I try not to think too much about this latest example of someone trying to leave Perth, albeit briefly, being stopped in their tracks.

Shaun, understandably, is quite freaked out, and the Sydney trip is on hold for the time being. He has a load of media interviews to get through anyways. Flowers are being organised by Cynthia, on behalf of all of us, though there's no card to sign, as for the life of us we can't find a suitable card nor construct an appropriate message for someone who's had a close encounter with a meteorite.

Suddenly the whole office is using astronomy lingo as if they were born to it. Water cooler conversation has switched from outrage that Madonna has dared rescue another African child from a life of poverty, to talk of falls, atmosphere booms, and the difference between meteoroids and meteorites. It reminds me of during the Iraq invasion when the terms 'sorties' and 'WMDs' rolled easily off even the most ignorant tongues.

This being my final day here is now old news, but it seems fitting somehow and I enjoy the office anonymity one last time. Appropriately I spend my final hours at IDS Googling, sticking with the topic of the day – meteorites. It seems there's no real proof any person has actually been killed by a rock from space, though a dog in Egypt copped it in 1911. The closest thing to Shaun's wake-up call was some lady in Alabama in the fifties who was badly bruised when one crashed into her living room and some debris slammed into her after it bounced off the radio. It's nice to think that in future our town will now come up when anyone, anywhere in the world, Googles this menace from beyond.

Even before I've had a chance to distribute my stapler and Post-it note pads to my nearest and dearest colleagues, my computer is given to Pet Problems, three cubicles down, whose own one has died – probably from complete boredom. As I'm wiping dust I've never noticed before off my desk, the IT guy setting up Pet Problems calls out to me to tell him my password so he can log her in more easily by not having to create a new one.

'I'll come down,' I whisper back, aware that Evan, Amelia and countless other sets of ears are in dire need of something interesting to hear.

'Just tell me – no need for secrecy now,' the polo-shirted one shouts back.

Oh, fuck it. In the decade I'd been here my login had changed with the times, even if I hadn't. But then you're forced to update your password every three months – no excuses or cop-outs allowed. Cobain, Eminem, Pancakes, Beyonce, Whopper, MySpace – the list is a tour through my changing obsessions over a lifetime in this place.

'Z (pause), O, E, B (another pause), R, A, D (final, humiliating pause), Y.'

Letters don't make words to the IT guy, who happily keys in the code, whereas Evan just looks at me. Luckily no-one else has bothered to unscramble the name, what with my clever use of pauses.

'I was stuck,' I say to Evan.

'Not any more, buddy,' Evan replies as kindly as someone completely unlike him might.

Cynthia presents me with my lame present and oversized farewell card in a hastily organised board-room ceremony at five minutes before five. I thank my assembled friends and colleagues without the suggestion of a tear from me or any of them. Maybe Miller was right in saying that it was a two-way street – I had remained as distanced from them as they had from me. Mutual ambivalence.

Thankfully Evan takes my cue that I don't want to drag this to the birthday bar, so I say I'll call him before I leave Perth, and the others each give me a final look of pity for wasting my opportunities at IDS before they head off to their superior lives. The fact that my farewell present is a twelve-month subscription to *Men's Health* magazine, including domestic delivery to my current address, seems final proof none of them believe me to be going anywhere.

Mercifully alone, I make my way to the birthday bar, over-compensating farewell card wedged under an armpit, to catch up with Miller. Things are very quiet when I arrive – I guess most everyone is on some sort of meteor watch. I catch Miller watching some senti-mental movie on the television above the bar and I swear he wipes his eyes clear as he spies me. It's going to take me a while to even partially understand this guy.

Miller grabs me a beer to celebrate my last day at IDS, then turns off the television and ups the sound coming from the jukebox a few notches. When I'd suggested we head further than car distance, as Jake had urged, Miller was all for it immediately, though he seemed reluctant to use the frequent flyer points. I threatened to back out if he didn't help me use them – the thought of all those miles for just me seemed way too daunting. I pointed out that he'd always planned to head north next – this was still north just a whole hemisphere extra.

Now Miller is completely excited about leaving Australia, and I've spent the last week trying to mimic him as best I can. When I start to waiver I've gotten into the habit of recharging my resolve by simply allowing him to talk up our plans. At this point we fly to Amsterdam via Singapore and then see what happens. Unless a meteorite gets us first.

# 16

If any of us are thinking that the only other time anyone from our family tried to fly somewhere they never came back, then they aren't mentioning it. Denise is making reparation pancakes and Lucy has come over early to wish me farewell. It still amazes me how fine Denise seems to be with the bond between Jake and his lingering physiotherapist. Maybe she's only as okay with it as I pretended to be about Evan and Zoe, but if this is the case she's a fine actress. She's been playing the role of a full-time worker all these years, I guess. Now when she sets off on Thursday and Friday nights at least she no longer needs to wear her casino-issue uniform.

The flight is not until this afternoon, but because Miller has worked every shift he possibly can, I'm going to help him do some collecting today. Collect his last pay, collect his last-minute passport, and collect the money he's getting for selling his car – to the same garage that fixed it.

My last days at work have allowed me time to organise my passport, and money-wise I have a reasonable amount without selling anything. As you do when you've worked for years and done nothing. Even though I've contributed my share into finally wrapping up the mortgage on this house, and I'm leaving a healthy account at BankWest with Jake's name on it, I still have the equivalent of nearly three thousand euros, and that sounds like a lot. And we're both prepared to work on our travels as well. As long as, for my part, it doesn't involve sharing cubicle space with Euro-Evan and Euro-Amelia.

When Miller arrives to an 'Ash, that Miller's here' from Denise, it's time for the dreaded farewells. There was no way we were going to do this at the airport – for Denise especially it still represents the loss of so much.

Lucy is the easiest of course – she's all smiles and asks if I can send her a postcard from Moscow. I say sure, even though I have no idea where she lives and whether I'll ever be in Moscow.

Denise hugs me for the longest she has since our parents' funeral. Our arguments since I decided to leave work and Perth seem finally to have had the same revitalising effect as land following a bushfire. This makes me feel way better about going, despite having no idea when I'll be back or what I'll come back to.

When Miller comes back inside to report that my backpack is now stowed, I go over to Jake's chair to hug him goodbye and my legs tremble like his can't.

'I love you, Jake.'

'Me too, buddy,' he tells me. 'Fly safely.'

After a surreptitious wiping away of tears I'm good to go.

Back at Miller's place there are less emotional farewells. Several drug-fucked flatmates wish him and me good luck, which in my delicate state I take to mean they have sold their portfolio of airline shares this very morning. Miller changes into fresh jeans and a white T-shirt in front of us and gives his discarded clothes to the only flatmate who shares his lean dimensions. I notice that Miller's backpack is half the size of mine, and I suspect it contains a black T-shirt – his evening wear – and little else. As we change time zones on the flight, will he change white to black and back again?

As we wait in the post office to collect Miller's passport from a guy with fewer teeth than fingers, I spot Zoe walking slowly up the street. It occurs to me that this is the first time I've seen her without blushing, and then, because I've thought about blushing, I do. Miller asks what's up and I tell him that Zoe is just outside.

'If you want to say goodbye I'll catch you up,' he offers.

'Nah,' I say automatically.

'You sure?'

'Okay, just to give me some *closure*,' I say in my weak attempt at an Oprah accent.

Rather than trying to call her name out on the street and risk my voice coming out shrill or broken, I chase after her and once in reach tap her softly on the shoulder. She seems genuinely happy to see me and we stand on the pavement facing each other.

'Evan told me you've left IDS and are heading overseas – good on you!' says Zoe.

'Thanks, Zoe – just saw you walk past and thought I'd say goodbye.'

'Don't make it sound so final, Ash,' Zoe tells me. 'We'll see each other again.'

'Yeah, I'll be back soon enough, I expect,' I reply.

'I don't necessarily mean here – our paths may cross somewhere else entirely.'

And this time I blush in full view of her but she kindly ignores the fact that she's now stood talking to Mr Beetroot Head, and Mr Beetroot Head reminds himself to move on.

'Good luck with the photography,' I say, then start to walk back to the post office as Zoe waves and takes a moment more than necessary to turn around and keep going.

Miller is waiting on the step of the post office and checks my face for distress.

'How'd that go?'

'Fine. It's worked out the way it was always destined to.'

'Destiny-schmestiny,' says Miller, adding, 'Did you ever tell her about not getting her message from your sister?'

'There's no point. She's with Evan, and even if I could fuck that up I wouldn't. And hey, we're going overseas, return date unknown.' That said, I promise myself that if time breaks them up at some point in the future and Zoe shows the slightest interest then I'd better fucking do something about it.

'Seems like I'm travelling with the right person,' Miller replies, and I feel better already.

Next we head over to the birthday bar so Miller can collect his final pay. We decide to have our last Perth beers, and as Miller grabs them I turn and head for the jukebox that sits by the bar's entrance.

'Where are you going?' Miller calls out.

Turning to tell him, I can see Miller as a little kid wondering where his mother went.

'Putting on some Goldfrapp, dude.'

'Cool,' he replies.

He should know – I wouldn't be going anywhere without him.

# PART 2
## WINGING IT

# 17

Twenty-seven years I have lived in Perth and not once have I been to the airport for the reason it was constructed – as opposed to my dodgy use of its shuttle system into the city. Until today.

My entire family had tried to ignore its existence until my parents took on the beast and lost. And since then, well, need I say more?

As the taxi dumps us at the mouth of the monster, I scan the tarmac trying to locate the bullet that's to be ours. There are a couple of planes in various states of undress and one fashioned for flying that's cruising down the runway, preparing to be fired.

'You know, it's just a short hop to Singapore and then you'll be an experienced flyer,' Miller reassures me.

I've gathered from hanging with him this last month that he's flown a few times before – furthest being to Auckland for some gigs. Aside from what drives him to make himself independent of others, I'd say Miller is pretty well fearless, though, as Denise has taken ample opportunity to remind me, I really don't know him that well and he could simply disappear around a corner at any point. Thing is, this morning I've come to understand that Miller might just be thinking the same of me and may have just as much to lose.

Denise has called us 'The Odd Couple' a few times recently, and it's a fair enough call. We seem to have as much in common as Liza Minelli and any of her husbands. I've tirelessly resisted change (until now), he embraces it; I tend towards thinking too much, he's easygoing. And of course there's a slight discrepancy in our appeal to women. Regardless, I don't reckon Miller particularly wants a clone and I'm not that fussed on hanging with another me.

Miller responds in kind when the luscious Singapore clerkette checks him out at check-in. An armful of tattoos screams either dirty sex or terrorist, depending on your general disposition. I'd already been warned several times by Evan not to carry nail scissors or knives in my hand luggage. This had not exactly altered my packing plans. We pretty well walk straight into the departure lounge after being untroubled at security.

When I'd told Evan that I was heading overseas, or attempting to, he'd seemed more interested in the electronics bargains I could get in the duty-free than what might face me on the other side of the world. For his sake, I wander through the immaculate displays of smokes, scent and booze, pausing at the mountain-range-sized Toblerone before realising that even without tax it would set me back more than I'm hoping a night's accommodation in Amsterdam might.

While Miller sits reading a book among the well-dressed Chinese and the loud-mouthed Aussies, I head to buy myself a farewell Whopper from Hungry Jack's. Miller has already explained that I'm likely to be mightily comforted by the familiarity of all the Burger Kings we'll come across overseas. However, I don't lose the opportunity to enjoy one last thousand-calorie heap of familiarity.

'So, where are you guys going?' a well-dressed lady with just a handbag for carry-on says to me. She's sitting opposite us and looks a little too posh to be flying economy, so I expect this will be the first and last time I see her.

'Singapore,' I say naively.

'I realise that,' she responds quickly, but without condescension. 'After the stopover, I mean.'

'Amsterdam.'

'Oh I love Amsterdam – have you been before?' she asks, leaning towards me so we can talk more easily.

Miller remains immersed in his book and the lady barely notices him, which is a rarity in itself.

'This is about as far as I've been,' I say, indicating the departure lounge.

'Well, you're in for a treat then,' she tells me happily.

'I hope so,' I say, meaning it with all my being.

'Where are you headed?' I ask politely, expecting that I should show as much interest in her trip.

'The great unknown,' she replies cryptically.

'Is that a direct connection?' says Miller with a smile, taking this opportunity to join in the conversation.

The lady laughs. 'I don't know where I'm going to end up – there's no real plan,' she says, taking no offence that Miller might be treating her like she's a whack-job, which if she knew him she'd know he wasn't.

'That's sorta like us as well,' I say.

Once Miller goes back to his book she really opens up. Seems she and her husband have been together for more years than not, and a few weeks ago, while they were both interstate on business, everything they owned had been stolen from their palatial house in the most exclusive suburb in Perth. Even their cars. The whole place had been completely emptied. Her husband cried and was close to inconsolable, she told me. Seems this got her thinking, and instead of immediately planning to spend the next few years dedicating themselves to recollecting the same stuff all over again, she took an entirely opposite view altogether.

'I felt this enormous sense of relief – we still had money in the bank and the stuff was insured, but I realised that none of what we'd lost was particularly what made me happy.'

'But what about your husband?' I ask.

'It became apparent that he was not going to relax, or be satisfied, until he had restored things to exactly where they were before,' she replies. 'But the thought of accumulating things that I could do without simply because that's what you do made me want to barf.'

I really never expected this genteel woman to use the word 'barf', and again Miller rejoins the conversation as if she'd said 'open sesame'.

'So you've just left him?' Miller asks, and now there really is a judgemental tone in his voice that doesn't match his generally cavalier demeanour.

It occurs to me that while Miller normally seems to take everything in his stride he has a raw nerve about anything that can be interpreted as one person discarding another. I didn't have to be Dr Phil to make some sort of link to his mother disappearing when Miller was Jet. Weirdly, I gain comfort from his unwavering stance on sticking it out.

'No, I invited him to come with me,' the lady tells Miller, 'but he wasn't ready to walk away from all he knew.'

'Do you still love him?' I ask, having as intense a conversation with a nameless passerby in a departure lounge as I've ever had with any work colleague I've known for a decade.

'Of course. How can you stop loving someone you've truly loved? Thing is, I've still got to do what is right for me, and if he wants to join me then I'll be doubly happy.'

'How will he find you in the great unknown?' Miller asks.

'If he looks he'll find me,' she replies.

We queue to have our boarding passes snatched off us, and then shuffle through the portal to another world.

After the chatty lady farewells us both before turning left to find her roomy seat to the great unknown, me and Miller turn right and struggle through the obstacle course of people trying to force too-big bags into too-small overhead lockers before squeezing their too-big asses into too-small seats. The interior of the plane is larger than I'd imagined, and I'd feel quite comfortable if it weren't planning on launching itself into the sky at any minute. For the first time in several weeks I have time to think about the last time a Lynch was strapped into such a fix.

'Dude, quit thinking,' Miller says.

'It's cool. Really,' I lie.

I appear to be the only person who pays any attention to the gymnastics presentation from the stewards as they attempt to mime what we should do in the event of trouble. Everyone else is either resigned to their fate or happy to wing it. The steward who's been allocated to our slice of the plane is pleased to have an audience, and focuses on me rather than making out to be short-sighted and glassy-eyed like his colleagues. In fact his expression is of a surprised raccoon, and I nearly get the impression that I'm meant to respond to his gestures.

Miller disturbs my viewing of the raccoon's performance by shoving a magazine in my face. He points to an article about Amsterdam's dope cafes and 24-hour party city image. How the in-flight magazine knows we're going to Amsterdam I don't know.

I'm not sure if I'll need to remind Miller at some point that I'm pretty well clueless about drugs, picking up women and generally being cool. These things are just everyday for him and sort of momentous and rare for me. Hopefully he really is fine with this. I'm counting on him being different to my other friends – able to truly cope with me being different to him.

So, we're surrounded by all the people you dread when you go to a cinema. Some guy hacking up a lung, already craving the time he can shove another fag in his face; a self-important woman talking at top volume into her mobile right up until it's yanked out of her hand by The Raccoon; and a precocious girl whose attention needs are being drowned out by her parent's conversation, which is intended for everyone's edification. Apparently they're very impressive – great jobs, successful friends and a fine collection of stuff. However, speaking loudly for Miller or my benefit is a complete waste of their valuable time. Why they're not sat at the front of the plane is beyond me, but I'm sort of hoping someone will ask them – just to bring them back down to earth.

Luckily, a baby starts howling, drowning them out pretty much – and it's the better of a poor selection of soundtracks.

'Did you hear what shit that bloke was going on about?' I say to Miller as I feel the plane tremble into motion.

'I understood the words – I just don't know why he'd say them.'

Listening to the baby's escalating cries, interspersed with the conversation of the idiots behind us, keeps my mind off the plane's insistence on speeding up and going through with this. Miller continues to distract me like a doctor about to surreptitiously jab you with a needle, and the plane is off the ground and packing its tyres away.

Ten minutes in, and just as I'm starting to realise I'm actually cool with being in the air, the plane starts to make like it isn't. The seatbelt lights go back on with a microwave 'ding' and The Raccoon scurries out of sight. Miller doesn't even notice, it seems, so I take some reassurance from that while begrudging the fact that both the baby and the loud family behind us have finally shut up just when I could do with the dumb fun of listening to them.

The plane is buffeted by some angry winds that shake us until finally giving up and letting us proceed to the next stage. When it's over, Miller ungrips his arm rest and I'm meant not to notice.

The rest of the flight is smooth sailing, as they say in the traveller's world. Miller enjoys double helpings of each meal while I continue to use my Whopper calories for fuel. It takes me a while to feel confident enough to iPod myself up, fearing I'll miss the screams around me that will precede our end. Once the captain announces we're out of Australian airspace I feel somehow empowered about being nowhere, and the prospect of landing doesn't bother me, even though that's probably as fraught with danger as any take-off.

Outside my mini-window I see my first foreign city, but we're only going to be in Singapore briefly before doing the flying thing again – and this time for a much longer stint. Singapore's airport is massive, and finding the right connection is probably going to be as big a challenge as any I've faced for a while. We head straight for a help-desk where a prim and meticulously attired white guy, balding in the English royal family way, and with the squeaky voice of a jockey, is being unhelpful to the lady ahead of us. She's overbred-looking – all lips, cheekbones and jaw – but still that's no reason for his attitude.

When the lady wanders off unsatisfied, Miller cops an immediate look of disdain from Fuckwit by bothering him and asking where we can find the fat-assed mother of a plane that's going to get us to the top of the world. He doesn't actually use those words, though.

'You'll need to find our European help-desk,' says Fuckwit snippily.

'So where's that?' Miller asks, ready to whack the guy.

'It's in Terminal 2,' he replies without offering any clue as to how to find Terminal 2.

'Where are we?' asks Miller, maintaining his patience. For now.

'Terminal 3.'

'Can you tell us where the Korean airlines fly from?' Miller asks. I have no idea why.

'Which one?' Fuckwit virtually snarls, looking at Miller's tattoos in the *not* dirty-sex way.

'Air Seoul,' Miller says.

'There is no Air Seoul,' the jerk replies, not getting it.

'Are you sure?' says Miller, looking the clerk dead in the eye before walking off.

Finally we track down where we're meant to be, and after a few hours of iPodding and checking out yet more sterile shopping experiences we're on our second plane for the day. This one is even larger, so we have to share our immediate space with a third person. He's much our age and tall and blond enough for us to presume he's returning home to Holland. As I'm sitting in the middle, I strike up conversation, and his English is okay – a lot fucking better than my Dutch anyways. Mögel lives in Rotterdam, which is apparently nowhere near where we're going, and he seems relieved. Catching a plane reminds me of picking up the phone before caller ID existed. You really have no idea who you're going to get.

About midway through the flight I seek out the large packet of chips I bought in case the airline food was as bad as television says. For some reason the packet has puffed up to near-bursting point. It must have something to do with air pressure and all, but if I leave it much longer it's going to explode. Fearing how that might freak out Dutch Guy and any terrorist-fearing travellers, I try and get a grip on it so as to prise open the seal, but it's so swollen this can't be done. The straining packet would make a perfect pillow, and if this plane does crash after the melee caused by an explosion then it's a shame that I don't have another to help me float about in the ocean while help comes – as the stewards would have you imagine it serenely plays out.

Eventually, without waking Miller, I grab a pen from his carry-on bag and decide to stab the packet as softly as I can so as to diffuse a complete explosion. I've heard about them having to do much the same with cows that eat too much clover, the gases blowing their stomachs to a sensational size. The 'pop' created by my timid stabbing with the pen is nothing like I'd imagined, and only Dutch Guy flinches for a split-second. After eating all the chips, I yawn my blocked ears clear and decide to go to Miller's happy place. Sleep.

# 18

Imagining I was going to alight from this huge plane completely overwhelmed by foreignness was some-what premature. Amsterdam's international terminal seems identical to Singapore's – the shops, the muzak, the sterility. It may as well be one of Perth's malls except the gift shops are full of clogs and windmills rather than celebrations of our local sporting teams. A Macca's easily finds me and I decide to commence my journey into the unknown, establishing myself early as a modern-day Indiana Jones by selecting the only item that doesn't also languish on the menu boards in Perth: the Chicken Mystic Burger. I have no explanation for its existence or its name, but it tastes more or less like you'd expect from a chain with approximately ten skazillion people served.

Miller has immediately switched into tour leader mode and advises that we can take a train direct from the airport to the centre of Amsterdam – Centraal Station. The extra 'a' promises further mystery so I encourage Miller to finish his generic Asian stir-fry, or 'lucky dip' as he describes it, and find the train as quickly as possible. As the train pushes to Centraal Station, I try to sort in my head what I am expecting to see. Recently my energy has been so focused on getting through the plane trip that I haven't had a chance to think ahead. I'm not just thinking of what to expect in this small part of this small country but in Europe as a whole.

It occurs to me that my brain has constructed a place already, like it does when you read a book. Seems my Europe is currently a blend of the experiences of Carrie from *Sex and the City* while in Paris, Elaine from *Seinfeld* in Tuscany, and the cast of *Friends* in London for one of Ross's weddings. *The Simpsons* also made it to Europe a bunch of times, but their colours are a bit too vivid to confer realism.

Though I'm not as tall as Miller I'm also not as dark, so it's me that people speak to in what I presume is Dutch. All I can say back is 'dank u wel', which apparently means 'thank you'. They could be calling me a slow-witted tourist for all I know and I'm thanking them like the tourist I am. Like with those Chinese-character shirts you see white folk wearing, to prove how travelled they are, that you imagine have Mandarin speakers laughing their heads off.

It is only as we exit Centraal Station for the first time that anything seems different and it properly sinks in that Denise, Jake and IDS are no longer near. Canals and bikes and cigarettes. Most everyone is on bikes and a lot of them are smoking. Take that, health Nazis.

It's still morning so there's no rush yet to find a place to stay, and anyhow my backpack is nearly as empty as Miller's now that I've eaten most of the comforting snacks I brought with me from home. We wander with the herd down the main boulevard, past buskers including Aborigines with didgeridoos and Peruvian guys bothering some wooden windpipes. Like most of the foreigners, we continually find ourselves walking across bike paths without realising, and the sound of the gentle bells the bikers use to wake us up and move us out of the way fill the air. One local lady who must have had her bell stolen is left calling out 'ding-a-ling' as people wander into her path.

'Dude, I think it's time for us to really get Amsterdammed!' Miller says as we walk past a busy frites vendor.

'Huh?' I respond.

'We need a coffee shop, and I don't mean for coffee,' he says, smiling.

We don't have to look very far to find one of the places that helps keep the city so mellow. Miller seems about the best person I could lose my pot virginity with, but I'm still a little concerned that he might be disappointed in his choice of travelling companion when he fully realises what a complete novice I am. Maybe he'll decide I'm a complete dud to enjoy these experiences with.

Thankfully he places the order at the counter and I'm happy just to take what I'm given – a joint that's twice as chunky and nearly twice as long as a regular cigarette. After lighting his similar-sized spliff as we sit in the window of the cosy little dope café, Miller passes me the lighter. I manage to ignite the right end, which has been twirled to a pencil point, and take a shallow draw back while scanning the other customers for signs of hysteria. Nobody, of course, is bothered to watch my attempts at making this look routine, and Miller's glassy eyes seem non-judgmental as well. I don't know if it's the marijuana but I suddenly feel completely without the fear that I might be making a mistake in leaving my world to follow this tour guide I barely know with his giant spliff held aloft in place of an umbrella.

Struggling to keep my joint alight, and not wanting to continually borrow the café's lighter, which is strapped to a big block of wood to stop it being either stolen or misplaced, I have to puff more furiously than I'd planned. Other smokers come and go, the more seasoned professionals sporting dreadlocks that make their entire heads look like they're sprouting the fronds of marijuana plants. Miller has no intention of walking out until it's virtually impossible for him to do so.

'How you doing, little buddy?' Miller asks after a while.

'I'm fine. Actually, I'm great!'

Miller laughs and shows the warmth of smile that I've begun to count on being there.

'What's the time?' I ask, as if it matters.

He looks around at the walls and says, 'Six o'clock.'

'At night?' I question, and he laughs again.

'Time to find a place to stay, buddy,' he says. We struggle to our feet and, only just remembering our bags, leave this dark and smoky place we've spent the best part of the day in.

Suddenly walking requires far more attention than I can ever remember it doing, and it's all I can do to not crash into the erratic people who continually speed towards me on the pavement. We find our way back to the Centraal Station area, where there are loads of cheap-looking hotels on the edge of the red-light district. Too trashed to negotiate much, we go into the first place that looks only moderately sleazy, and for 90 euros per night we get two single beds in a room that seems barely big enough for one. There's also a small bathroom that Oprah could fit into now but not then. Or is it then but not now? There's a dripping sound, and what floor space there is could do with a drying out. Other than that, our euros have got us some carpet you wouldn't want to walk on, a window showcasing an identical room just feet away, and a couple of hooks for hanging our meagre possessions from.

'This is just how I pictured my honeymoon with Zoe,' I say, trying to make light of the squalor.

'Let's dump our stuff and head out. It's time to leave your baggage unattended for a while!' Miller says to me.

After he's put on the black T-shirt that signifies evening, we make our way into the clubs and bars district. The cobblestoned streets add some charm which is completely sucked up by the smell of piss. We decide to keep walking until the smell dissipates, and we come upon a bar that has a huge deck area over the junction of two canals. Suddenly Amsterdam is looking like the brochures, and we celebrate by ordering a jug of beer that we'd never drink in Australia. The waitress – blonde and European slim – asks Miller how many glasses.

'Actually, make it two jugs,' Miller says, smiling his way into her favour.

'And how many glasses?' the girl asks again.

'No glasses, just straws,' Miller replies and she laughs as she turns to head off and fetch the beer.

'Dank u wel,' I call, and Miller repeats it but loaded with Aussie accent.

'Ash, check out the Eurotrash behind you,' he says.

I try to casually swing around on my stool and there they are – so many Donatella Versaces dressed in what looks to be ski gear even though the weather is far from frozen. Like everyone in this city, they are smoking as if their lives depend on it, while their unsightly bling catches the last light from a tired sun. There's no need to hide my interest in their species since they're completely oblivious to ours. Or maybe feigned lack of awareness is all part of the look.

'Where's the ski-lift?' Miller says to our returned waitress, nodding slightly towards the beautiful people.

'I've been trying to work out exactly where they are from, actually, but their accents and languages are such a jumble maybe they truly are the new Europeans,' our waitress replies, making me wonder where *she* is from.

'Are you Dutch?' I ask.

'No, originally from Copenhagen, but I am now studying in Amsterdam for two years. My name is Anita, by the way,' Anita responds.

I introduce myself and Miller and realise almost immediately that she's interested in Miller and that he's only human. We drink our jugs, and some more, using the glasses Anita insisted on bringing us. She begrudgingly services the Eurotrash with their vodka every now and then while looking over at Miller at any opportunity. Once her shift ends, Miller invites Anita to join us. She's lots of fun and runs through what we should see in Amsterdam. Our conversation gets me to thinking about the fact we really have no plans as to where we might go next or how long we're going to stay anywhere. I guess that's sort of how I've lived the previous part of my life too, but before it meant staying still and no change whereas now it means being free and the opportunity for constant change.

'I'm not sure I should cycle all the way back to my place tonight,' Anita says to Miller as we leave the bar and skirt around the Eurotrash, who are farewelling each other with extravagant multi-cheek kisses.

'Maybe you should stay at our place,' Miller says, and I wonder whether to enquire how she feels about sleeping standing up.

'Thanks,' Anita says, and I'm just glad I'm well drunk as I'd be freaking out about trying to sleep less than a metre away from this horny couple. Back at the hotel, the old guy on the desk gives us a raised eyebrow as we fetch the key and make our way up to the room I can only hope has given birth to more space since we left it a bunch of hours ago.

Anita shows no surprise at how diminutive the room is and asks to use the bathroom.

'Dude, I hope you don't mind', says Miller as I hear Anita struggling to find elbow room in the closet with plumbing.

'It's fine. I plan to fall asleep fast,' I say, shedding the same clothes I've been wearing since Perth and leaping into bed with my face turned towards the wall.

'Thanks, buddy.' Miller musses my hair and turns the light out as Anita joins him in his bed.

For purposes of making my strike rate with women seem the best it can, I've always counted blow jobs as sex. This definition helps my score to just below respectable. I'm guessing Miller is well past counting as I try to do the impossible and force myself into sleep. However, I can't avoid hearing Anita gnaw away on Miller's cock for what seems like hours.

Though I appreciate Miller saving me the ignominy of listening to them fully smearing each other with their DNA, it sounds like Anita hasn't eaten in weeks. All the while Miller must be working hard not to groan, but I think I can hear the smile on his face. Finally our friend from Copenhagen retires and it's pretty clear I am going to be the last one to finally fall asleep. I focus on counting Eurotrash in my head, roll over and try to ignore my hard-on. Unsuccessfully.

# 19

This morning I wake to the sound of pealing bells rather than departing planes. This signifies two important things: that I'm elsewhere and that somehow I got to sleep at some point last night. In the end it wasn't Miller and the very hungry Anita who kept me awake for the best part of the long night but some guy snoring on the other side of a really thin wall. It wasn't even snoring so much as that noise contented cats make, only magnified. Human purring. That's it.

The controlling part of me hopes that Anita will make herself scarce so Miller can devote his day to making sure I do something with it. Once they realise I'm awake they get out of bed and get dressed.

'Morning, buddy,' Miller says, leaving out the 'How'd you sleep?' bit.

'Hey,' I reply. 'Hey Anita.' I use her name in case Miller has forgotten it.

'Anita's going to get going,' Miller tells me, for her benefit.

As I sit up in bed, Anita comes over to kiss me goodbye. She makes for my lips, but given where her mouth has been recently I turn my head quickly and she does three rounds of my cheeks like a good European.

Miller happily takes her phone number, though neither of us ended up bringing our mobiles. I guess he could use a payphone, if they still exist. Not having a phone makes little difference to me and I'm not sure how many people Miller has even told he is no longer in Australia. As Anita is the first person we've met here, I suggest we might come and see her at work in the next few days, and she runs us through her shifts. Miller walks Anita away as I busy myself getting dressed and gathering our maps, brochures and other crap that will help steer us through a day.

After grabbing some pastries studded with chocolate, we walk along one of the main canals that the map swears will get us to one of the best street markets in all of Europe. Once we come upon the kilometre of complete crap that has been piled along both sides of a closed-off road, we decide there'll be no need to bother searching out street markets again for the rest of the trip. If you ignored the occasional wayward car pushing stragglers up against the stalls you'd swear this was unchanged from what it would have been like during the war. World War Two, that is, not this current Iraq thing.

Having grown up helping out in my parents' grocery shop, I am not mesmerised by the fruits sitting uncut and unpackaged in the morning sun. But Miller is. Though he'll try anything, unlike me – the old me – it seems Miller's experiences of food, though varied, have all been mostly of the sort you can collect from takeaway joints and 24-hour convenience stores.

'It never occurs to me to eat actual fruit – like with a skin,' he says.

It gets me thinking again about the differences between growing up Ash and growing up Jet. I'd written down the spelling of Miller's original surname in the notebook Jake gave me just before leaving. At some point I plan to do something with it, though I'm not entirely sure what. Miller certainly gives the impression he wants nothing to do with the woman who vamoosed when he was five, leaving him expecting everyone else to do the same. Maybe he silently wants to know more about her but doesn't want to be the one to do the looking. Giving his mother a second opportunity to ditch him is something this tough-looking guy is likely to want to avoid. It could be that vetting that possibility might just be how best I can repay Miller for all he's done for me in the way of widening up my world – figuratively and literally.

'Do you ever think about looking for your mother?' I ask boldly as he sets to choosing some uncanned fruit.

'Did that. Every morning for a while. And she wasn't there,' Miller replies, not looking for sympathy. 'If she wants to find me then that's up to her,' he adds before changing the subject.

From an old guy who doesn't appear to have moved from his stall since the German tanks rolled through, I buy a peach with a furry skin that makes me feel like

I'm taking a bite out of a rodent. Miller chooses a huge green apple that looks just like it must have when it fell out of the tree. He passes it to me to take the first bite, given my previous experience with actual fresh fruit and all. So while Miller is fast introducing me to a world outside my own, all I can lead him through is the world of unpackaged fruit.

'It took guts, you know,' Miller tells me, and I'm not entirely sure who or what he's referring to.

'What, biting the apple first?' I ask, mocking him.

'No, coming here.'

'It's just a market,' I say, remaining obtuse.

'Very funny. No, I mean Europe. Leaving Perth.'

'Well, you did it as well.'

'It's different. I wasn't leaving anything. And you also had better reason to think you were risking life and death by just getting on the plane.'

'So, am I your superhero?' I ask, trying to keep it light.

'Nah, but you're more than you think,' he replies, before dropping the core of his apple into some loud-mouthed American tourist's open backpack as it meanders ahead of us.

In fact, for almost the entire length of the market Miller points out what he refers to as 'pig people'. These are people who take up more than their share of everything. By pig he doesn't mean fat, but those people who speak loudest, demand more, and basically remain oblivious to those they step in front of, knock over, race ahead of, and push past. After Miller has sprayed the crowd with a bunch of 'fuck offs', 'blow mes' and sarcastic 'you're welcomes', we leave behind the market and the rustling sounds of a hundred tourists' cheap parkas, Miller declaring that pigs are no real use alive.

'At least sheep give you wool, cows milk, chickens eggs,' he says.

'Goats cheese, horses rides, dogs loyalty,' I add, continuing a theme that has never occurred to me before. 'What about cats?' I ask.

'Well, I suppose they give old people company, so let them live,' Miller replies kindly.

'Birds?'

'Hope.'

'So it's just pigs that must die?' I ask the guru.

'Uh-huh. And then we got bacon.'

Given we've made a pact to stay well away from art galleries, museums and cathedrals, we debate whether Anita's suggestion of checking out Anne Frank's house breaks the agreement. In the end we decide it's a house and so we enter. It's hard not to be affected by the photographs and the diary excerpts on the walls. And being in the actual house makes the movie depiction seem ordinary. Hearing the same bells that they must have heard every hour while being stuck in this place is something you can only try to imagine, knowing you'll never truly relate. Recalling that the last bell count we've heard means we're in the fours, somewhere between four and five, makes it time to consume something more than fruit.

Nearby there's a small café where the patrons are all out the front watching the passers-by while soaking in the afternoon sun. None of them face each other. It reminds me of television sit-coms where scenes in restaurants have the characters sitting in a line or a semicircle booth formation so there's room for the camera crew.

We take our places out front, also sitting beside each other rather than opposite, and enjoy the break from filling time with conversation. The waiter brings fresh beers at just the right intervals and again I am thinking nice thoughts. Not all routine sucks, or so it seems.

Miller gets chatting with the girl next to him and introduces her to me as Karin. She's even cuter than Anita and enjoys beer as much as us, so is pretty well perfect. Her accent is American and she explains she's just completed college in Oregon and is spending the summer travelling before returning to the US to work as a vet. You've got to love someone who fixes broken animals, and Miller seems to already. By the time she's done explaining to Miller exactly where her hotel is, I'm pretty well decided that I should make myself scarce soon, as I know Miller is unlikely to leave unless I do. Karin leans into his ear and whispers,

'Do you want to come back for some coffee?'

Miller surprises me, and Karin, by saying 'No', but then adds, 'However, sex would be *very* nice.' They both laugh. Time to say my goodbyes. Miller subtly checks his wing-man is cool. And I am. The thing is I'm actually looking forward to having some time alone. I kind of need to sort myself out.

As I head off, Karin is saying to Miller that she doesn't normally have one-night stands, and I hear Miller assuring her that it's still daylight. They both laugh again and so do I.

Walking around the streets and along the canals in the general direction of our hotel, but with no reason not to get lost, feels unreal and I take longer than necessary because it really doesn't matter.

Back at the dump, I lie on my bed listening to my iPod until it's dark enough outside for me to feel cool about devoting the rest of the night to jerking off. When, I wonder, will I tire of fantasising about Zoe? I try and steer myself to Salma Hayak or that blonde chick in the Heineken ad, but my head's Zoe-screensaver overrides all others. Either way, having the room to myself for the night so I can enjoy a masturbate-a-thon is far superior to listening to Miller being blown to sleep.

# 20

I awake for the second morning to the sound of bells – it's starting to feel like something from a sentimental movie, if you ignore the squalid surroundings. That and the persistent smell that I've not quite identified. It suddenly occurs to me that it's sewerage – or is it sewage? Either way it's shit and it stinks.

There's no Miller in the other bed, and though it feels quite early, I'm too slow-witted to have counted the number of bells, so the only thing I can be certain of is that it's daytime. I decide to beat the crowds and hit the streets.

Being a creature of habit is a hard thing to shake, and I find myself already establishing routines in this new place, returning to the same patisserie as yesterday and consuming an identical puff of calories. Though I have no real plan for the day and no way of hooking up with Miller other than waiting in our room, I revel again in having no set schedule and spend the morning wandering, sitting by canals, and people-watching.

With my legs dangling over the side of a small, shaded canal, I drop bits of chocolate-studded pastry onto a posse of ducks cruising by. The ducks don't share well at all. Once the pastry is gone they continue to busy themselves pecking around my feet to remind me of the purpose of my being here at all. To feed them. Showing them empty palms is not a language they're familiar with, and so they continue to nip at my shoes. For a long time.

I try and calculate what time it is back in Perth, and think about what Jake, Denise, Evan and Zoe will all be up to today. It's about time I checked my emails and at least let Jake and Denise know I survived the flight and all is well.

Without Miller I would be completely anchorless, and questions of how reliable my new friend is and how much I should depend on him buzz about me like small aircraft around an Empire-State-Building-hugging King Kong. There are no guarantees from him, no assurances, just his continued presence. Then again, he could say the same of me. I think about my friendship with Miller. It's fair to say neither of us is inundated by close connections, though he's always maintained that's of little concern to him. It's hard to know if anyone really feels that way, but I'm the first to admit I want friendships more solid than those built of mere convenience.

Thinking about why I'm travelling, I realise that I'm not so much here to get away from Perth but to get something more than I've had – to find something real, something of my own. It would also be nice to have sex occasionally, with someone else preferably. Sex is like magnesium in the diet: I don't need a lot – but some is vital.

Thinking too much is as good for you as drinking too much, so I dump the ducks and break my agreement with Miller by heading for a museum.

The Dutch Resistance Museum sits in the shadows of Amsterdam Zoo. The zoo has a line of excited animal gawkers out front, whereas the museum is queue-less and as empty inside as it sounds. I wander through the winding exhibit and find myself lost in the stories of individuals caught in way bigger things than I can imagine.

Just as I'm coming to the conclusion that birds were really only good for eating, I come across the story of the carrier pigeons. Apparently, during the height of the Nazi occupation of The Netherlands, allied planes would drop baskets containing pigeons into villages throughout the countryside and along the coast and borders. The baskets each floated down, beneath small attached parachutes, to hopefully be recovered by resistance-keen Dutch villagers.

The pigeons had small canisters fastened to their sinewy ankles and in the canisters there were notes in Dutch asking for the finder to feed back information about troop numbers and locations. The locals were asked to write answers to the intelligence-gathering questions, put the paper back into the canister, and release the birds, who then amazingly found their way back to England. I'll never swipe at pigeons the same way again.

Now that I've been through a museum I feel like a bona fide tourist and decide to top it off by seeking out a Burger King for the purposes of comparing their menu to Hungry Jack's and, of course, to stuff my face. Most of my BK cohorts are wearing confidence-promoting banners on their T-shirts such as 'Princess' or 'Sexy Thing'.

'Hey, buddy!'

It's Miller.

'Where'd you come from?' I ask as Miller plonks himself next to me and my Whopper Meal.

'Just caught sight of you as I was walking past. I went back to the hotel but you'd gone already.'

I look at Miller and it's as if his face has only recently been wiped clean of anxiousness.

'Yeah, actually got up early to do some stuff,' I say, nearly adding 'How was Karin?' before deciding that would sound real wrong.

It's just now that I notice that Miller is in neither his day-white nor night-black T-shirt. In fact he has some fresh tourist shop T-shirt that boldly announces '9.25'. Miller sees me looking at the shirt and says, 'I've run out of clean clothes. Oh yeah, had to borrow your deodorant as well. And some toothpaste. Shampoo too.'

'No worries,' I say, and it isn't. In fact it's sort of a relief he's not beyond needing something from another person.

His T-shirt is working some magic as most of the women in the place seem to like its message. A couple of the guys as well.

'This T-shirt is pretty effective,' he says. 'You can borrow it if you like?'

'It's too long,' I respond.

'I can change the "9" to an "8" if you like,' Miller says, smiling.

'No, I meant *the shirt* is too long,' I reply, laughing to mask my blushing.

Miller finishes off my meal, then he and his grande T-shirt guide me through the tourist-laden streets in search of a coffee shop to waste the rest of the afternoon in. Before finding a place with the right ambience for Miller, we literally run into, and knock over, a cute-looking chick backing away from some guy collecting money to save dolphins. She apologises profusely, in English as we help her to her feet. She has dark shoulder-length hair, olive skin, and teeth as white as most anyone on television.

'My name is Cali,' she says, smiling and shaking us both by the hand.

'As in California?' I think this question while Miller actually asks it.

'No,' Cali says kindly, oblivious to Miller's T-shirt.

'I'm Ash, and this is Miller,' I say as she finishes dusting herself off.

'Why are dolphins so special?' she asks softly, looking back at the fish fanatic she'd swerved to avoid. 'I mean, we worry about dolphins caught in nets but we are busy taking a bite out of a tuna. Poor old tuna, I say,' she says in her delightful take on the English language.

I'm just enjoying listening to her, immediately attracted to her sense of humour, but Miller has to add, 'Whales too. They're all fair game!'

Cali, you can tell, thinks that's a bit much but says nothing.

'Where are you from?' I ask. I rarely asked this question in Perth because the answer was pretty well always the same. Oh, and I never really met anyone new anyhow.

'Antiparos,' she replies, and I don't know whether to fake knowledge of it or just go 'Huh?'

'Huh?' Miller says, beating me to it.

'It's an island from Greece, south of Athens,' says Cali without a hint of judgement about non-Europeans and their famed aversion to the world geography category.

Cali tells us she's here visiting her sister, who lives in Amsterdam with her Dutch husband, and I tell her where we're from and where we're staying and she says she knows it, again without looking horrified. After a while, with my pleasure at Cali's humour and smile rising exponentially, we say our goodbyes and continue on to find our place for the afternoon sun. Miller works his T-shirt as I joke with him that we've just met our first person he's not immediately slept with.

# 21

Today I wake, on what seems to be the first morning ever, without Zoe in my head. Of course she's in my head now, but it was still quite an achievement.

And another first: Miller is in his bed, by himself. It's quite nice just lying here waiting for him to wake up, so I daydream between bells. Sort of like being at school again.

'Hey, buddy,'

I quit staring at the ceiling and roll over to face Miller.

'Hey,' I reply.

'How'd you sleep?' he asks.

'Fine. Any jetlag is now well gone,' I say.

'So what are we gonna do today – whatever fuckin' day it is!' Miller says, more like a statement than a question.

'Let's just see what comes.'

This is a new policy for me but I love it already.

'Cool.'

Neither of us is in any rush to get the day going, so we just lie in bed and talk the morning away.

Miller opens up more than he has before, even more than when he's been drunk or stoned, and gives me additional information about his mother, like her first name. It occurs to me that Miller mightn't be averse to me searching her out but is too proud to directly ask me. This way if she's untraceable or disinterested then he'd never know. Also, to his knowledge, she won't have been given the opportunity to dump him a second time. This is mostly unsubstantiated conjecture on my part but I'm quite good at that. I decide I'll Google her when I eventually make it to an internet café and see if that leads to anything. If nothing transpires, Miller will be none the wiser but will be saved the possible ignominy of getting fucked over again. I really have to write to Jake as well.

We also talk a bit about what work we might be able to get, and decide that hospitality is probably going to be the easiest and most transportable. Tourist places probably only require English and might be a bit lax about working visas. Our money will last a while but I'd sort of like to meet some other travellers, and finding work may be as good a way as any to do this. Miller should have no worries getting work in a bar but I'm going to struggle given I've never done anything other than IDS, and that hardly jumps off the résumé. So I'm on the lookout for a particularly easy job to get. A place with low expectations, to match my own.

Miller says, 'Set your expectations at zero and it's impossible to be let down.'

I assume he's talking about more than just working a McJob.

By the time we're done talking, the bells have started back at one. As we attempt to get through the hotel's foyer before being asked again to set a definite check-out date, the old guy calls out that we have a message. I immediately think of some sort of problem with Jake, then realise this would be impossible given Denise has no idea where we're staying.

The note is from Cali, the Greek girl we met yesterday. She must have remembered our names and where we're staying. I'm already impressed by her listening powers. Apparently her sister is having a bit of a cocktail party tonight and she thought we might want to meet some locals. My first reaction is that Miller and I are not very cocktail party. Miller, on the other hand, is immediately into it.

'It sounds very adult,' I say, sounding truly lame.

'Dude, you're 27. In a few years you'll be 30,' he says.

'Good at maths, huh?' I respond.

It's okay for him – he has a black T-shirt. Without Miller around I would easily justify ignoring the note, avoiding anything unfamiliar.

'Hey, little caged animal, howsabout you just dip your toe in the wild and see what it's like!' Miller returns.

'Well, okay, so long as you don't fuck off with the first Euro-chick who wants to see the rest of your tattoo,' I counter.

'Deal,' Miller concludes, and so cocktail party it is.

We ask the old guy if he recognises the address and he gives us vague directions, so now all we need do is be sure to get nice and wasted in a coffee shop beforehand. Hopefully that'll help make me even partway confident enough to last however long a cocktail party lasts.

# 22

Luckily, Miller, as it transpires, travels with several black T-shirts at his disposal, as I imagine the Queen of England does. Depending on age and the cumulative hours they've spent in laundromat dryers, some of his black Ts are still Miller size, but others have shrunk, by varying amounts, to better fit the rest of us.

I fuck around with hair product and cologne in front of the miniscule mirror in the tiny bathroom. Again, I note that Miller doesn't even check himself in the mirror. He knows what he looks like.

The directions the old guy gave us to Cali's sister's place hold up well and we arrive at the apartment building not long after the bell announces the time Cali put in her note. I try to block out my fear scenario for this evening, which has Cali not being there when we make our way into the party and us having to explain who the fuck we are. Miller, on the other hand, looks as relaxed as Paris Hilton in front of a camera.

I buzz the intercom and a female answers. I tell her who we are and we get buzzed in. By the time we make it to the right door, on the fifth level, Cali is there to greet us and I feel heaps better about coming. She shakes our hands and welcomes us into the spacious and ultra-modern living room. The furniture is sleek and expensive-looking. Like the people.

It's extremely bright inside but there are no lights on – it's just that the sun is still up and virtually the entire apartment is walled in glass. Seems the interiors depicted in *The Jetsons* have finally arrived and it's in Amsterdam of all places. A wide balcony runs the entire far side of the apartment, which overlooks the street and gives a view of a large section of Amsterdam itself. I see several people in the room we enter wearing sunglasses and normally I'd be quick to ridicule them, but I can feel my own retinas narrowing while making the noise a camera makes when its zoom lens retreats.

Cali is in no way surprised that we've actually fronted, and introduces us immediately to her sister, Alexa, and Alexa's Dutch husband, Emil. Alexa is obviously a bit older than Cali but shares her rich, dark looks, while Emil wears a stiff suit and looks like he most likely sleeps in one as well.

'So, Cali tells me you are Australian,' Alexa says without a single reference to crocodiles or sharks.

'Yes, I think my family pretty well goes back to the original convicts who were shipped out there. They were the last ones to have travelled, too, it seems,' I reply in my best cocktail party banter copied from Niles and Frasier.

Cali smiles and I'm immediately glad that Miller dragged me here.

'Miller looks like his family could easily come from the part of the world Cali and mine does,' Alexa says, nodding at my friend in case we're confused as to who Miller is.

'Can't say, really,' Miller responds.

'They're Greek,' says Emil, misunderstanding Miller.

'I know where *they're* from. It's me I'm not sure about,' Miller replies.

Following that conversation killer, Cali offers us some drinks that are the colour of blood, and shuffles us onto the balcony to check out the view as the sun lowers. I make like I'm mesmerised by the horizon and city panorama and junk, like you're meant to be, but I'd prefer to check out some of the other guests, who appear way more interesting. At a distance anyways.

Cali spots me checking out an older couple further down the balcony and says, 'I should introduce you around.'

'It's fine,' I reply, preferring to people-watch over people-meet.

'Come on, buddy, you're no longer stuck in Perth,' says Miller, who's still a bit stoned from our session this afternoon, whereas I'd been a bit too nervous to really draw back on my joints.

'Ash, Miller, this is lady Marcia and this is partner Herman,' says Cali, introducing us (in her own special way) to the middle-aged couple who've been keeping their own company on the balcony. I'm certain Marcia is a lady but doubt she's got the title, though she holds herself in that manner.

We all shake hands, though Marcia – as aloof as a cat which has just eaten, and smoking a cigarette in the manner of a forties film star – can barely muster the effort to look at us as she proffers her cold paw. Herman is a lot friendlier, with a shaved head and a thick gold earring he's stolen from a pirate, though I can feel Miller suffering the sight of his crisp lilac polo shirt, the collar at attention, and his loafers without socks.

'Ash and Miller visit us from Australia,' Cali says to Herman, since Marcia's attention has long since wandered. She makes it sound as though we've come all this way just for this evening. Maybe we have.

'That's okay,' Herman says nicely enough, though you've got to wonder what he means.

Cali struggles to build something to bond us with, and offers, 'Herman and Marcia are also in Amsterdam for this first time. They live in Berlin.'

'So you're Herman the German,' Miller says, as Kramer might.

Cali laughs, so I do, and even Herman does, though he's probably heard it before. Marcia doesn't. Then again, she likely wasn't even listening.

Miller offers to get the lot of us some drinks and Cali guides him to the bar, so I continue to talk with Herman as Marcia feigns a lack of familiarity with any of the pop-culture topics I choose to initiate discussion about. Herman and I finally settle on film and, like a lot of Europeans apparently seem to, he has a great interest in movies.

'Does Germany have its own Oscars?' I ask.

'We do but it is much less important than the American ones. In fact, it is better for a German film to win a best foreign language film award in the US.'

'Do German films cover the same sort of genres as American ones?' I say, continuing the interview.

'Yes, but we do not do so much the blockbusters and it seems that Oscar judges prefer to reward portrayals of people with disabilities or impersonations of famous people like Virginia Woolf and Truman Capote. Our actors are asked to do more with less, I think. For less money as well!'

I notice that Herman's speech is a bit slurred, though not in a drunk way, and it's sort of cool that he doesn't allow this imperfection to stop him talking. And he can talk, which is a relief, since Miller is stuffing around at the bar, and without Herman I'd be totally entertaining myself. Herman tries to bring Marcia into the conversation, but she's now holding her mobile in her non-cigarette hand and says she can't talk as she's expecting a call. Nice.

Finally Miller brings out four large vials of blood and I look back inside to see Cali with other people she needs to help mingle. As I watch her, allowing Miller to take up the conversation with Herman, it occurs to me that I've yet to find out how long she will be in Amsterdam and even whether she has a job back in Greece. Or a boyfriend.

I decide to wander inside, where it has actually got dark enough for pretty well everybody but the genuine wankers to be sunglasses-free. With extra blood in my veins I find myself going up to a Russian-looking lady and commenting on the beautiful view that is gradually disappearing.

'I'm sorry, I do not speak your language,' the old lady says in English.

Just as I'm about to challenge her on that, a tough-looking guy I presume is her son walks up to me and adds, 'That's about the extent of my mother's English, unfortunately. My name's Marat, by the way.'

'I'm Ash. How do you know Cali?' I ask, suddenly hoping that the response does not include the word 'girlfriend'.

'My girlfriend is Emil's sister,' he says, and that's a perfectly acceptable use of the word.

Cali appears from nowhere and seems happy that I've blended into the group.

'Would you like to tour the rest of the apartment?' she asks.

I have little interest in the apartment.

'That'd be great,' I say.

Both bedrooms, in contrast to the rest of the apartment I've seen, are window-free. The main bathroom is littered with candles and coloured soaps, and the kitchen, at the far end of the living area, contains a giant green bird in a slightly larger cage.

'Anders can talk,' Cali declares while stroking his big head, which must be crammed with brain.

'Hello, Anders. How are you?' I say politely.

'He speaks Dutch,' Cali says for Anders. 'Oh, and Bird as well, of course,' she adds with a soft laugh, leaning slightly into me. She must have had a vial of blood as well.

'So this dumb animal speaks one more language than me,' I mock protest.

'And he can fly also,' Cali says admiringly.

'So can I now,' I declare, and then fill Cali in on the fact that this trip is really the first time I've left my home town – information which leads her into telling me a little about Antiparos and the rest of her family back there.

By the time I've finished hearing about the small restaurant her family runs on the island and discovering that Cali is actually at the end of her visit and returns to Antiparos tomorrow, the apartment is even darker and yet still no-one has put any lights on.

Alexa has been in and out of the kitchen as Cali and I have been talking, ferrying food out onto small tables in the living area. This has been a popular move and most everybody in the room has dived onto the snacks and canapés with boundless enthusiasm. So much for the notion that cool Europeans refrain from something so ugly as the consumption of food. The exception is a very slim and elegant lady Miller pointed out earlier, naming her Lara Thin Boyle. She avoids the food altogether, though she has the strength to speak, unlike Marcia on the balcony, and talks at whoever has the fullest mouth, which is mostly me.

Most people in the room are probably Dutch – sharing a certain formality with Emil and avoiding the use of English, unlike those from further-flung places who've been forced to use any English they have so as to fit in.

In the dim light I grab what looks to be some sort of exotic nut from a small white bowl and am about to eat it when Cali grabs my hand and tells me I'm about to devour somebody's discarded olive pip. Thankfully no-one else has seen, except for Anders the bird, who says something in Dutch, and I swear a couple of people look at me with barely restrained smiles.

'You're not really a cocktail party sort of person, are you?' says Cali, hitting the bullseye in one.

'Yeah. Not real suave am I?'

'No, thank goodness,' Cali replies gently.

Reinvigorated, I dip a mini meatball into a bowl of sauce that Alexa has just laid out.

'Great sauce, Alexa – is it Greek?' I ask.

'It's ketchup,' she replies, and gives me the same soft smile her sister shares. Thankfully Anders misses this latest faux pas.

Cali grabs me by the arm and drags me back to the kitchen, where she finds a Post-it note. She writes down an address and tells me that if Miller and I make it as far as the Greek islands we should come and see her.

This Post-it note might just be more precious than the one Denise intercepted from Zoe. I flash it at my nemesis, the bird, and say, 'Oh, that's right, you can't read.'

Cali laughs and pushes me out of the kitchen so Anders and I won't bicker any more.

Returning to the balcony, I find Miller still talking to Herman and tell them there's food inside but that it's pretty dark so to be careful what they eat. Marcia gets up to go inside and stumbles briefly, and Miller whispers 'mad cow disease' in my ear.

Herman follows her, after telling us that it was nice to meet us, and when he's gone I ask Miller if he'd noticed the way Herman the German slurred.

'Probably from a lifetime of biting his tongue,' says Miller.

I don't get much of a chance to talk with Cali again as she's pretty well busy talking to the United Nations of guests, but the best part of the evening is when Miller and me are making our farewells and I catch Cali telling Marat that she's really glad she'd invited us.

To overhear someone say something good about you is loads better than to have them say it to you.

# 23

'Between the two of us we're down to less than four thousand euros,' Miller concludes a few days later, after we decide to take a break from spending and spend a moment counting.

Finally Miller is referring to our total, rather than continually reminding me he started with less while steadfastly refusing to allow me to help him out. I had told Miller the other day that if he was going to get a job then so would I.

'Well, I guess we've had a fun break but it's probably time to look for that work now,' I say.

'Here, in Amsterdam?' he says.

'Why not? We haven't really thought much about where we want to go next anyways,' I say.

'Fair enough – so how do we go about it?' says Miller, who has had even more jobs than women, and that's saying something, yet is asking *me* how to get employed.

'When I went to the internet café the other day, among the skinny ferals who spend more money there than on food at real cafés, there was a bunch of notices on the board about working in bars and hotels and restaurants. They're obviously pitching those sorts of jobs to travellers, so maybe we should start there.'

'Let's do it,' Miller agrees, and we leave the coffee shop we've spent the last couple of hours in and head towards the internet café I'd recently used to write to Jake, and Denise, and even Evan.

Miller makes his way straight to the noticeboard, ignoring the internet, which I have a suspicion he's completely clueless about. Meanwhile, I log onto a PC to check my emails. Jake and Evan have responded but there's nothing from Denise.

I check the message from Jake, who sounds really upbeat but doesn't mention my big sister at all. There's lots of local news, and he talks about Lucy, as well as questioning me about my travel plans.

Evan's email, of course, is all about work. I get the impression he actually believes I might be missing it and regretting my decision to leave. The fact is I can barely remember what IDS stands for despite how long I worked there. Evan only mentions Zoe in passing, just as she appears in my thoughts now. But it's not like my head is empty when Zoe's not in it – I find myself mentioning Cali more and more, and Miller has lots of fun ribbing me each time I finagle her into any random conversation.

Handing me some of the torn-off contact numbers from the job notices, Miller says to me, 'Here you go – these are yours.'

'But what jobs are they for?' I ask.

'That's part of the fun. You just gotta ring up and ask about the position they have going and wing it from there. It's called Job Surprise.' Miller laughs, thinking I'll have a conniption.

'Fine. What the fuck do I care? What about yours?' I say, surprising Miller by accepting the challenge.

'Same sort of places as yours – only bars instead of cafes. This way we'll meet double the number of people.'

We both hit the payphones and Miller sorts himself an interview for later in the week at the very same bar we met Copenhagen Anita in the night we arrived. She didn't speak Dutch either, so obviously English alone is cool, and Miller, like me, pretty well has that covered.

It takes longer for me to score a meeting, but eventually someone who sounds like she trains hit squads agrees I can come by right away.

'Ice & Slice' is in fact a gelataria and pizza restaurant, though from what I can tell as I enter, not a single Italian works here. The fact it is up front and centre in the main tourist strip means any degree of cultural authenticity is not required. Already I'd had plenty of Chinese and Japanese food in Amsterdam cooked and served by people who'd likely never used chopsticks or eaten raw fish in their lives, so this place is no different.

I wait at the counter till Doris, the manager I'd spoken to on the phone, is finished berating a cool-looking worker with dreadlocks for letting one of his dreads drop into the mango sorbet as he was reaching to scoop from the chilli-chocolate tub. Doris is actually Dutch – one of the few I've met here in Amsterdam, other than at Cali's sister's place. She's very tall for a woman, not much shorter than Miller in fact, and has wavy hair the colour of the hazelnut-coffee gelato. She speaks in English so she can be understood by staff and tourists, though I can still barely make out what she's saying. The accent she serves her words in is very unforgiving but I do ascertain she wants to give me a trial, starting immediately, as several Austrian girls working here have chosen today to decide life is too short and head back to the Alps.

'Madness – you go out back. Clean! Give me Lars.' I think she's talking to the mango-dipped dreadlock dude.

'It's Magnus, not Madness,' he mutters as he saunters off to the kitchen, and I'm guessing he won't still be here when Doris is handing out gold watches for ten years' service.

As Doris runs me through how to scoop and serve the ice-creams without any part of my body falling into them, I ask about the pay rates and she shouts something about five euros. I hope this is the quarter-hour rate but assume it's not. A guy about my age comes out from the back of the restaurant and Doris introduces him as Lars. He seems more to Doris's liking than Madness, and she lets him take over my training so she can stalk Madness some more.

Lars is Nordically good-looking, with short blond hair, matching stubble, and standard-issue blue eyes.

I tell him my name and where I'm from, which is pretty well a ritual now.

'I'm from Iceland,' he says in perfect English.

'Do your family all live back there?' I ask, doing my best not to mention Björk.

'Yes, my dad's a weatherman on television and my two sisters and brother are all older than me but live still in Reykjavik.'

'Your dad's famous then?'

'Well, in Iceland, yes.'

'And so there are four kids in your family?' I make polite conversation to help pass the time as I head towards earning my first five euros.

'Yeah,' Lars replies. 'One of each.'

I have no idea what that means but decide to leave it. We talk a bunch more about Iceland, and his questions about Perth have me a little embarrassed about how ordinary my hometown sounds.

'Don't worry, Iceland is pretty barren as well,' Lars says to make me feel okay about my uninspiring description of where I come from.

Doris breaks up our running conversation intermittently over the next three hours as Lars serves approximately ten times more customers than me. I do get better as time passes, and the warm weather certainly pushes a lot of tourists through the doors. The pizza side of the business is pretty well on hold till the evenings, apparently, and only if the customer seems really to your liking do you bother saying anything other than 'Unfortunately the ovens are not yet hot enough.'

As I'm starting to tire from working for the first time in weeks, well years really, Doris again joins me and Lars and asks him, right in front of me, if he thinks I should be kept on. Lars tells Doris that he reckons so and she informs me I'm to come back tomorrow at ten in the morning.

I shake Lars's hand goodbye as Doris approaches a customer with 'Can I introduce you to some ice-creams?'

This makes me laugh and I can see Lars behind Doris, his back quivering with laughter.

Heading towards the hotel, I start to calculate how many hours I'll need to work to make some decent money, and it really doesn't bear thinking about. The quickest way to feel better is to find a zebra crossing and stop some traffic.

# 24

'Four sausage and egg McMuffins, please,' I say to the Burger King lackey, who doesn't bother to reprimand me that at BK you're encouraged *not* to call them McMuffins.

'Dank u wel,' I tell the probably non-Dutch-speaking attendant, and ferry our breakfasts to the table Miller is diverting attention towards.

I'm reminded of the literally hundreds of times I'd bought my dinner at Hungry Jack's back in Perth, preferring to eat it as I walked home rather than have complete strangers contemplate my lack of company and dull life.

Today, however, I relax as people I will never see again glance over at our table. It's Miller and his tattoos or Miller and his casual good looks they can't ignore. And the thing is, he doesn't see them at all.

If I went back to Perth tomorrow and had to sit alone in a Hungry Jack's, without the aid of Miller absorbing all the gazes, would I be any better placed to deflect the opinions of the Perth folk? Have I learnt anything from

Miller, who swears that they all care far less about me, about anyone else really, than I think?

'So what time is your interview?' I ask Miller, who is already onto his second McMuffin.

'Tonight, actually. I guess I'll just hang out today while you work and we can catch up later. Maybe Copenhagen Anita will be working,' he says with a smile.

Working at Ice & Slice hasn't been as bad as I feared, and the week has gone pretty fast. Lars and I are on the same shifts and we get on well. And Doris provides lots of laughs. Unintentionally of course.

'No Doris today. I'm in charge so let's close the doors,' Lars announces, joking unfortunately, when I arrive after leaving Miller to another day on his own.

'If only,' I say. 'But I wouldn't be surprised if she walks past behind dark glasses every hour to see what's happening.'

Doris, however, as far as we know, doesn't come by until we're both about to leave, just before six. She does an inspection of the entire restaurant with only a few complaints before letting us go, and readies herself to make the also-just-arrived Madness's night a misery.

'You have me tonight, Madness,' Doris says with the hint of a smile, 'This is good, huh?'

'No, it's great,' Madness mumbles just loud enough for me and Lars to hear and sets to tying his dreads back, though I sense he'd rather be wrapping them around Doris's throat.

'So what are you up to this evening?' Lars asks me as the sun hits our faces out on the street.

'No plans. Jet has his interview about now and he'll probably hook up with a girl we met who works at the same bar,' I reply, using Miller's first name, which Lars thinks is the bee's knees, though he pronounces it 'Yet'.

'Cool. Let's grab some food and bask in this sun,' Lars says, and it sounds like a plan.

Obviously Italian food is out, so we locate a place on a sidestreet that dispenses cheapish warmed snacks via a huge bank of vending machines and decide that the impersonal nature of the service is just what we're after. We walk until we find a canal that has a small jetty sitting just above the water line and dangle our feet into the abyss. The packaged salmonella snacks taste better than they look.

'So where are you and Yet going to go next?' Lars asks.

'Not sure. We haven't really got the map out, but with our frequent flyer points we can go almost anywhere,' I reply. 'What about you?'

'I'm going to drive to Berlin. Leave in a week.'

'You have a *car*?'

'No I booked it on an internet site that lists cars needing to be driven somewhere for whatever reasons. If you drive and deliver it to where it needs to go, then you only have to pay for the gas,' Lars explains.

'Sounds cool,' I say, before it occurs to me the only friend I have in this part of the world, other than Miller, is going to be gone soon.

In Cali and Lars I've already met two people in Europe the like of whom I've never come across during decades in Perth. Add in Miller and suddenly I'm clocking up people I'd like to hang out with faster than a nymphomaniac on a porn set. People who I like, and who seem to like me, at the rate of one a week! It's like I'm on the other side of the world. Of course as I'm recounting this trip, in a few months time, to the glazed-over eyes of my old work colleagues, I might by then barely struggle to remember Cali and Lars's names, having never seen them again after Amsterdam. I hope not, though, and I can't imagine forgetting Cali, let alone her name, even if I never do get to her island.

On the path behind our jetty, a stream of bikes continues to roll past with their riders talking on mobiles, smoking cigarettes, and doing most other things people driving cars in Australia do. The warm weather and clear light of the early evening has also brought people out on the streets to take slow walks, seemingly without any real destination in mind. On the water, small craft and the occasional tourist barge ply along, sending floating ducks towards us on patterns of ripples.

We both lie on our backs, legs still hanging over the edge of the jetty, causing the hungriest of the ducks to nibble our toes. And it occurs to me that, for the first time, I actually feel like a joint. A few weeks and suddenly I'm a drug addict.

After nearly falling asleep I sit up and continue to rattle on to Lars about whatever the fuck comes into my head. And then Lars sits up, leans over and kisses me on the lips. I kiss him back and then stop.

'I didn't know you were gay,' I say, 'or *a* gay as they call it back in my home town.'

'I didn't know you weren't,' he replies.

'Was it that bad, huh?' I ask, trying to make light of the awkwardness.

'No, it was cool. A bit shorter than I'd hoped, though,' he says smiling.

I don't want this to be some weird moment that will fuck up our fledgling friendship, so I choose to push aside the fact I'm a little freaked out that I'm not really freaked out, and I make light by listing the stereotypical things he ain't.

'You're meant to be humming show tunes and gasping a bunch while clutching at your throat,' I protest. 'And instead you're into ice hockey and decent music. You don't even go to a gym!'

'Yeah, I know, I'm not a total caricature. I've seen *Moulin Rouge* about a hundred times, though!' smiles Lars, clawing back some of the gay territory he's lost. 'Anyway, I did tell you that my siblings and me are a mixed bunch – that should have clued you in,' he adds.

'Oh, the one of each thing, what does that mean exactly?' I say, still a bit clueless.

'Well, there's me – the gay son, my straight brother, straight sister and then there's the lesbian!' Lars explains.

'Wow. Must make for some interesting family get-togethers,' I say.

\*\*\*

164

Later, as I walk back to the hotel in the dark among the drunk and stoned to see where Miller is at, I contemplate the fact that my only kiss in Europe so far has been with a guy from a place called Reykjavik!

Miller thinks it's hysterical, he being, of course, impossible to shock. This is sometimes nicely comforting but at other times reminds me of the level of my unworldliness. Miller hassles me to define the length and passion of what he's already referring to as 'The Kiss'. The best I can do is rank it on the Kiss Richter Scale as more than 'Goodnight Gran' but less than 'Brokeback Mountain'.

'So are we talking Britney and Madonna?' he says, continuing to laugh at me.

'Close enough,' I say, and change the topic. 'How'd the interview go?'

'No good. I think Copenhagen Anita was pissed off I hadn't contacted her, and dissed me to the boss,' says Miller, not unduly perturbed.

Leak-taking in the leaking broom cupboard complete, I lie in bed waiting for sleep to wash over me, and it occurs to me that I hadn't stopped to think what the people watching our kiss might have thought. Cool.

# 25

'So when is your boyfriend going to join us?' Miller asks, lighting both of us up.

The coffee shop we're in has become a favourite of ours, mainly locals but no attitude.

'Very funny,' I respond, drawing back like a professional – if there's such a thing as a professional dope smoker, that is. 'Lars said he'd get here about seven.'

I'd mentioned to Miller that Lars was driving to Berlin in a few days and he immediately decided we should tag along. I'd always assumed we were going to fly our way from place to place, but Miller had pointed out that we'll see a whole lot more by sticking to the ground like most people. It also got me thinking then that I should conserve the frequent flyer points in case Jake might ever be persuaded to use them himself one day and hook up with us – maybe sooner rather than later. I'd not mentioned this to Jake but Miller thought it was an excellent plan, which means it likely is.

My only two male friends in this entire continent have not yet met, and while there won't be the same confusion that Miller is anything but straight, I weirdly do not want Lars to be attracted to him despite the fact most every man-loving person seems to be. Even though Lars was not for me, I'd still actually been complimented that this cool, good-looking person was attracted to me, even if he is the wrong sex. I am, however, keen for the two of them to get on, recalling the way Miller and Denise loathed each other. Given the fun Miller has been having at my expense since The Kiss, it's clear he's not in the least bit homophobic. In fact, he reckons the less competition for women the better.

When Lars arrives I can tell he's right at home in such places as he orders himself a joint before joining us in the window booth, where I introduce him to my already-stoned mate.

'So where are you from?' Miller asks Lars, and I realise I haven't told Miller much about my work buddy.

'Reykjavik,' Lars replies, without asking the same question of Miller – given I've already told him loads about my travel buddy.

After Miller follows up with a confused look, Lars adds, 'Iceland.'

'But *no-one* comes from Iceland,' says Miller with a smile.

'Björk does!' says Lars, finally mentioning the Icelandic equivalent of Belgium's Van Damme or Kazakhstan's Borat.

'I thought she was from Brazil,' Miller replies, though I'm assuming he's taking the piss.

'What?' Lars exclaims.

'You know, where the nuts come from,' Miller says and laughs.

That's a great start, I think to myself, but I soon realise Lars is not precious and in fact has enjoyed the exchange.

The initiation ceremony over, Lars asks us if we definitely want to split the cost of the petrol to Berlin. Miller nods and has us quickly on board. It's decided that we'll head off in two days, which means Doris is going to have to do without me as well as Lars. Poor Madness.

'So how are all your girlfriends here going to cope with you leaving?' says Lars, deciding to have some fun at Miller's expense.

I hope he knows he's dealing with the master.

'I'm over dating girls for a while. Copenhagen Anita has seen to that,' says Miller, denouncing the girl who cost him the job at the bar. A job he'd be ditching now anyways.

'What about a guy?' says Lars, trying to rattle Miller's cage a bit, which I quite enjoy, given the shit Miller's been giving me about The Kiss.

'Oh yeah. Or maybe a goat,' Miller replies.

'You'd prefer a goat over a guy?' Lars asks, perfectly reasonably.

'Is the goat a chick?' Miller responds, straight-faced, and I laugh for what seems like two full minutes, eventually bringing Lars and Miller along for the ride.

# 26

'So how'd you go last night?' I ask Miller as he clambers out of our tiny bathroom for the last time, wearing jeans and wet hair.

'Yeah. Okay.'

Miller was never one to boast about his successes with women, and he was bound to have had more of the same last night.

'What about you?' he asks.

'Nothing much,' I reply.

In actuality I spent my final night in Amsterdam at an internet café. I Googled the name I'd gleaned from Miller – of his mother who'd never returned since leaving him when he was five and called Jet Balcescu. The fact her name was so obscure – Drina Balcescu – was in search engine speak a real gift, especially once I narrowed my search to Australian sites only. A name like Jane Smith would have scored more hits than 'big tits'. There was just the one result, though I couldn't be certain whether it related to Miller's mother or to some other unfortunate destined to spell her name out for the term of her natural life. It made me grateful that although I had a rare enough first name it never required spelling out.

While Miller probably also enjoyed the easy flow of letters in the name he'd taken from his subsequent family, as I got to know him better I realised he'd have preferred not to have had to make the switch. Ditching his mother's name had probably been some sort of proof that he could discard her just as easily as she had him. But in fact it proved nothing.

Anyways it turned out that somewhere in Sydney there was a club that over a year ago had presented the unique singing talents of a lady labouring under the tag of Drina Balcescu. There was no image provided so I couldn't see if any resemblance existed. And as you didn't have to pay to see her, and the venue had never again advertised her presence, I was not surprised when she didn't appear on iTunes. It seemed sort of fitting, or maybe just ironic, that Miller's mother might have done some work in the same industry that her long-since-discarded son has dabbled in.

Miller had told me that he and his mother had been quite transient during the few years he could remember spending with her, so it was entirely feasible that she'd made it to Sydney and also possibly that she'd long ago moved on. The club, which I'd visualised as being as smoke-filled as Amsterdam and as dark as its coffee shops, still advertised gigs, so I decided to email the address given for general enquiries, after setting up a hotmail address with a generic music-biz sounding name.

Assuming the identity of a music agent, creatively called Mr Smith, as in *The Matrix*, I fabricated some story of having seen a singer called Drina at the club a while back and being interested in contacting her. I kept it vague, but if the club did forward the message on to Drina, as I'd asked them kindly to do, then it might be intriguing enough for her to respond to. The downside was that even if Drina did get the message, and responded, she might either not be Miller's mother or she could disappear again when I mentioned the real purpose of my contacting her.

'So what time is Lars collecting us?' Miller asks.

'Midday – from out front of the coffee shop we met him in the other day,' I reply, packing the few clothes that deserve to see Berlin.

'Cool, I'll grab some grass for the trip,' Miller says as he packs his even lighter requirements.

As we stand on the street, backpacks at our feet, it occurs to me that we're about to throw our lot in with someone we still barely know. But then I'd done the same with Miller and it had turned out fine.

'Lars and car,' Miller declares as a bland sedan stops on the narrow street long enough for us to throw ourselves inside. Without thinking, I find myself in the front, and therefore the navigator. Seems an oversight but I do not want to tell Lars quite yet that in addition to having no licence I've never even travelled in a car outside my home town before.

'Hey guys,' Lars says. 'Ready for adventure?'

'Bring it on!' Miller replies from the back, already rolling the first spliff of the many we'll need to smoke before we get to the German border.

'Do you know anyone in Berlin?' Lars asks me and Miller.

'Nah,' I say.

'Dude, you're forgetting Herman the German and the lovely Marcia,' Miller laughs.

'Oh yeah, I forgot,' I reply, then explain to Lars about the couple we met at the cocktail party.

'Unfortunately we don't have their address,' I conclude, then check my bag to ensure I still have Cali's.

'Do you know anyone there?' Miller asks Lars.

'Just a guy on MySpace called Jarmo who I've been corresponding with for about a year. He can show us around if we want.'

'Not a very German sounding name, is Jarmo,' Miller says.

'He's Finnish originally. He's just working and living there with his packet.'

'Packet?' Miller asks.

'Packet of fags. I think his friends are full-on.'

Herd of sheep, flock of birds, packet of fags. Makes sense I guess. I wonder about what lesbians come in. Lars reckons it's a dumpster of lesbians, but we end up settling on an argument of lesbians.

'Pretty gay these guys then, huh?' Miller asks.

'So gay it hurts,' Lars replies, reminding me how cool it is when someone caught in a minority makes fun of themselves.

As we head in what feels like the right direction, the spliffs go around our triangle formation, with Miller the apex, commanding the centre of the back seat and thanking us in Dutch – 'dank u wel' – each time a joint is returned home.

Lars allows me to hook my iPod into the car speakers but insists I run each track selection past him first. He tells me it's not that he presumes I've got bad taste (which of course I don't believe I do), just that he's been burnt before. Oh the agony of enduring anything on the ear that may be even the slightest bit passé.

'Welcome to Zwolle!' Miller declares from behind us.

Lars and I have been mindlessly chatting about names since he asked me what Ash was short for and I'd explained it was short for nothing. Ash was the all of it.

'Are we meant to be in Zwolle?' Lars asks me.

I check the map, trying to look like I have a clue. 'We might have detoured slightly but I can get us back in the general direction,' I say.

Neither of my travel companions cares either way.

Sleepy windmills and colourful houses are scattered across the town's welcome mat, but as the buildings get closer to each other we're already looking for the bypass.

'So you've never been in a car outside of Perth but you've got us to Zwolle, buddy,' Miller says after I reveal my virgin navigator status.

Lars gives me a well-done whack on the arm as he tries to find a way out of Zwolle.

Later, with the border barely minutes away, Miller smokes the last of the weed and then hands around some gum to help rid us of drug breath. We all wind down the windows, despite the intemperate weather.

'Fuck me dead,' Miller says when we see the line of cars waiting to get through the border that we'd – well Miller and I – thought we'd only have to momentarily slow down for.

'What does that mean?' Lars asks Miller. 'Fuck you to death or fuck you when you're dead?'

'Either way,' Miller replies.

As the line of cars waiting to get approval to proceed on their journeys reduces in front and increases behind, we try and make out what the procedure is. It seems that the two strong blond-haired guards, who both look as though Hitler himself wrote their DNA codes, take turns to train their steely-blue eyes into each car before deciding whether they need to check passports. Lars suspects that as our car has Dutch number plates we might come in for extra attention, what with The Netherlands being one big opium den and all.

When it's our turn for Fritz and Jürgen, as their badges claim they're called, to pay us some consideration, it becomes clear that Miller's un-Germanic looks are of the most interest. His tatts probably don't help much either. And then there's his general demeanour when hassled.

Fritz just glances at Lars's passport, barely pauses on mine, but decides to walk off with Miller's as the other grown-up child of the corn asks Lars to release the boot. I discover as a result that Lars understands German. Bloody European know-alls. This is quickly followed by another revelation when Jürgen holds up an instrument he's found in his brief search of the boot. Lars has brought a violin along. The expression on Jürgen's face asks who owns the violin, and Lars points at himself. All the while Miller is watching Fritz in the glass-walled checkpoint booth trying to get Miller's passport to give it up. Jürgen motions for Lars to get out of the car to play the violin, which he does, effortlessly bowing a short stretch of 'La Marseillaise' out of it. I presume the clear sound proves the instrument is not packed with cocaine. This, of course, disappoints Jürgen, who ambles over to the next car. The choice of music may not have been his favourite either.

Fritz also seems like he's lost a bet on a sure thing, glumly returning Miller's passport and waving us on as if *we've* been wasting *his* time.

'He can suck my cock,' Miller says a bit too loudly.

Lars laughs and says, 'There's no need to reward him.'

Now we're out of The Netherlands the weed is replaced, temporarily probably, by peanut M&Ms which Miller pulls out of his backpack.

'Dank u wel,' I say, grabbing a handful, and thinking about how not only are we driving into more fun but we're also, as it happens, getting closer to Cali.

'It's danke schön now,' Lars corrects me.

# 27

I guess we could be saving on petrol costs by not keeping up with the other racers on the speed-limit-free autobahn, which shoots across the centre of Germany like a comet. However, Lars has taken up Miller's challenge of pushing whoever's car this is we're in to its limit.

As we reach the city of Hanover, all eyes strain for the familiar golden arches, and thankfully this dull and orderly city has also lain down before the advancing armies of American fast food. As the car catches its breath I go the McRib, Miller has something called Beef Lang Zu, which looks like a fried burger in a bun with wasabi cream, and Lars makes his way through a chicken burger smeared with curry sauce and the grand title of Chicken Fernköstlich. *And* they sell beer. Danke schön very much, Ronald!

I spy an internet café a few doors down from Macca's so slip out briefly during our McFeast, battling the office workers busying themselves with their daily cigarette quota, to check my emails – specifically, even though it's extremely unlikely, given I'd only written to the club just last night, to see if Drina the Diva has responded. There's nothing from Miller's faux-mother, but Jake has written and it makes me feel a little anchorless to read about my so-familiar world from such a distance. I experience a wave of that stupid blend of sadness and gratitude that causes you to smile as the tears threaten. Not for a minute, in any of the emails he has sent me, does Jake insinuate that I've abandoned him. And he writes of Lucy, and even Denise this time, in such a glowing way as to reassure me he's surrounded by love.

After we've all disposed of the Macca's, much like the car has disposed of the easily digested autobahn, we make for the final leg of the journey to Berlin. This gets me thinking about where exactly we're going to stay.

'So what's the plan when we get to Berlin?' I ask Lars.

'Apparently Jarmo has a huge apartment right in the bohemian part of East Berlin and his roommates are all travelling for the summer, so we can stay there,' Lars replies, saving me and Miller who-knows-how-many euros, not to mention a load of hassle.

You sure know it when you cross over from what used to be West Germany into what was East Germany. Huge trees suddenly line the autobahn, which Lars tells us were planted so official visitors to the communist state could not make out the ugliness of the vista beyond. Behind the arboreal splendour, grey buildings cluster in shivering rows to create even greyer cities, though Lars says it will all change back again once we hit Berlin.

He's not lying. Berlin is like an explosion right in the centre of Europe. Luckily Lars has been to this city before so I'm saved having to navigate our way through the formal western part on to the funkier east. The sprawling city is full of grand, wide boulevards and a sense of structured chaos. After traversing the city, the whole time watching the huge variety of tribes that seem to blend easily, we park not too far from where Lars's MySpace friend lives. Luckily the tired car does not need to be delivered to its patient owner until tomorrow.

We walk our meagre possessions to what looks like Mr Sheffield's apartment block in *The Nanny* and take the elevator to the third level. It's only when Jarmo, stocky and cheerful-looking with the gentle eyes of a lovesick cow, answers the door that I fully appreciate that he hasn't actually met Lars in person before. In real life, as Denise would say. He welcomes us with the same feverish excitement one Japanese person greets another with, and waves us in. Though the apartment is not posh inside, like the Sheffields', it's massive and full of enough furniture and assorted knick-knacks to make collecting dust no problem whatsoever.

'This is my friend Toby,' says Jarmo, introducing yet another northern European.

Toby has obviously dedicated an enormous amount of time to creating a look intended to appear as if he's spent no time on his appearance whatsoever. The opposite of Miller. Toby's fair hair is immaculately ruffled and his tan smoothly applied. I assume this fluffy ball of nonsense is Jarmo's boyfriend as he seems right at home, offering us all drinks from the kitchen side of the huge open-plan living space.

'I only have Heineken or vodka-pops,' Toby offers.

'That should do,' Miller jokes.

'Greedy as a bisexual,' says Toby, flirting with the oblivious Miller.

'So how long you guys been going out?' Lars asks Jarmo.

'Three weeks,' Jarmo says proudly.

'In our world that's a diamond jubilee,' Toby jokes to Miller, still wasting his efforts.

Toby is entirely one-dimensional. And that dimension is gay. Jarmo can do better, I think to myself.

After the customary tour of the apartment, Miller and I cool our heels for a polite period, though I can tell Miller is itching to hit some bars. Eventually he kindly offers to allow Lars and Jarmo time to catch up in peace and we get ready to head out and give them all even more space.

Jarmo gives us a spare key and easy directions on how to find the main entertainment area, while Toby writes us a note in German that we can give to a cab driver if we get lost. It includes the apartment's address, but from what I can tell commences with something like *Hello, our names are Miller and Ash and we need to get to* . . . It might just not translate well or it's his sense of humour, but it makes it sound like we're retarded.

After he warns us that beautiful people don't go out till after midnight, we finally escape him.

Back on the street it smells like a blend of imminent rain and exhaust fumes. It smells like Europe. Apparently it's only a couple of blocks to the main nightlife, and from what I can tell it's still a couple of hours until tomorrow.

'That Todd is bizarre,' says Miller as we make our way to where the action is meant to be.

'I think his name is Toby, actually,' I respond.

'Oh well, it should be Todd, with a silent T,' Miller says.

Jarmo's directions get us to the heart of the situation, and now we've found it we immediately know we'll be back, probably each night we're in this city. No two locals seem to bother replicating the same look. For once, more than one fräulein manages to resist Miller, maybe because he's now the same as everyone else, in that he's different.

The main entertainment strip is lit up like I imagine Vegas to be, but without the highrise and the billboards. The bright, colourful lights dazzle you at eye-level instead. So without the need to look up at anything, people mostly acknowledge your existence as they pass you. Smiling all the while. And it's not just those who cast themselves meekly who smile; even those dressed for a night of chicken strangulation seem friendly.

'Hello,' says more than one passerby as we amble through the growing crowd looking into the neverending string of clubs and bars.

'Hey,' I push myself to reply each time so as to blend in with the general spirit of familiarity and bonhomie.

It's as if we're all headed to the same party and are taking the time to acquaint ourselves in case we might find ourselves sunk into the same sofa together at some point later in the night.

There's loads of tourists also, but it's not too skanky – more Asians dressed in Hello Kitty gear and Europeans insisting on making the peace signal with their fingers as they take photos of each other with their mobiles.

'This place looks alright – I can see pool tables,' says Miller, indicating a bar which does not have a steady stream of leather-clad guys falling into it. The bar is set just below street level and has two neon-lit blue-felted tables in the centre of a reasonably empty room. There's a jukebox, rather than a DJ, so Miller puts a euro in and selects The Hives for me and The Killers for himself. I expect they'll come on as soon as the Madonna tracks are done with.

Both pool tables are occupied, so Miller says we need to put a coin on the edge of one to signify our intention to challenge. He chooses the table with the two girls playing, not because he thinks them easier beats than the two guys playing the other table but because the blonde girl is particularly awesome. Unfortunately the girls do not take this well as they must want to keep the table strictly for themselves.

'Why you choose this table – it's because we girls and you think you beat us,' the blonde girl says to Miller almost immediately after he has placed the coin down.

'No, it's because you're playing better than the guys on the other table and will therefore finish quicker so we can play sooner,' Miller says, which is amazingly quick thinking even for him.

The feminists consider this and gracefully get off their high horses, allowing Miller to buy them some drinks as we await our opportunity to challenge them to doubles.

They end up being a laugh and we play several games. The discussion is pretty elementary as we can't find a language we're all proficient in and we don't even get their names – then Miller's interest fades completely when he catches them making out as he's taking a shot.

Our music selections never do come on, the music videos being interrupted by the screening of an episode of *Queer as Folk*. Suddenly the whole place is quiet and all heads turn to watch the big screen, which has German subtitles.

'You'd think it's the fucking moon landing,' Miller declares. 'Let's find some food.'

We ignore tourist-filled restaurants with names like 'Reef n' Beef' and follow a group of Asian college students into an area thick with the smell of jasmine. The rice, that is. Most of the restaurants in the Asian quarter are Thai, but they're also the most popular and we're way too hungry by now to demand quality. And while Miller warns that Indian takeaway is probably riskier than any drugs you might try, the smell of curry soon overpowers the jasmine and in turn has us overpowered.

As we decide which vats we want our dinner to be scooped out of by one of the elegantly attired family members, I notice a young guy come in quietly and take a seat at a stool someone's just vacated and finish off the meal's remains before it's been cleared away. The girl serving us reminds me of Marcia, who must be in this city somewhere with Herman the German. She doesn't bother to look at us but glares unkindly at the starving interloper before coolly accepting a small tip from us, ignoring our danke schöns and throwing the items into a plastic carry bag. As we leave, Miller makes me laugh by declaring, none too softly, that butter chicken wouldn't melt in her mouth.

The food might not be traditional German fare or even decent Thai, but as we sit, eating from plastic containers on the steps in front of the lazy fountain that lights up the middle of the main square, it doesn't matter. Our spot is perfect for watching the crowd, which only gets larger as the night grows older.

I'm quickly realising that there could only be one Berlin, and right now I'd rather be nowhere else.

Ich bin ein Berliner.

# 28

After drinking about two litres of water I ready myself to leave Jarmo's silent apartment, following what seems like half an hour's sleep at best. The room I'd scored was already announcing a fresh day as I fell into bed, and soon it was too warm and bright to do anything other than get up again. Wherever Miller is, he at least has the note Toby wrote with Jarmo's address on it. The hot Lithuanian girls I left him with, at about the tenth bar we descended into, were happy to look after him – which was entirely what he was counting on.

It's fast becoming tradition that, whenever Miller gets laid or just waylaid, I take the opportunity to do that other touristy activity of sightseeing, given Miller's aversion to checking in with history. The only place apart from bars that he expressed an interest in seeing as Toby ran us through Berlin's sites was a place called the Erotik Museum.

I try to wake Lars to see if he wants to join me in entering the outside world, but he's been vodka-popped into oblivion and most likely will give this Friday a complete miss.

Jarmo has lent me a travel guide to Berlin and I use the map to help find the closest subway station, which I take to get me to the Brandenburg Gate – apparently the symbol of Berlin. Much like shopping malls are to Perth.

A short walk from the gate is the Holocaust Memorial, which was designed to commemorate the six million European Jews killed at the hands of Hitler and his forces. It consists of thousands of grey stone slabs bearing no markings such as names or dates. Each slab, according to the guide, is unique in shape and size. Some come just to ankle height and others would dwarf Miller. The slabs undulate in a wave-like pattern across a huge open area. Apparently the architect wanted to create a sense of disorientation, and as I wander through the maze I agree with the guide that he's succeeded. Not since The Kiss with Lars have I mislaid my orientation so much. People are walking through the arrangement in all sorts of directions and it appears that many locals use the memorial as a shortcut for getting to work and home again. Clearly they have a better sense of direction than me. Or they just know where they're going.

After escaping the Holocaust Memorial I find my way to a patch of remaining Berlin Wall and read the stories of those who successfully escaped from East Berlin during the communist regime, as well as those who failed. Hot air balloons, gliders made of scraps, escape tunnels, and cars modified to hold stowaways are but some of the modes of transport that were chosen by escape-attempt makers. It makes me feel truly lightweight, given my lifetime of staying caught inside Perth's unpatrolled and invisible walls.

In the late afternoon I return to the apartment, weary after my long day of war and fighting. There I find Miller, tired from his long day of sex and loving.

'Hey dude, you been sightseeing?' Miller says, lying on a sofa watching Euro-cable.

'Yeah, loving this weather – wish it would never end,' I say, and though it sounds like I mean the sunshine, it's more than that.

'Summer might leave but it'll be back,' Miller says knowingly. 'That you can rely on.'

'Guess so. I need a drink. Where's Lars?'

'He and Jarmo just went out to get some food.'

'So how was your *trade?*' I ask Miller about whoever it was he ended up with last night, using the term I'd gleaned from Lars.

'Cool. She didn't live far from here.' Miller uses the past tense so I guess she's been classified as a one-nighter.

'What do you wanna do?' I ask my real travel guide, tossing Jarmo's guide book on the coffee table.

'Let's go back to the same area as last night. It's Friday, apparently, so it should be twice the fun. Lars and the others are heading for some club later, so we can meet up with them when we're well tanked.'

Miller's plan makes good sense to me.

The first bar we squeeze into is packed with end-of-working-week revellers. The place is alive even though it's full of office types, and compares favourably to the birthday drinks sessions the IDS gang either endured or enjoyed. The bar's soundtrack is the continual ringing of mobiles as people try to locate the rest of their friends, lost not just in the crowd but in this part of the city, which has more places to drink than Amsterdam has places to smoke dope or ride bikes.

'Jarmo gave me something to get us started,' says Miller when we've found our section of a wall to lean against.

'Huh?' I say, partly because of the noise, partly because I'm slow.

'A pill, dude. Jarmo reckons it's a strong one, so we should split it.'

'So where do we take it?' I ask, imagining all eyes are immediately trained on us.

'I'll pass it to you to nibble and then I'll have the rest,' Miller replies as he shakes my hand and I take the tiny pill into my fingers without looking.

My heart is thumping like it's meant to *after* you've had ecstasy, but for not the first time in the last month I'm driven by the what-the-fuck part of my brain. In fact I think I'm going to be sick, but as soon as I've brought my hand to my mouth and bitten off and swallowed what feels like half, it's too late to change my mind and the nausea subsides. I pass the remains of the pill to Miller, who downs it quickly and tells me to stay put while he gets some drinks.

I've forgotten to ask him when I'm going to start convulsing and swatting at swarms of bees, so I await his return before my freak out.

Some random guy comes up to me and says, 'You need a drink. The drunker *you* get the better *I* look.' I literally just stand there and say nothing. I mean, what's to say? Anyway I'm busy concentrating on myself. Eventually I drift away without a word and find a better place to lean.

Miller has bought four large beers, I guess to avoid having to line up again for a while, and heads back to where he left me. I motion to him from my new resting place but he doesn't see me and starts scanning frantically in all directions other than mine. The crowd is now too tight for me to move much, and without a mobile I can only wait until he finally spots me and becomes the cool dude again.

'You okay?' he asks when through sheer force of his height and general demeanour the crowd has parted enough for him to join me.

'Sure. So when exactly am I going to feel this pill coming on?' I ask.

'By the time we finish this lot,' says Miller, nodding at the brewery load of beer he's got for us, 'you and the pill will be the best of pals.'

I sip away at my first beer as I'm still a bit nervous I'll simply melt to the ground and be trampled like some slow-witted Indian guy at an elephant festival. After a while I start to decide I must be pill-resistant and begin to feel a little ripped off and envious of the others around me who all seem to have raided a chemist's. That said, I really don't know what I'm expecting to feel, like a pregnant woman waiting for her first baby, I guess.

By the time Miller has drunk and chatted his way through his two beers, I complain that I feel entirely unaffected and MSG remains the strongest chemical I've ever ingested.

'You're there already, buddy,' Miller says with a smile after checking my eyes, which used to be blue.

'I don't feel any different,' I say, and decide to give Miller a big hug before mentioning something about how beautiful the world is and then adding, 'I don't know if I've told you this, but you are the best friend I've *ever* had.'

'I think you're his favourite person,' some small-eyed guy standing alone just near us remarks to Miller.

'Cheers, buddy,' Miller says, cutting him off, not planning to make any new friends in this place.

'Nope, it ain't working,' I conclude and again tell Miller he's the best friend I've ever had.

# 29

Hours seems to have rushed through me and all I know is that Miller, who thought he understood where we were to meet Lars and his friends, has been dragging me in and out of places that have all definitely been *it*. And now we are standing on a dance floor that's dressed in more leather than a cattle station. The music won't quit and has the hundreds of identically attired men – the difference principle seems to have bypassed tonight's crowd – and small scattering of fag hags hypnotised. The sweat and heat of the packed dancing bodies causes condensation to form on the dark walls.

I've lost three kilos since we fell down the steep stairs barely minutes ago, and even if Lars is here the chances of finding him among this gyrating crowd are not good. It also really doesn't seem like Lars's sort of gig. Miller reminds me not to move as he heads to the bar for some bottles of water. I keep my feet still and my eyes fastened on him as I'm not keen to lose him either.

'I don't think this is the place,' Miller says, for the seventeenth time tonight, if I've counted correctly, so we take our waters to the place next door. More stairs, more stumbles.

Someone's turned down the music, upped the lighting and scattered the bodies. Wherever we are it's a world away from the other side of the wall, and we catch up on some breathing as we sit, actually sit. I can tell almost immediately that our friends are not here, but it's so calm and inviting we're in no rush to proceed to the next stage of our epic search. As usual, there are few women, and the men, all in their early twenties and clean-cut like Mormons or IT professionals, are pretty well each sitting by themselves, watching. Probably shy.

'I'm going to do a lap to make sure Lars is not here,' Miller says.

'Don't move,' I tell myself to save him the trouble.

I notice on the bar that there's a platter of what appears to be quartered cucumber sandwiches. Miller's seen the food as well and grabs a fist of them, which no-one seems to expect you to pay for, before making his way down a corridor to what I imagine is another bar. The barmen just smile and busy themselves doing little.

Immediately some tall guy with thick, jet-black hair gelled to attention comes up to me and says, 'A hundred euros.'

I decide just to smile at the beggar but he looks at me directly and offers, 'You and your friend. I do you both. A hundred euros.'

'Uh. No. Cheers,' I say, suddenly getting a handle on the sort of place we're in.

'Ninety then.' He thinks I'm bargaining.

'We're about to go. We're meeting friends,' I say, like he wants to hear my life story, and he wanders off empty-handed, as it were.

Miller returns, cucumber-sandwich-less and Lars-less, but with the same knowing grin that I'm trying on for size.

'Some guy offered his services for ninety euros,' I tell him.

'Ripped off, dude. I met a guy who'll do it for seventy-five!' Miller laughs and we leave the comfort of the bar where loving comes at a price, and head back to the bars where all you need do is look at someone for more than a glance and they're yours.

Back on the street the first person we see is Lars, who's been wandering up and down looking for us for the best part of an hour he tells us.

'Where have you guys *been*?' he says, keen to return to where he's come from.

'Around the world,' I say, and ask him where the others are.

'A place just fifty metres down the road,' he says as Miller and I follow him past a bunch of places we've already totally covered and into pretty well the only bar we've missed.

I've generally stopped, by this time, paying much attention to the layout of the drinking spaces we push into, but this place seems relaxed, with a mixed crowd.

Best of all, it signifies our search is over. Like everywhere, though, you have to get past the whole crowd going silent momentarily and staring at you as you enter.

Jarmo and Tobias – apparently he only goes by Toby at home – are both pleased to see us, and I offer to buy a round of drinks as soon as the crowd at the bar dissipates a bit. As soon as we sit down, Lars immediately recommences talking with a dark guy (clearly the reason for his earlier exasperated impatience) on the table next to us who looks a little like Miller but not quite. Jarmo informs us the guy is Turkish and he and Lars have been hitting it off nicely.

Also at The Turk's table, which Lars is edging closer to by the second, are an American couple who've already twigged that me and Miller share their first language so start to drag their stools towards us. The woman introduces them both and I swear their names are Randy and Sandy. Sandy is actually pretty cool and she suggests that we save all the leaning-into-each-other's-tables and actually drag them together, which Miller does while Lars ensures he doesn't lose proximity to The Turk. Randy is less cool, in fact about as humourless as communism, and insists on listing the cities and countries they've 'done'.

'So what places have you guys done before Berlin?' he asks Miller, confident that he's out-citied us.

'Bars and dope cafes,' says Miller flatly, not playing the game.

'We've eaten some amazing food,' Randy responds. 'What about you guys?'

'Sure, we've tried a bunch of stuff,' I reply, to avoid Miller snapping his head off.

'Even fruit,' Miller helpfully adds.

The bar has cleared so I go to get what I think Jarmo and Toby asked for but the barman has not heard of: Vodka Rebels. Eventually he decides I must mean Vodka Red Bulls and I say, 'Okay.' Our pill has long worn off so it's back to serious beer for me and Miller. As the drinks, no doubt priced as if they are luxury items, are released into glasses I take a better look at the crowd. There's the usual posturing and matching ensembles you get anywhere. The coolest-looking group of dudes all have their names printed on their shirts: Hugo Boss, FCUK and Diesel. The label junkies search the crowd for someone worth moving towards, but seem unsatisfied.

In a corner a drunk girl, dressed to horrify in an outfit so tight I can feel her pain, is pleading with some model-looking gay guy. 'Surely you prefer my tits to any guy's here,' she insists, flashing her cleavage into his unappreciative face. Her friends drag her away, back to dignity. It all feels a little like the bar of freaks on Mars from *Total Recall*.

I return with the drinks, passing some flibberti-jibbets with Emo hair who insist on disco dancing although the jukebox implores them to sit down by playing Nirvana's 'Lithium'. The Turk is at the jukebox so I get a chance to steal Lars's attention back briefly.

'So, how *you* doin?' I ask a happy Lars.

'Real well. He's *exactly* my type!'

And then it happens. The Turk has selected Mariah Carey. Lars blanches as he returns to the table and immediately I can see him picking faults with The Turk that were not there mere moments ago, as the pop diva insists on dragging her voice through some forgettable track for over three excruciating minutes. Lars's face has turned from sheer delight to utter horror as quickly as the cheering crowd who watched the Hindenburg airship attempt its landing in New Jersey.

'So how many tracks do you get for a euro?' Lars asks The Turk, and I know that he's holding out for the fledging relationship to be salvaged by something slightly more hardcore than Mariah.

'Two,' the Turk replies, clueless that he'll most likely be going home alone tonight unless he pulls something decent out of the fire.

Whitney Houston. It's all over. Lars makes his way to our side of the table, and The Turk, sensing the change in mood, heads towards Hugo Boss and gang and their tapping Converse feet.

'What happened to your trade?' Toby asks Lars.

'Not a good match,' the music purist replies.

'What a waste – I love a bit of Turkish!' Toby exclaims, ignoring for the moment that his boyfriend is Finnish.

'Bread? Delight?' Miller fires at Toby, and then proceeds to tell Toby that liking someone simply because they come from a certain country is as irrational as disliking someone for the same reason. Jarmo is saved further ignominy. For a short while anyways.

Miller and I decide to walk home before the sun comes up, and we farewell the group. Lars and Sandy are sharing the burden of listening to Randy, while Jarmo is doing his best to try to keep Toby's attention from wandering.

'Goodnight, Toby,' Miller calls back as we reach the stairs.

'It's Tobias!' Toby shouts back.

The morning air is surprisingly warm, and the sparrows that apparently prefer Berlin to pretty well any other European city are spreading the word that the day has started. We talk about the night and agree it's been great, and I mock-console Miller that he'll be sleeping alone.

'What about you, buddy? Don't you want to see some more action?' he asks me.

'It's not that I don't also want to shag someone every night. It's just that I want it to be the same person,' I reply.

'I can guess who that is,' Miller says knowingly.

'Cali,' I reply.

'Fuck, I'd have sworn you'd have said Zoe,' says Miller, surprised.

'Me too.'

# 30

Until now I hadn't fully contemplated the fact that at some point I'd stopped whacking off to Zoe. Penelope Cruz, Scarlett Johansson – even Mischa Barton – had all got a run as masturbation fuel. And now even these celebrities are off the list. I hadn't kept Miller up to speed at how Cali had suddenly invaded the place previously reserved in my thoughts for Zoe – probably because it had blindsided me as well.

Evan's surprise-free though lengthening emails – occasionally over 40kb in return for my measly less-than-30 – rarely mention Zoe and finally it seemingly doesn't bother me at all. I know the exact moment I fell in love with her and yet am hazy about when the pain eased to nothing. Could I be this fickle? Instead, Evan tells tales about the office intrigues at IDS – all of which seem funny to me now rather than just plain dull. His battle with Shaun, his office nemesis, continues, though I wouldn't be surprised if Shaun is not even aware that he's at war. Evan lists the occasions he believes he's scored points over Shaun, and they're so lame I'm not sure whether to laugh or laugh harder. I expect Evan thinks my emails to him are proof that I want such updates. I guess it's better than an entire inbox of spam, though I'm now finding myself reading the spam first.

Now, weeks after meeting her, I'm suddenly lost in thoughts of Cali. And I'm hanging all this emotion on a piece of paper with her faraway address and a vague suggestion to call in if passing through what seems like the ultimate cul-de-sac. A Greek island at the very end of a string of islands, at the very end of the tip of a country, at the very end of this sprawling continent.

Miller has been playing me well, like Lars with his violin, since my shifting affections became apparent. He mentions Cali regularly and then just lets me rabbit on as I trap myself deeper in thoughts of this girl who's the total opposite of Zoe and has struck me entirely differently. No bolt of lightning, no one moment I could calendarise forever, but now she has me all the same.

A couple of days after our long Friday night out, an invisible wave knocks me over and just the very thought of getting up is exhausting. Miller tells me that I'm not in fact dying but suffering, as he is, from what is known as 'Eccy Tuesday' syndrome. The comedown pretty well voids all the short-lived benefits of the pill and has me declaring that I'll be 'just saying no' with good old Nancy Reagan in future.

As we lie around the apartment, pleased that Lars and the others have headed to some music festival in Denmark for the best part of a week (Jarmo happily leaving us the apartment to ransack if we're so inclined), I navel-gaze my way to how we found ourselves here together, especially since we've only known each other a short time.

My mind wanders to how Miller never seems to bother emailing anyone – in fact I assume he has no email address, to match his lack of a physical one – and how he always seems to act as if the fun need never end.

Mostly we both muse in silence, me uncharacteristically ignoring the existence of a television and the both of us each swamping one of the matching sofas, but occasionally we verbalise a thought out of nowhere like when you're sitting with someone reading a newspaper.

When I refer to the fact that I'd initially considered Miller would be too cool to befriend someone like me, Miller baulks at the term 'cool' and stops me dead, saying, 'Ash, you're twenty-seven years old – cool and uncool, that's completely redundant.'

'Well, did you think we'd become friends?' I ask, transparently fishing for a compliment – the reason Miller is here with me – but will be happy to settle for simple validation.

'I like you because you're *not* cool,' Miller replies, heavy eyes closed as his hand blindly dips into the huge bowl of cheese snackettes that's emptying faster than the single platter of precious oysters at a crowded seafood banquet.

'Gee, thanks,' I say.

'That's a compliment, buddy. You're not too smug to be yourself, to admit you're not the best at everything, to make mistakes and to fuck up. I like fuck-ups,' Miller explains, and though I'd never have figured it for a compliment, to Miller this is a big one I reckon.

# 31

Having the apartment to ourselves means no more polite conversation with our hosts, and the best thing about my strengthening friendship with Miller is the ease with which we can enjoy silence together. But Eccy Tuesday has faded into the distance, the weekend approaches and the sofas need a chance to re-puff their flattened cushions.

Jarmo, the perfect host, has left some acid for us, and though Miller is a bit wary on my account, and suggests maybe I should take it a bit slow with the rollout of new experiences, I'm all bravado for setting out on another trip into the unknown. This unlike-Ash mode of thinking is turning Miller into the sensible one.

'Sure you survived a pill relatively unscathed, but maybe you should consolidate your gains before further conquests,' Miller tells me as we wait, with the vampires and albinos, for the sun to descend so we can get outdoors. In our case, though, just long enough to cosy into a string of bars that will get us through till daylight again.

'Well, just bring it along and we'll see how we feel once some beer has disappeared into us,' I say.

Miller nods that that is enough due caution on his part and he's back as the one most likely to be referred to as the bad influence.

I chatter, along with the feeding birds, as the twilight drifts to night and we stride towards the bar district that now feels like we own it.

'You got your key?' I ask, fully expecting that at some point he'll be hijacked by a girl or few who can't believe their luck.

'Sure do,' Miller replies, knowing why I ask, though he's never once openly alluded to his ability to score more often than the entire West Coast Eagles put together. But then he's not bothered by sports.

In what will probably be the only bar that we'll remember much about tomorrow, we buy a couple of jugs of beer, which seem to be much the same price as regular glasses, and position ourselves close to the action but far enough away from the most obvious freaks. This means joining a guy, lost on his way to some 1960s anti-Vietnam War protest, who welcomes us to his table. He looks just like Axl Rose from Guns N' Roses might nowadays.

Miller introduces us both and he puts out a bony hand and says, 'My name's Axl.'

'You're joking?' I say, before I've had a chance to run my response through the good-manners filter.

'You know me?'

'Fill up your glass, Axl?' Miller asks so we don't have

to argue with this guy as to if he and Axl Rose are one and the same. I'd like to imagine that the real Axl is not still wearing the bandana and has put a bit of weight on to comfort him through his midlife crisis.

'Sure. Thanks,' says whoever this is and conveniently forgets his unanswered question.

'I'm going to need that trip now,' I whisper to Miller, half-joking, but he's already tearing the tab in two and, with half a pill already on my drug register scorecard for this city, I slip the little cardboard square into my mouth as inconspicuously as someone who's just picked their nose.

'No going back now, buddy,' Miller says to me, then tells me to stick with him and to expect the unexpected.

Axl wafts in and out of conversation with us, never once saying definitively that he was in a band but somehow continuing to allude, very subtly, to having lived a life smeared with fame.

'It's not him,' I protest to Miller when Axl heads to the jukebox.

'Does it matter?' Miller replies.

And on comes 'November Rain'!

Over by the bar, the first contestants willing to try their luck at the Miller game are flicking blonde hair and giggling among themselves, and it's definitely not on account of the guy charading as someone from the early nineties. Or for me, who's yet to find a decade that fits me.

The bar is crowded now and our table requires a lot of holding on to and is receiving as many affectionate and longing glances as Miller. I've lost track of the blonde girls, and as I scan the length of the bar I lose them in the billowing mist.

'Miller, can you see mist rising out of the bar?'

'There's no mist – you're tripping. Accept that there's no mist, dude.'

'Are you sure? Even though you say there's none, and I know there can't be any, I can still see it.'

'Enjoy the hallucination – you're fine so long as you know that's all it is.'

'Do you see anything I can't?'

'I can see your stupid face,' and even though I'm meant to laugh I don't. This doesn't feel like the pill. If this is a trip, it's a bad one. Like to the dentist.

'It was a joke, buddy,' Miller tells me, and I can see his worried expression but I don't want to ease it. People are now packed around us so that if we wanted to get a drink we'd have to clamber over their heads like Crocodile Dundee. I'm starting to feel hot and nauseous and the mist ain't helping things.

'Just chill out and take a deep breath – I'll help you through this, Ash,' Miller says, reminding me of how Evan once mocked me for being a joyrider, a non-instigator – always letting things be decided for me.

Of course it was as true then as it is now, but suddenly I resent Miller for making me reliant on him. As if it's his fault.

'I do stuff for you too – it's not just you looking after me,' I snipe back, knowing how stupid I'm being but wanting to lash out nonetheless.

'Sure you do,' Miller replies, no doubt without a hint of sarcasm but that's not going to stop me.

'I'm going to get your mother back for you – that's how much I do for you,' I announce.

'What the fuck, Ash!' Miller shouts at me. 'She ain't coming back. Your mother ain't coming back and neither is mine.'

His attempt at tough love is wasted on me, and as he makes to put his arm on my shoulder I shove him away, knocking beer all over myself. The beer doesn't cool me down and I smash my fist right into Miller's mouth. My clench breaks but my heart hurts more.

This time Miller is speechless. The punch has surprised me but it has Miller entirely stunned. I don't prepare for a retaliatory strike and Miller doesn't even seem to consider hitting me. He is silent and dark as night, and it feels like I'm waiting for the first plane to depart and get things back on path.

Miller's face is not cut or even marked, but his eyes belie the weakness of my jab. And still he says nothing and the crowd around us has barely noticed, given we're both still seated and you don't expect to see a bar-room brawl carried on at knee level.

I know that I should reach out now to try and save this somehow, but I simply get up out of the chair and push through the people with more might than my stupid punch packed. The mist has gone now but it feels foggier somehow, and the exit is hard to find. Tears are running down my cheeks and the turned backs are like waves of zombies I have to eliminate before I can get where I need to be. Out of this zombie-infested night.

Behind me I know Miller will be trying to catch me up, but he doesn't call out and so all I hear, above my thumping heart, is another Guns N' Roses track and I nearly laugh. Like some people do at funerals. Tourette's-like.

Somehow I'm in a kitchen somewhere and some fräulein ushers me out into a back lane where I vomit more than I've eaten. This makes me feel a bit better until I remember that I've punched Miller and – acid-induced as it must have been – our friendship might just be fucked once and for all. My trip has fucked this trip I think as the idiot that I am shivers in the warm night. Still, I choose not to seek Miller out and start the walk back to the apartment. Much longer this time. By myself.

# 32

For the briefest time I'm happier than I reckon I've ever been, but once sunshine eventually drags me into full consciousness it hits me. That I'd hit Miller. Lying in my bed with no planes to distract me, I run through last night. So much is a blur but one thing is very clear: I'm a total fuckwit.

Jumping out of my anguish suddenly seems a good idea, but my body isn't ready for sudden movement and collapses to the floor like some imploding building. I drag myself to a sitting position and take it more slowly this time, raising myself up like I'm making some yoga movement but without any of the flair a swami might employ. Out of all the things I could wish for – world peace included – the thing that ranks first is to find Miller in his room. Maybe the acid has burnt my stupidity out of his brain – that's a lot of burning but Ozzy Osbourne has shown it can be done.

Walking gingerly down the hall to Miller's room, I can see the door is open and it all looks just as he'd left it last night. The living room is quiet – in fact my whole world seems more silent than I can remember. Back in Miller's room I look about for his passport or anything worth him returning for – now that I'm not enough. T-shirts, coins, a couple of paperbacks. He travels more lightly than a butterfly, and even more so now.

Most days, after a night out, you could expect Miller to come home well past the time most people have already ticked off several meals, hours of work and a mall visit, but this time I fear he isn't just going to turn up like an errant dog who finally realises he's hungry. He has no mobile, no email, no blog, and no frigging microchip in his neck.

I lie on his sofa and ignore the remote. The more of last night that filters into my memory the more I feel certain Miller is not just going to waltz back into the apartment. Where does he spend his time, other than with me or a succession of eager women? We have no mutual friends, no meeting place, and no telepathy.

The selfish part of me, that great big slice, starts to consider where I'll be if Miller has gone. In Berlin, by myself. Exactly where I am now. Across the room I see the guidebook to Berlin that Jarmo had given us, so I fetch it and fling myself back onto the sofa. Flicking through the index, I recall that the only place Miller had shown any interest in was called the Erotik Museum. But page 43 is missing. Torn roughly out of the book. After checking Miller's room again for the missing page, I cross-reference my way through the remaining pages of the guidebook and find a map that includes the museum. If Miller is avoiding coming back to the apartment then he might just pull the missing page out of his jeans and spend his own downtime among the corset and dildo displays. And it seems the only proactive thing I can do is to go there and hope to see him. While it's probably in vain it'll feel a whole lot better than staying still, waiting for nothing to happen. Where has that got me before?

After walking to the U-bahn station and waiting the standard tiresome five seconds for a train, I enter a spotless carriage and sit down next to a middle-aged woman who looks as lonely as an Australian Democrats voter. For the entire trip I contemplate Miller returning to the apartment while I'm gone. Of course I know that if I'd waited there he wouldn't have come back. On a less pessimistic note, I hope that if he *did* return then the note I've attached to his white T-shirt will give him pause to wait long enough till I've given up staking out the museum or better still come meet me there. In the note I say things I've never said – I speak boldly and am decisive. If he doesn't disappear on me now then I'll never leave him so long as he wants me about. I tell Miller he's the best and most valued friend I'd ever had. All that emotion without a pill or a tab of acid. Feels like real to me, and I hope Miller gets the message.

Just outside the garden that leads into the museum entrance, a Turkish man is selling currywurst, small discs of sausage floating in spicy sauce on a paper plate. What would the new me do? Would he look around for a McDonald's or try something different?

'Can I have a plate of the sausage?' I ask the currywurster.

My mouth and the small plastic toothpick I'm given race against time as the paper plate sags, becomes translucent, and starts to disintegrate under the gooey weight of the only food I've eaten for the best part of twenty-four hours. I decide to save myself a few euros and stay in the garden outside the entrance to the museum proper. If Miller is inside he'll have to pass back this way, and if he's yet to arrive I'll see him before he's had a chance to get salmonella from the currywurster. Given I've been such a huge prick, it seems appropriate to sit in the shade of one of the huge cock sculptures that spring up throughout the heavily flowered gardens. If I have to sit here all afternoon without any joy, at least I'm protected from the sun by a great metal schlong. I lean against the thing and watch the passing parade of horny couples, drunk lads and embarrassed novices – but no Miller yet.

'Why are you sleeping up against an enormous outdoor cock?' Miller is standing over me with a smile I'd thought was lost.

'Hey,' I say with delight, and get to my feet much quicker than I had this morning.

'I can't believe I found you,' I exclaim, shaking the grass off my ass.

'I think I found *you* actually, buddy,' Miller says, and although he's called me buddy a hundred times, this time it makes me beam.

'Are you leaving or did you just arrive?' I ask through my great big grin.

'I'm just here to get you. I've been back to the apartment and got your note.'

'Shit. What's the time? I must have been asleep for hours,' I say.

'Well, from the long shadow being cast by this prick you've been dozing beneath, I'd say it's time to leave.'

'You can hit me now if you like – I deserve it,' I offer, fully aware he'd never take me up on it, and even if he did it wouldn't knock the smile off my face.

'No more hits for you, Acid Boy – let's go.' Miller grabs my shoulder and I upsize it to a hug.

'I reckon Lars would love this garden,' Miller says with a laugh, and we make our way back to the U-Bahn, stopping for some currywurst on the way. This time the food tastes a whole lot better.

# PART 3

## THE ISLAND

# 33

Today is D-day. D for Dream-come-true or more likely D for Disaster. After cramming more new experiences into the last month than I'd had in the previous hundred, we are heading south. Like the birds seeking warmth. Literally. Miller, having ignored my persistent protests that people don't mean it when they say come on by if you're passing their way – especially when they live at the end of the line – has sorted us some early morning tickets to Athens using Jake's frequent flyer points.

We have no phone number for Cali even if we wanted to see how our imminent arrival might go down, giving her the opportunity to feign her grandmother's death or the island's swamping due to global warming. Miller says if we get a bad vibe then we'll simply enjoy island hopping like we'd planned to do anyways. This despite us never having mentioned such a possibility before – neither of us being particularly surf and sun dudes.

And though we have no real reason to rush down to Antiparos, where Cali enjoys life oblivious to our plans, we agree that we can't really afford to hang in Athens longer than passing through. Our combined euros are down to just over a thousand.

I'm glad we held off leaving until the guys had returned from their music festival in Denmark, looking years older but with great tales of music, drugs and instant friends. Saying goodbye to Lars reminds me how he's offered the possibility that my friendship with Miller might not be just a one-off fluke or a passing phase. Lars, in this short time, has also become someone who just might miss me if I weren't around.

I hug him hard enough to show that I don't want this to be a short-lived and easily forgotten connection, and he says he'll stay in contact and it sounds real. We thank Jarmo for putting us up, and just as we leave them all standing out front of the apartment block and start the walk to the subway that will get us to the airport that could get us to who knows what, Miller calls out, 'See ya, Tobias.'

'It's Toby!' Toby shouts back, adding in his best Lars accent, 'See you, Yet.'

The flight to Athens is cram-packed with my day-dreams, and the highest rotation one is our arrival at Antiparos. Cali just happens to be sitting on the beach by herself, looking forlorn, as the ferry drops me and Miller off and Cali's delighted expression immediately means this is not the stupidest idea ever.

The Tie Rack, Body Shop and Benetton stores, and a bunch of other generic chain outlets, have followed us from Singapore airport to those in Amsterdam, Berlin and now Athens. If we're greeted at Antiparos by a Starbucks, I'll just about puke.

The Greek metro map offers the excellent news that it will take us directly from Athens airport to the port of Piraeus. On the metro I realise that Miller is no longer the standout tourist but rather it's me, given my lighter appearance. Miller, in fact, seems quite at home, except when he's saying 'dank u wel' or 'danke schön' to the ticket inspectors. They reply 'efcharisto'. As Hallmark insists, there are many ways to say 'thank you'.

At Piraeus we check out the ferry vendors' stalls and discover that we need to get to an island called Paros first and then catch another ferry from there to Cali's Antiparos. The next ferry to Paros is not for a few hours, so we decide to wander the streets and soak up the local culture. Then find a Macca's. I'm trying to mix it up but I ain't going cold turkey.

A soft warm rain has started to fall, and umbrellas appear from nowhere, though some of the pig people with them still insist on walking under the covered sections of the pavement. Most everyone is smoking, possibly due to the anxiety caused by the anti-cigarette billboards attempting to frighten the fuck out of them. The streets are crowded, as are the cars. I see five adults in a small sedan and it occurs to me how weird it is that this appears weird.

Again, the McDonald's is right next to an internet café. What are they assuming about us geeks? I suggest Miller surprise me with something exotic to eat – which is so unlike the last season – as I make a quick check of my emails. As I'd half expected, still nothing from Drina. I don't even know if the club has passed on my message to her. Evan has written yet again, which really surprises me, but the contents are much the same as the other recent ones: IDS, IDS, IDS. Back at the home of consistent dining, Miller has got us both something called The Greek Mac, which is two burgers in a pita pocket with yoghurt sauce, tomato, onion and lettuce. Seems a perfectly reasonable combination.

In case the islands have the same infrastructure as Gilligan's, we decide to grab some stuff from a small old-fashioned supermarket we passed on our way from the docks. It's sort of fun buying foreign brands of deodorant and shampoo that haven't advertised you into submission. Some tiny old Greek lady gets me to reach for something for her and then, rather than offering an 'efcharisto', actually rips the item out of my hand, drops it into her basket and continues on inspecting the lower shelves. As if I worked here. Not that that would make it okay either.

I tell Miller, who wanders up behind the head-to-toe-black-covered midget and slips a large box of studded condoms into her basket. We make sure that we time it so that we're behind the cranky old lady at the checkout, and then give her our best judgemental looks as the cashier pulls the packet of knob gloves out of the basket. And while whatever the cashier with the confused expression and diverted eyes says to the old lady is all Greek to us, we enjoy every word of what seems a totally awkward exchange.

Even closer to the port is a small string of businesses, and we decide to choose one to loiter in as the rain is heavier now and the ferry still has an hour's rest before heading for Cali. The best option is a small pool hall that owes its existence, I assume, to bored tourists. The attractive woman looking after the place changes Miller's ten euro note into coins and says something to him in Greek which he has to merely smile and nod his head at. She switches smoothly into English and says we can order coffee or beer. We go for the beer and end up talking to her a while rather than immediately heading for the rows of tables – about ten in all – half of them entertaining backpackers while the other half take a break.

Her name is Georgina and she apparently runs this place all by herself. Every day it's just her until closing around eight in the evening when the last ferries depart. She has a small glass-walled office behind the service counter that she has made into a home away from home, with a couple of sofas, a television, a fridge, and a bunch of toys that I presume are for her kid, a photo of whom sits by the espresso machine. She asks after our schedule, like everyone in Europe does, and we tell her about where we've been and where we're headed, and she approves immediately of the Cali expedition Miller has blurted on about. Georgina declares Antiparos is the bomb. She doesn't use those words exactly, as her English is not entirely contemporary. I suspect she also thinks Miller is alright as well, and she's quick to point out that she's freshly divorced.

The phone rings, and as Georgina takes it we saunter to a spare table and deposit a euro, which drops the balls for me to set up, Miller having paid for the game. We can hear Georgina on the phone and she's in quite a state – it seems to be bad news and I hope she won't need to be reaching for the black in her wardrobe. It's all in Greek, of course – the language and the flailing arms – but hopefully it's just that her cat is ill or the electricity bill has arrived or some such thing.

After she's done receiving the bad news, Georgina looks around at the small crowd of customers and rushes over to our table.

'I need to go to pick up my son George from kindergarten,' she tells us, which initially I think means we'll need to leave so she can close up.

'Is he sick?' Miller asks.

'No, it is finishing time. Normally he comes here but today I need to take him home,' she says, her mind elsewhere, racing about.

'We can go,' I say.

'No, I need you to stay! Can you look after things?'

This seems bizarre, to say the least. We've only just met her, speak no Greek and she wants to leave us here, with the money and all. Not to mention we're going to be out of Athens in less than an hour.

'Why don't you close for the day?' Miller asks her.

And so she explains that it was her sister-in-law on the phone, who she's obviously close to. Seems her ex-husband, who now lives up north in a city called Thessaloniki, is trying to get custody of their only child,

George, from Georgina. The husband has hired a private investigator to try and catch George spending time in an insalubrious place such as this pool hall. Georgina therefore needs to collect George and take him home, rather than here, until the private investigator gives up.

'I cannot afford to hire anyone to look after the shop at the evening and I can't afford to close as evenings are the busiest.' Georgina is now tearing up and already she's clued in to implore Miller's eyes as a priority. I'm immediately trying to work out what the scam is.

'We'd like to help but we're off to Paros shortly and we've nowhere to stay if we miss tonight's ferry,' I explain.

'Please help me!' she pleads. 'You can sleep here on the sofas as long as you like, and there is food in the refrigerator and a bathroom out the back.'

'But we don't speak Greek.' There seem so many reasons why this is a bad idea, but she seems determined to combat them all.

'Coffee, beer, change, everybody knows these words,' she says.

'Surely if you close for a couple of days, just while the private investigator is around, that won't cost you too much,' I say, looking at Miller, who may well be thinking about how he'd wished his own mother had fought like this to keep him.

'My sister-in-law says that they might also check that my business is open the hours I said when I try to prove that I make enough money to support George. If someone comes by you will have to say you work the nights all the time.' Georgina is now speaking as if this is agreed.

'How many days?' Miller asks.

'Just a few, no more than a week,' Georgina promises.

George is much the same age as when Miller was de-mothered, and though Miller might be as suspicious as me, he wants this story to be real. I look at him to gauge the effect of Georgina's plea. Sold.

After hugging us both and running us through the till and the keys and lights, Georgina is gone. Miller looks at me, shrugs his shoulders, and we both laugh.

'Let's check out the fridge' I say, finally accepting I won't be seeing Cali quite yet, and we make ourselves right at home.

# 34

As the light fades and closing time closes in on the pool hall, it seems the tide has taken our few customers with it, saving us the need to hurry anyone out. We therefore close the place without disappointing anyone, and just after we've locked up Georgina calls on the office phone to check all is okay and to thank us for the millionth time. I ask her if she saw anyone watching her as she collected George and took him home, and she says she can't be sure. That makes two of us.

Miller and I decide to hit the streets of this part of Athens that most foreigners only pass through. The rain has stopped and Piraeus basks, somewhat, in the shadows of evening. The town looks a lot better at night, like those ageing actresses who supposedly order the camera lens be filtered before capturing them. There's no McDonald's and I'm actually glad of it. Since we're now running a local business, I think we should eat like locals as well. We both keep our eyes out for Miller's favourite four words – 'All You Can Eat' – but no luck. Miller points out that we should look for a place that has Greek-looking locals in it, rather than tourists who've just missed their boat.

'I guess a Greek restaurant in Greece ain't actually going to call itself a Greek restaurant,' I observe wisely.

'No, Einstein – you're probably right,' Miller replies, looking for just the right place. Cheap and full of people that resemble him.

Finally, amid the tourist ghettoes is a small restaurant with enough Greeks inside to make us feel adventurous. Typically, everyone looks at us as we enter, but once they see I'm with a local they go back to their lamb. The business is completely run by guys, and it makes me appreciate a bit more that Georgina runs her business all by herself in what seems a pretty bloke-centred town. Lars would fit right in.

The least lazy waiter comes over to us and speaks to Miller in Greek. Miller does what I had to do in the northern part of Europe – smile, shrug and apologise for speaking English. Our waiter is unfazed and goes off to rummage through a stack of stuff behind the till, returning with their single English-language menu, which is handwritten. The table we sit at is bare aside from two ashtrays, presumably so neither of us need stretch further than our fucked-up lungs might permit. The waiter offers us a light even though neither of us has a cigarette at the ready, or are likely to. Miller blows it out and the waiter laughs – at us or with us, who can say?

Recalling that Lars had recommended we try something I can't remember the name of, I look for a dish approximating lamb meatballs with yoghurt and cucumber sauce, and that description is matched to an item named keftedes. I point at my choice and Miller points at some other variation of lamb, and the waiter seems satisfied with our selections.

'Retsina?' the waiter says, to which Miller responds, 'Yes.'

'What did he say?' I ask as the waiter wanders off, turning the television up on his way out to the kitchen.

'No idea, but we're having it,' Millers says, smiling.

The food is unreal, the retsina is some sort of wine, and I find myself about to proudly declare to Miller that I'll never eat junk food again once I'm back in Perth. This very thought of our trip coming to an end and becoming a memory rather than in the now suddenly takes the wind out of me more than this entire restaurant's daily quota of cigarettes ever could. Miller, noting that I've stopped ranting about keftedes briefly, asks me what the matter is.

'Nothing,' I say.

'Are you thinking about Cali?'

'Sort of, I guess. But more about what happens after Greece.'

'You can't plan that until you've seen how this all works out,' Miller responds, adding, 'Ride the wave you're on, dude.'

'Ride the wave you're on, dude!?' I mock Miller's hip-surfer speak and Miller pours more retsina into both our tumblers before whacking me across the back of the head. Exactly what I need.

We lessen our dwindling load of euros even more and head back to the pool hall and our sofas.

'So, you think Georgina will be here in the morning?' I ask Miller, suddenly conscious of his mother's failure to be, and wishing I'd kept my mouth shut.

'I reckon so,' Miller replies, inexplicably in a cowboy's languid drawl.

I hope she is, for his sake most of all.

As I lie on my uncomfortable sofa, listening to Miller trying to fit into his, a small noise scratches at the calm. It sounds like gnawing and it's not my stomach this time. The small, persistent creature is getting no closer and I'm too tired to bother getting up to turn the lights on to put a face to the thing.

This rodent's going to chew for as long as I'm awake, it seems. Thinking in turn about Cali and Perth is doing me no favours either. The Cali thing is so flimsy and unlikely and Perth is so solid and consistent. I wish Miller would whack me across the head until I fall asleep.

What the fuck is that gnawing?

# 35

The many reasons why Cali will not be mine wait for me, again, to wake this morning, like reliable friends that never leave you. I've no idea what time it is but it's already way warmer than comfortable. And still with the fucking gnawing!

The rodent's all-you-can-eat buffet has continued through the night and into breakfast. Miller must be having a shower – either that or it's heavy rain I can hear and he's vanished. Reappearing, Miller tells me that while the shower has only cold water, which is for once nothing to complain about, the towels are magically warm despite there being no towel warmer.

'Fuck it's hot,' Miller announces, searching for a fresh T-shirt.

'What's the time?' I ask him.

'No idea.'

'How long till this place is meant to open?'

'In seventy-six minutes,' Miller responds immediately, straight-faced, and I laugh loud enough to scare the rodent out of gnawing briefly.

'Once Georgina turns up,' I say confidently, 'I'm going to *do* the Acropolis,' scratching inverted commas into the air around the tourist love-verb. 'You wanna come?' I waste my breath.

'Nah, I'm going to find a girl with air-conditioning and settle down,' Miller jokes.

'She sounds nice,' I reply.

We sit around, neither of us openly considering what we'll do if Georgina doesn't materialise, and instead talk about our travels to date, with the comfort of hindsight. This is effectively my first chance to discover if Miller is getting as much out of all this as I am. I'm too embarrassed to admit that my recent thoughts about the trip's imminent end have my sleeping hours receding, so I steer clear of going out on that limb and casually mention that it's been fun.

Miller tells me matter-of-factly, and without a hint of sentimentality in his voice, 'This is the best time I've ever had, buddy. You're a primo friend.' And though the statement is delivered a bit like Arnie Schwarzenegger's couple of lines in *The Terminator*, I'm suddenly real happy to feel this warm.

We hear a knock at the door and I hope that it's not Antoine from Antwerp, Didier from Dijon or Molotov from Moscow wanting to kill some hours before their ship comes in. It is in fact Georgina, and she seems not at all surprised to see us here and her office unransacked.

'Did you sleep okay on the sofas?' she asks Miller.

'Not a problem,' Miller replies for us both.

'That is good. Now you can have some fun in Athens and I can take over,' she tells us, and Miller asks when we need to return so she can continue her charade for the private investigator.

'Two o'clock.' Georgina shows two fingers, in case we'd forgotten English.

I've been hankering for some more keftedes so we farewell Georgina, who from what I can tell doesn't immediately check her till, and make our way towards an early lunch.

'I remember when you used to eat anything just so long as it was pancakes or burgers!' Miller proclaims. I smile, realising that already Miller and me have some sort of history together – things we can look back on and I hope more to look forward to. For a lot of folk, this last month or so would have been a mere blip on a permanently stacked social calendar – for me it's been a total irregularity.

'Maybe food is my TV replacement,' I proclaim, but in fact maybe it's more than that. The ambivalence I once felt for food was not without company.

The sun drives us into choosing the first place that looks reasonably authentic. There's only one guy working the small cafe and only one other customer, an older deeply tanned guy in a tank top who immediately reminds me I must try and age gracefully.

For once Miller's looks have not fooled the waiter, who asks in English what we'd like. Maybe the fact that I'm sitting here with a huge tourist map of the city laid across the table has clued him in.

Once I've satisfied my passion for keftedes, I leave Miller to do whatever he does and head for the nearest metro station. The walk from the stop conveniently located near the Acropolis is short enough but, given the heat, is way too long. By the time I've clambered to the remains of the Parthenon, the temple at the centre of the Acropolis, the sweat is dripping off me at such a rate there's a real possibility I'll cause some extra erosion at this ancient site.

This place is by far the oldest and most awesome thing I've seen so far, and it gets me thinking about what parts of Perth might be preserved in thousands of years. Maybe back when this place was constructed it seemed ordinary also. I find some shade and decide to people-watch a while as I rehydrate myself with some expensive water.

Soon I get listening to a tiny old Greek guy, better than any museum, who tells me something about his country's proud performances in the great battles of World War II and Euro 2004. Apparently the Greeks initially defeated the Italians, in the war that is, and both Mussolini and Hitler were real pissed off. It caused the Germans' planned invasion of Russia to be postponed for six weeks, by which time winter gripped Moscow and the invading forces, not used to the freezing conditions, were halted. Like most older folk, who are familiar with more successful wars than recent ones, he doesn't mind that I'm a foreigner, and is pleased that I might spread the word of how influential the Greeks have been, not just when this place was constructed but also in his very lifetime.

Other tourists start to gather around the old guy as if he's holding an umbrella in the air, and I'm crowded out of my own shade. Now that I've got my dose of history first hand, I'm pretty well done with looking at what was, and sweat my way back to the metro. Once I'm back in Piraeus I make for the internet cafe so I can be disappointed by the shy Drina one more time. Even after what happened between me and Miller in Berlin, something tells me that some good might come out of knowing more about his mum.

Dear Mr Smith,
Thanks for your message that was forwarded to me. I am still available for bookings and hope to have the opportunity to perform in your club soon. Below are all my contact details.
Best regards, Drina Balcescu

I read the email several times, in amazement that it's worked. She's even given me her phone number and home address in Sydney. My initial reaction is to call her immediately, but I take a moment and remind myself there's still the possibility this Drina may just be a singer and not the real deal. Like a Las Vegas Elvis.

How exactly can I establish if she's in fact Miller's mother before she hangs up on discovering that there's going to be no cabaret set for her to wail through? As I steel myself for making the call, I check for other email messages. Apart from the endless spam about making it bigger and keeping it up longer, there's nothing. I stall some more by Googling around on the internet and then send a general blast to all the IDS addresses I can remember: Evan, Amelia, Modern Bride, Practical Parenting, Fortune, Pet Problems, even Cynthia. Somehow I stuff up the message and instead of my upbeat note about the sights of Athens being complemented with a link to a cool site about the Acropolis, I've instead attached a link to a recipe for keftedes I'd been checking out. That should reassure them that I remain a loser, irrespective of what country I'm in.

Finally I purchase a phone card and take a shot at calling Drina. Thinking too much about exactly what I'm going to say might seem like a good idea, but I steadfastly ignore it. The phone rings a bunch of times and then, 'Hello.' The drowsiness of her voice suddenly reminds me that this world is too large to squeeze into one time zone. Fuck. Too late now.

'Drina Balcescu?'

'Yes. Who is this?'

'My name is Ash. I'm a friend of Miller's.' I decide that the whole thing about Mr Smith's nightclub and a possible gig is just not going to cut it, given it's probably two in the morning or thereabouts.

'Who?' She is very tired and not up for overstretching her vocabulary.

'Oh, I mean Jet.'

And now I wait.

'Why are you calling me?' The way she says this, her head becoming clearer as she becomes closer to awake, tells me she is the right Drina after all.

'Jet does not know that I am calling you. I just wanted to make contact on his behalf,' I say, realising that I'm not really going to be able to establish if she's better in or out of Miller's life by talking to her on the phone, in the middle of the night, half a world away.

'How did you get my number?' Drina is now well awake.

I don't want to come across as a stalker, so I say I used a phone directory. Like in the olden days.

'I ain't listed, fella,' she says, and being called fella has me flummoxed for a second.

'The internet,' I say crisply, to avoid further questioning.

'Do you know what time it is?'

'It's half past one,' I say, 'but I'm in Greece.'

'The musical?'

Oh, man! 'Athens, Greece,' I reply.

'Why?'

*Well, since you enquire, we're in Athens because Miller wants to make sure some other five-year-old gets to stay with his mum.* I think but don't say. *And in Greece because I want to take a shot at something I haven't succeeded at before.* I keep this thought to myself as well – I'm sure Drina couldn't care less about my love life.

'Me and Jet are travelling around Europe,' I tell Drina, and hope that this will personalise things to the point she'll offer me more clues as to what she's like, other than vague when drowsy.

'So how is he doing?' At last, some interest. She's taking the hook.

'He's doing good. He's really happy and loving the trip,' I say excitedly.

'I mean how is he doing with work and all?' She may not care so much for his mood as for his finances.

'He does really well,' I say, presuming this will keep her on the line.

'Well that's nice. Get him to call me himself. During the daytime preferably.' And out.

It's going to take me a while to get my head around that exchange and decide if that's what I wanted or not.

Miller is already running things by the time I arrive at the pool hall, Georgina having gone. As he keeps his eye on the only table that has chicks playing, a couple of friendly New Zealand backpackers apparently, I fill him in on my day without mentioning the fact I'd just chatted with the woman who chose to leave him to pursue a life singing in cheap clubs.

'Let's rack them up – we have six hours to fill,' says Miller, all the while watching the healthy-looking Kiwi girls make one euro last till their boat is ready.

'I know what I want for dinner,' I proclaim.

'Let me guess. Keftedes?' Miller suggests.

'No surprises from me today!' I declare, taking the opening shot and scattering the balls without sinking any just yet.

# 36

Athens shrinks behind a mist of sea spray, providing me and Miller with the warmest shower we've had in this country. I can no longer make Georgina out but assume she's still waving, so I make one last grab at the empty sky in case her eyesight's better than mine.

We never did establish if the whole private investigator thing was a scam, but that doesn't seem to worry Miller. No-one ever came by the pool hall, so far as we know, to make sure it was not closed in the evenings or to meet her staff, and we never even saw George. If it was all an elaborate ploy to get some time off then she probably deserved it. She tried to pay us this morning for our week of playing pool and sleeping on sofas but Miller refused the euros, though our own collection is fast disappearing. Maybe this afternoon a couple of lads from Luxembourg will be trading shots when Georgina gets a frantic call from her sister-in-law.

I look at our remaining handful of hundred euro notes, the very same ones we'd got from the bank in Perth. Luckily we've had no accommodation costs in our last two cities and so the rate of cash-dwindle has slowed down – which it certainly needed to. If we avoid work much longer, though, it will have to be back into the sky one last time for us. Me, I'd rather take work at the IDS branch office in Siberia than return, once and for all, to Perth just yet.

Miller has put me in control of the cash on the condition I don't spend it all on keftedes, which is now most unlikely since I'm totally over them. I've eaten them right from instant passion, through certainty of everlasting love, followed by sudden complacency, and now to boredom and irrelevance. Maybe this is my signature process – I immediately obsessed about Zoe night and day, feasting on thoughts of her, and now I rarely think of her – and it appears to be the same with lamb meatballs dipped in yoghurt and cucumber sauce.

The few notes we have left will get us to Antiparos plus a couple of days of hanging, if there's anything to hang from, and then all we'll have left is our remaining frequent flyer points. It's fortunate that we've never once had to change currencies on this whole trip, even though Amsterdam is a world away from Athens. As a result I've started to think in euros rather than converting to dollars.

The Greeks are real proud to be thought of as part of Europe, whereas I got the impression that the German Government is a little annoyed that their club's membership has been opened up so widely. In turn, the Greeks are now looking down their substantial noses at the really new kids on the block – Bulgaria and

Romania. Some guy we met in a café a few days back pretty well suggested that their inclusion in this special club, the European Union, virtually heralds the end of civilisation as we know it. Wait for the bitching when Kazakhstan's application gets approved.

Miller spends the hours to Paros sleeping on the deck as I watch our stuff and prepare myself for serious disappointment. Today is gonna be brilliant or it's gonna suck big time. My money, what's left of it, is on the latter result, but everything else of value that I have – my heart, my head – is all on today working out as I've daydreamed it a hundred times. I remind myself to prepare for what in fact is the most likely result when black battles white – grey. The scenario where Cali will show just enough to keep me guessing but not enough to make me feel comfortable is something I'm gonna torture my brain with for the next few hours at least. That's a guarantee.

Apparently Paros is a reasonable-sized island, and it's only a thirty-minute boat trip to the much smaller Antiparos. Why it's called Antiparos will be up for discovering, I guess. The salty spray keeps drying on my skin so that my face feels repeatedly stretched and then loosened, like Joan Rivers'. Most of our fellow buccaneers are passed out on the benches inside the boat, so the sea's spit and the sun's scorch have very few others to compete over.

As we push closer to Paros, the midday sun is amplified to extreme as it bounces off the brilliant whitewashed cube-shaped houses, blue-domed churches and tangle of dazzling white alleys. I wake Miller so he can take this picture into his memory. He's a little dozy on being woken, reminding me of someone else recently. I have no idea what the next step should be with regard to his mother. All I'm sure of is that he wouldn't want to know unless I could guarantee she wouldn't be given the opportunity to fuck him over again.

Getting even closer to Paros, I now see fishing boats with actual fishermen selling a catch that's never known the inside of a refrigerator. The village is a living postcard and I want to stamp all over it. We have less than an hour here and, not just because I'd happily delay the impending embarrassment of meeting Cali and her boyfriend or Cali and her memory loss, I wish it weren't just a place we were passing by.

Now that we're docking into the port I can see that the village centre and the alleyways, which rise up softly through the hillsides of white, have all been overrun by cats. They laze in the sun as if they've never encountered a dog in their lives. Miller grabs our packs as I'm too busy being blown away by all the happenings in this still place. Fuck, there are more cats than people. There are more cats than in *Cats*.

'Can you believe we're still in the same time zone as Athens?!' says Miller, now getting up to speed on the beauty of this place I'd never even heard of just a month ago. Which other amazing places have been hiding all this time?

'Yeah, it's not bad I suppose,' I say, dripping with understatement.

'So, you're finally over keftedes, right?'

'She's outta my head for good,' I reply, getting a confused look from Miller.

'I've sorta linked my love-at-first-sight thing for Zoe with my love-at-first-bite thing for lamb meatballs,' I explain, yet again proving that I ain't a friend of Shakespeare's language.

'I'm sure any girl would love to hear that, buddy,' Miller laughs, adding, 'So I presume your slower march towards other Greek delicacies like calamari is mirrored in this quest for Cali?'

'Actually calamari does make sense now that you mention it, given we're in a fishing village,' I respond, hoping to deflect conversation away from the real reason we're here.

We sit on the edge of this world, our legs dangling above a sea of food, and delight our way through as many rings of squid as our budget can handle. The miniature woman in the takeaway shop fried the calamari right in front of us and packed our lunch as carefully as if it were her life's blood. She smiled even though she knew we'd most likely never be this way again, and I tipped her because she didn't expect it.

Antiparos moves closer to us with less dressing than Paros, and as the small ferry drifts to the jetty I realise that only a handful of people are joining us in visiting this dot on the map. A stocky man around seventy, dressed as if it were winter, is pounding a large octopus against a rock that's stained black from years of soaking up squid ink. Once the octopus is tenderised he throws it into a rope basket and it's not alone. We think about asking the guy to look at Cali's note with her address but instead just follow the other arrivees, presuming they'll be heading for where the rest of the locals are hidden away.

A sick-sounding bus putters just behind a wall of trees that's been hiding the rest of the island from our sight as well. The bus waits patiently to see the catch from the ferry, and the guys we're following clamber on as if they know where they're going. I put my head inside non-committally, leaning Cali's note into the bus driver's view. He nods us onboard, and when I hold out a hand of euro coins he waves them away. This has us confused until he stops after just a few minutes and gestures towards a single taverna that looks out over a secluded and virtually uninhabited beach. We could easily have walked – hopefully the driver puts it down to naivety rather than a severe dose of tourist laziness. I gotta stop worrying what a complete stranger may think of me and get back to worrying what a virtual stranger, Cali, thinks of me.

The taverna, unsurprisingly, is painted stark white with soft blue window and door frames. It has two levels, presumably Cali's family inhabiting the upstairs. The inside and outside dining areas are both empty, but I recall Georgina telling me that everything on the islands closes for a few hours after lunch until the air cools.

'So, am I going to do this?' I ask Miller as we're just metres from entering Cali's life.

'Do it!' Miller replies as if we're contestants on some extreme sports show, preparing to leap from safe to risky.

We walk into the dining area, where it's cool and dark. There are about ten tables, and the walls are decorated with images of Greek islands in case you forget where you are. I can hear someone singing in the kitchen and realise that it could be Cali. Miller calls out her name and the song gets louder and closer.

# 37

Like some sort of paparazzo, I want to capture Cali's unguarded reaction to seeing us and not some hastily posed shot. I'm desperate for her face not to show disappointment or indifference before her brain has a chance to correct it back to polite. Miller has reminded me a bunch of times, when we've talked about this moment, that I should give Cali a chance to place us as we've only met twice and naturally she'll be surprised, irrespective of how she might feel about me.

'Ash!' she screams. 'Miller!'

With my eyes set to a shutter speed that's been responsible for the embarrassment of a club-load of celebrities, I will forever record that her face was coloured with actual delight. It also did not escape my notice that she called my name out first. Surely she didn't have enough time to consciously alphabetise. My day has already been made and it's really just beginning.

The three of us hug simultaneously as she escapes the kitchen and we drop our packs onto the floor.

'I guess you're surprised to see us?' I ask as we stand in the middle of the taverna looking at each other.

'Yes, but it is a good surprised,' Cali says and for the life of me I believe her. It's that or her acting ability makes Cate Blanchett look like Hilary Duff.

'Did you just arrive?' she asks.

'We've been in Athens for a week and now here,' says Miller.

Cali can't keep the smile off her face, and it's the same one that's refusing to budge from mine.

'Did you expect we might come and see you?' I ask, interested to know if she'd given us a thought since Amsterdam.

'I know if it's meant to be it will happen,' Cali replies, sounding a bit New Age but not so much so as you'd start to worry.

Miller gives me a 'told-you-so' look which I'm more than happy to accept.

Suddenly, as if she's experiencing a burst of Tourette's, Cali screams out a word in Greek and soon we hear someone descending the wooden stairs that finish by the side of the kitchen. It's a very refined-looking fifty-plus woman with greying dark hair scooped into a bun. Her bright-blue dress suggests she's never had to bury a husband.

'Guys, this is my mother, Melina,' says Cali, and the woman shakes us both with a soft hand.

'Mom, this is Ash, and this is Miller. They're the Australian guys I told you about who came to Alexa's party.' She uses the American 'Mom', I guess like anyone who's learnt English from the TV.

'It's nice to meet you both. Are you hungry?'

You've got to love Greek hospitality.

'We don't want to put you to any bother,' Miller says, not meaning a word of it. Those calamari are already feeling like they were a long time ago.

'It is no trouble. This is a taverna after all,' says Melina kindly and goes into the kitchen after telling Cali to get us some retsina and take us to a table outside. Glorious smells of lamb, squid, and untold herbs that Colonel Sanders has ignorantly left out of his mix waft from the kitchen, through the inside eating area and out to us. We update Cali on what we've done since meeting her and she laughs heaps. The retsina goes down steadily as we talk non-stop. A few tourists who've chosen this small and secluded beach over the more popular ones elsewhere on Antiparos drift about in the still, crystal water.

'It will get much busier later this afternoon,' Cali says, nearly embarrassed about the lack of people. Maybe she thinks tourists are lost without the noise of a crowd.

'This is great,' I tell her.

'It is flavoured with pine resin,' says Cali, thinking I mean the wine.

'Do you like squid?' Cali asks as Melina brings out a huge platter of it, gently fried and splashed with lemon juice.

'Absolutely, we had some this morning in Paros,' I reply, and then thinking that this sounds a bit rude add, 'and it wasn't nearly enough.'

Miller, reminded of Paros and its legions of cats, asks Cali, 'Do you have any animals?'

'No. We do have Milou, though,' Cali replies curiously, before another Tourette's-like shout, this time of 'Milou'. There's a sudden thunk as a skinny cat with funeral-black fur jumps from one of the upper level's balconies. Milou nuzzles his face into Cali's shoulder before being distracted by the squid. He flashes a paw into the platter and springs onto the ground to eat his catch.

'Quite a mover, that Milou,' I say, and Cali laughs so freely and fondly that I want to nuzzle my face into her shoulder myself. And purr some.

The food keeps coming until Melina eventually joins us to help with the eating of it all. Cali and her mum seem like good friends and relax into the afternoon, listening to our travelling tales, laughing at the same stories, and ignoring their chores. A friend of Melina's, Elektra, drops by and takes a place at our table. She's a lot larger than Cali's mum, with hair that's remained as black as Milou's. She likes squid a whole lot as well.

'Are you staying in Antiparos for long?' Elektra asks me innocently.

I have no idea what to say.

'Not sure yet,' says Miller, saving me from stuttering through a response.

'You must stay here, of course,' Cali announces, and her mum looks to be in total agreement.

'Cool,' Miller replies.

'Do you have the space?' I ask, trying to impress with politeness.

'There's the room Elektra uses when she's had too much retsina,' Melina replies, smiling at her friend, who in turn throws a calamari ring into Melina's bun. It's like these ladies are from *Cocoon* and have found some sort of fountain of youth.

'I will show you, and we can put your packs in there and maybe take a walk into town,' says Cali.

We follow her back into the taverna and up the wooden stairs. There appears to be a whole lot of rooms, and Cali shows us to one where both beds are set so as to present their occupants with a view that insists on getting you up and into it. I throw my pack onto a bed and am immediately drawn onto the small balcony, through doors which appear permanently fixed open. Melina and Elektra are just below this room's balcony, chatting in Greek and seemingly in no rush to prepare for reopening. There's a balcony on either side of this one, and it must be from ours that Milou launched himself onto Cali.

'So who else lives here?' Miller asks.

'My brother Thanos. We are the twins,' Cali replies with her turn of phrase I can't get enough of, and then explains that her parents were long ago divorced.

'Do just the three of you run this place?' Miller continues.

'Mom and I make the cooking. Thanos and a friend of his, Simon, are the waiters. Elektra helps out too sometimes, like when I go to Amsterdam.'

We say farewell to Melina and Elektra and walk back in the direction of where we joined the bus for our short ride here. As we pass the jetty I mention the old guy we saw giving the octopus a tough time when we arrived, and Cali says it would have been a family friend called Yorgos, who supplies their taverna with some of his catch.

We take the road that Cali tells us gets you to the chora, the main town area. The fields on our left are dotted with olive groves and oak woods, and dusted with wildflowers that provide insects for the migrating songbirds, who still take time to perform as they feast on the all-you-can-eat buffet. Cali points out small birds called shrikes, black and white with yellow underbellies, who visit the islands every summer.

'Antiparos is a stepping stone for many types of migratory birds. Just like the tourists,' says Cali.

'Do any of the birds like it so much that they stay?' I ask.

'Sure. The linnet is an island bird that never leaves,' Cali replies, keeping an eye out for one to show us while she describes their mixed colours of olive green, orange and yellow. She seems to enjoy the role of tour guide, reminding me of the ancient guy I met at the Acropolis in Athens.

Along the right side of the long road into town are whitewashed houses with colourful hibiscus and bougainvillea trimming their balconies. The flower names are courtesy of Cali, who continues to describe the island with such detail you'd nearly think she thought us blind. The late afternoon sun shyly slips behind the odd cloud and offers some relief as

Cali-power walks us right into the chora, which basically consists of three squares in a row and is, she informs us proudly, a traffic-free zone. The middle square is where most of the nightclubs, bars and tavernas are situated, and in the centre is a massive eucalyptus tree. In fact there are plenty of trees around the whole town centre providing shade for both the locals and tourists, who are about equal in number.

The tavernas in the village are very different to Cali's family's place. First up they actually have customers despite their massively inferior vistas, and secondly they all seem to have boards out front shouting the standard items and prices in more languages than the United Nations recognises.

'Are your menus in Greek or English?' I ask Cali as we cross through the main square.

'We don't have any, actually,' Cali replies, sending Gordon Ramsay into another right fit.

Cali explains that we're going to take the back way for our return trip so that we can get a complete picture of this side of the island. The back road is less certain than the road into town and ducks and weaves, never quite sure which direction it wants to go. Occasional buildings litter the fields and are set further back, probably, I imagine, because cars doing faster than donkey pace might just leave this track at any moment. Many of the trees that line the road have their trunks painted white, which not only reflects light at night but also acts as an insect repellent, our friendly tour guide tells us. Cali could easily get a job with Lonely Planet.

'How are you going, Miller?' Cali asks my friend, who has less need than me to act as if this is a casual stroll and not in fact the most exercise we've taken this entire trip.

'I need beer,' he responds simply, and Cali laughs.

'Not so far now. Maybe can stop at Yorgos's place for a break. He lives just a short way further,' Cali says.

A rumbling sound behind us turns out to be a bus struggling to simultaneously keep both sides of its wheels out of the roadside grass. The bus comes at us at about the same speed as a dog being enticed towards its bath. We step right off the road and wait for the battered blue behemoth to pass us. Just as it does, the at least thirty darkly dressed Greek ladies on board all make a sign of the cross in virtual unison. Even the driver lets go of the wheel briefly to do the same. I mean, I know we're foreigners but that seems a bit much.

'Is there a 666 on my forehead?' Miller asks us both.

Cali doesn't understand the question for a second, and then points out a small Orthodox church behind us and tells us that most Greeks bless themselves whenever they pass a church or if they see something terrible happen. Like a car crashing as the distracted driver makes to cross himself, perhaps?

As we continue, Cali runs us through a short update on her family, including the fact that her twin brother Thanos is thinking of redressing the imbalance in Australia's population with me gone, by travelling there in the next month or so. Further along we come upon two old detached village houses set among the shade of a clutch of oak trees. Neither house is in the best shape. One of them looks like it is still a work in progress, though it's probably older than anyone on the bus that just dissed us. Both are two-level, though each only looks big enough to house just a couple of rooms. Made of stone with wooden doors, they have white stone stairs on the outside that connect the upper level with the lower. I guess it never snows here, or even rains for very long; otherwise going upstairs to bed might be a real hassle. Small shady yards in front of each house soften the simplicity of these traditional village homes and I can also see gardens out the back of both. The balconies on the upper floors are draped with grapevines and I imagine they offer spectacular views over Cali's taverna and beyond to the blue-green sea.

'These are Yorgos's houses,' Cali announces as we approach the more complete building in the octopus-beater's real estate portfolio.

We follow Cali, who doesn't knock, through the open front door and find ourselves in a large room that's modestly furnished and doesn't contain Yorgos. I look around and am surprised at how inviting this place is, basic yet homely. There is, in fact, a large-screen television underneath a dated framed photo of a couple and their son, so comparisons with *The Flintstones'* house are not entirely fair. To the right is the only other downstairs room, a sizeable kitchen where I assume a lot of octopi have copped a marinating. Cali leads us into the back garden, where we find Yorgos hanging out sea creatures, like so much washing, onto long lines of thin rope that connect the house to what appears to be its outside bathroom.

Yorgos welcomes us with a big smile and waits to see what language Cali is going to choose. He is totally adept with English and offers to fetch us some retsina from the kitchen as we sit down on the mismatched chairs that are scattered in the small garden. Once our glasses are full, our host calls out 'yasou', which means 'to your health', and Cali leads the response of 'yamas', or 'to our health', and we all drink to that. Yorgos tells us about how he dries the octopus, squid and sardines and prepares them for delivery to the local tavernas, and Cali points out the weathered gargoyles on the house's tiled roof which in medieval times were believed to ward off evil spirits. Miller seems particularly taken with the house and asks if he can take the outdoor staircase to have a look at the upstairs room.

'From the balcony you can see further than I've ever been,' Yorgos tells Miller, who returns and assures us the view is way more than adequate. After Yorgos has given us an insider's account of when this island was occupied during World War II by Italian soldiers, we select the parts of our travels that might be of interest and recount them for this master storyteller.

Sparing him tales of Amsterdam's coffee shops and Berlin's clubs, Miller instead runs with our adventure in Athens with Georgina and her pool hall. When I question out loud whether Cali or Yorgos can make out what the scam was, Yorgos simply assures us, 'You did good.'

Like most old men, Yorgos happily leaves most of the entertaining to the women, and Cali is certainly up to the task. It's clear Yorgos lives a pretty simple existence, and his happy demeanour reinforces the concept that simple may just be a pretty cool path to choose.

'So how long before you finish fixing up the other house?' asks Miller as we linger in the garden of Yorgos's official residence before setting off again with the inexhaustible Cali.

'For me it takes longer as I'm too old to spend much time on the roof like a mountain goat,' says Yorgos. 'It will be finished when it's done.'

This sounds like the cooking instructions for Melina's slow-cooked lamb.

Yorgos seems immensely pleased that Cali included this visit as part of her tour of what is worth seeing on this side of the island. And so Cali has us stay longer than I reckoned she'd planned to.

'Are you staying in Antiparos long?' asks Yorgos.

'No fixed plan,' Millers says simultaneously with Cali replying 'I hope so' and me saying nothing. Works for me.

The final part of our round trip through the eastern side of this tiny island back to the taverna is quite short and we're unbothered by any cars.

'There's one!' Cali calls out, pointing into a heavily leafed tree just metres from the back of the taverna. I stare, unsure what I'm looking for, and finally make out a bird swathed in olive green, orange and yellow.

'It's a linnet – the bird that decided to stay,' Cali reminds me.

'Looks quite happy,' I say.

'How do you tell if a bird looks happy,' says Miller, deadpan, and I laugh.

When we approach the front of the taverna I'm surprised that the place is full and most of the customers look like Cali, or even Miller. Like locals. As we make our way through the outside section, Cali introduces us to various people, including an attractive woman, immediately transfixed by Miller, who'll be played in the film by Jennifer Aniston.

Inside we meet Cali's brother, Thanos, who is also, not surprisingly, very good looking. It occurs to me that if he does go to Australia soon it'll be Miller he'll be filling in for rather than me. Thanos offers to roll us cigarettes, but as neither of us smokes, regular cigarettes anyways, we politely pass. I get the impression that his consumption makes up for the rest of us, given there's one behind his ear, one between his not-yet-yellowed fingers and a third in preparation. The other waiter, Simon, seems shy and keeps himself busy covering for Thanos, who insists on getting to know us immediately over some beers.

'Yasou,' Thanos calls out and motions for Simon to join us, though I can't imagine who he thinks will wait on the tables if he does.

'Yamas!' the three of us respond simultaneously.

# 38

As our first night in Antiparos drifts to its end I can't stop smiling, thinking that, of all the possible scenarios I'd imagined on the boats over here, this feeling is pretty well one of the better results – short of me and Cali exchanging vows at this moment.

Cali and Simon have been doing most of the waiting tonight, though I'd put up my record of waiting against most anybody. Thanos has been keeping me and Miller entertained, and well drugged with retsina, a Greek beer called Mythos, and second-hand smoke. Melina and Elektra have cooked the food that has no menu to praise it but is simply recounted if required by Cali and Simon, or occasionally Thanos, as they welcome guests more like personal friends than mere customers. Most everyone already knows what to order, and they all seem immensely pleased with what lands on their table before it quickly, and completely, disappears.

'So you happy you are here?' asks Cali between charming diners and taking empty plates back to the kitchen.

'How does he look?' says Miller, mocking my poor poker face.

'Happy,' replies Cali laughing, and I just keep on grinning.

She should know the look, I think; she sure wears it a lot herself.


'So did you two sleep well?' Miller asks me from his bed, just a metre away.

'Huh?' I say, confident enough that I would've known if Cali was beside me, and surely if Elektra was.

Miller motions towards the end of my bed, where Milou has curled himself into the form of a Russian mid-winter hat.

'Hey, scat cat,' I call, and Milou, clearly emotionally intelligent if not adept at English, jumps off the bed and bounds onto our balcony.

I look out at the unbelievable view and am transfixed. Again. While Milou is probably thinking about all the tasty creatures laughing at him from the safety of the water, I decide today is as good as any to take my own first step into the sea. I mean, I don't want to be a pussy and all. Dangling my feet over the edge of the Mediterranean in Paros yesterday was the closest I've been to saltwater, having only ever glanced at the Indian Ocean as it crashed into the side of Perth. My mother had so scared me and Denise about the threat of rips dragging us away from her that neither of us ever did throw ourselves into the ocean. I want to conquer this before Cali and her family gets clued in on what an unworldly alien I truly am.

'How do you feel about taking a swim at the beach?' I ask Miller.

'Who are you and what have you done with Ash?' Miller replies smiling, and adds, 'When will this junkie finally get his fix of new experiences?'

I assume this means he'll accompany me to make sure the tiny waves at the taverna's doorstep don't steal me away.

'What do we need?' I ask.

'A shovel, plenty of rope, and a nine-volt battery,' Miller replies with a smile before he drags me out of my bed. We quietly head down the stairs and make our way through the silent taverna in just our boxers. Unsurprisingly, neither of us had had much call to pack boardshorts, even if we did own any.

The terrace's tables and chairs, left out overnight without a single one disappearing, pretty well lead right to the sand, which is the colour of custard and just as comforting and warm. I follow Miller as he walks directly into the water with as little fanfare as Virginia Woolf in *The Hours*. Hopefully Miller's armour of tattoos will scare away sharks in the same way it does skittish employers. The water is just clear enough for me to see any slimy seaweed before it attaches to my legs, and warm enough for me to pretend like it's a bath. Just with loads of bath salts. Once I'm half wet I realise I've no idea what to do next and so, still not quite ready for my own independence day, again look to Miller for inspiration. Miller's dark hair glistens as he comes up from beneath and shouts for me to take a dive. Initially

I'm too scared to open my eyes under the water after I sink myself completely, but then decide I'm too scared to *not* open my eyes. Of course I see nothing that Milou would happily eat, and surface again reasonably certain that Miller and me are pretty much alone here on the very edge of the ocean.

'Last night was fun, huh?' I venture.

'You wanna talk about Cali?' says Miller, reading me like a book.

'Yeah,' I reply.

'Dude, she's great and I think she really likes you. You're going to have to let her know you feel the same way. Don't Zoe this one.'

'What's the point, though? We can't stay here for long without money and no permanent visas, and even if we did get it together she's hardly likely to leave this place,' I say, listing a few more excuses for not having the balls to take a chance.

'Forget all that, buddy. Test the waters, just like we're doing now,' says Miller. He never seems to get exasperated by me. I wish I were the same.

'This all seems too good to last,' I say, standing in the ocean, for the first time feeling the sensation of water pushing me. Gently towards Cali. I look back at the sleeping taverna, bathed in early morning sun.

'It's too good to end, I reckon,' Miller replies thoughtfully before we head out of the seafood broth and back to where we can see our feet more clearly.

# 39

The smell that meets us as we drip our way back through the awakening taverna is so amazing I start drooling like Homer Simpson when he's thinking about doughnuts. The air is filled with the aroma of fresh bread, and Melina gives us a peek into the beehive oven at the sunbaking loaves, thick and crusty, browning before our eyes.

Cali, who I'd presumed was still asleep, returns on a moped with a basket of flowers that come without packaging, ripped directly from the earth.

'Is it some sort of special day?' I ask, standing in a puddle of salt water and drool.

'Yes. It's Saturday,' Cali replies and offers to fetch us some towels, without once ogling Miller's tattooed body. Hurrah!

'The sun can do the job,' Miller says, and so we dry off as we tidy the furniture on the terrace, scattered from the previous night, and listen to the songbirds who love summer so much they follow it wherever it goes. What with the bread, flowers, birds and all, not to mention Cali, it wouldn't surprise me if Bambi makes a sudden appearance.

Thanos joins us, cigarette for breakfast, and asks us questions about travelling in Australia. I allow Miller to make suggestions about where he should go, given I've already seen more of this place than my own country.

'When are you leaving?' I ask.

'As soon as possible,' he replies vaguely.

'Have you travelled much before?'

'Just around Europe. Not to the New World,' he says, and it amuses me though I can't exactly explain why. Thanos, with dark eyes that he shares with Cali, laughs along but probably for entirely different reasons.

Cali comes out with some warm bread and honey. This most simple of breakfasts beats the shit out of any I've had in the longest time, including Denise's pancakes and Starbucks' frappe mango chiller combo thingamees.

'I thought maybe we should explore more of the island today,' Cali announces.

Though I'm totally up for hanging out with her, the thought of keeping up as we walk for hours in what promises to be a day as hot as every other delays me from making an immediate response.

'We can take the mopeds,' she adds, and that's all I need.

'Cool!'

'I actually might head over to Yorgos's and help him with his renovations,' Miller says.

I'm not sure if he is doing this to give me time alone with Cali or because he actually wants to work on Yorgos's houses, but either way I'm grateful.

As we get dressed for our separate days, Miller runs me through a few basics: do not presume she can do better than you and do not imagine you're the only one who might be nervous. Sound advice from someone who surely could never have experienced such feelings.

'And on a more concrete level, have you ever ridden a bike powered by something more than your legs before?' Miller wisely asks me.

'Nope.'

'Well you've already conquered the beach today so you're on a roll. Just don't think too much,' Miller advises, and the thing is I'm not nearly as freaked out as Redcliffe Ash is meant to be. Seems the more firsts I complete the easier it gets. Who'd have thought?

Elektra has arrived from somewhere, apparently without being formally requested to stand in for Cali. It amazes me that there's always someone around to make sure this place opens on time and runs smoothly, but without a roster or any apparent fuss. Haven't they heard of stressed managers and grim-faced clock-watching? Total anarchy.

I can hear Simon's moped pulling up outside, so while Cali, with Elektra's assistance, rummages through the kitchen for some supplies, I catch him before he has a chance to alight and get him to run me through the basics.

'Do you like working here?' I ask Simon, whose casual yet shy demeanour makes him appear as if he's arriving for a relaxed family barbecue rather than a tough shift of minimum wage.

'I'd probably turn up even if I weren't being paid,' Simon replies, then adds, 'Don't tell them, though.' He smiles for the first time that I've seen, and I think, as Miller says about my firsts, that he should do it more often.

Elektra has packed so much food it's as if she's joining us *and* we're expecting to lose our way and be missing for the rest of summer. Simon waits for us to depart, subtly reminding me of the moped basics when Cali's not watching. We haven't had a chance to talk about exactly where we're headed, but I'm getting used to starting days like this.

After about two kilometres Cali slows down to a stop ahead of me and I pull alongside her, my short hair no doubt a little less manic than her beautiful dark mess.

'You hungry yet?' she says, and laughs as I take her seriously for the shortest of moments.

'We can turn off not so far ahead and make our way to the caves that are full of stalactites and such very old engravings. Sound fun?'

'Sure does,' I reply, still a bit suspicious that she expects Miller and me to be disappointed by this island's modest offerings in contrast to our lives of malls and car parks.

We leave the mopeds propped up by a sign that points down a narrow passage. Once we've followed the passage for a while we come to some rope ladders that we clamber down to find the opening to a natural cavern. The entrance has inscriptions and engravings which Cali explains to me before we head into the large cave to look at the stalactites – large spikes glistening with subtle, opaque colours under a veneer of soothing water. It's all pretty amazing I guess, but to be honest I spend most of the time looking at Cali. The cavern is all ours, and as Cali looks at my face, hoping to see me enjoying this place, I decide not to avert my eyes but to look directly at her so as to say more than I can verbalise.

'Can I kiss you?' I ask, more direct than I've ever been in my life.

'I think you should,' Cali replies softly.

Cali's lips taste even better than fresh, warm bread and honey. I move closer into her as the kiss refuses to end, and she holds onto me as if challenging me to never let go. We say nothing but continue standing there, holding each other and trading kisses on lips and throats, while above us a particular stalactite looks down. In fact, it seems some drops from the nosey stalactite have gotten into my eyes. Cali's too.

The moment ends when a cheerful blond guy bounds into our space.

'Hello. I thought it might be empty in here – I couldn't hear anybody,' the young interloper says, offering his hand. 'My name is Erick.' His baseball cap tells us he's from Stockholm, or at the very least loves the place. After introducing ourselves we wish him a good day and he does the same in return. But for me that is now entirely unnecessary.

# 40

It's less than an hour before the taverna officially opens for dinner, and like you see in some Asian restaurants back home, the workers are all eating together while they have the chance. It takes me back to the overpriced management consultants hired by IDS during my seemingly never-ending stint there who came up with this very idea – staff sharing a meal, like a family – and labelled it a team-bonding exercise. Our compulsory Friday lunch get-togethers lasted but a week. But here it's natural and unforced.

We start with mezes – platters of breads and morsels and things to dip them in. Melina and Elektra join us after ensuring what needs to be simmering in the kitchen is. I gather that this relaxed meal happens every evening and is the forum for sharing the day's exploits among this extended family. Like some families do on television.

Of course I'd already filled Miller in on my kiss with Cali the instant he returned from spending the day helping Yorgos bring his second house a little closer to liveable. I wanted Miller to be pleased for me, proud of me, that I had taken a chance. And he genuinely was.

Thanos, who somehow spent the entire day at the island's main tourist beach even though he was meant to be working, brags to his audience about how many kilometres he's swum.

'How did you keep your cigarette lit?' Cali asks with a smile, and Simon, who presumably had had to cover for his buddy, laughs till he cries.

Miller, who seems to have turned Greek since I last checked, describes the progress with Yorgos's renovations as he pours retsina and then slices the lamb to give Elektra a chance to join in the eating.

'So why does he have two places?' I ask the table, not sure who exactly knows the old guy best.

'The other place was always intended for the son, but he is now in Vienna as a very successful trader,' Cali explains. 'There is no way he ever leave all that to live back in this small place, that tiny old house.'

'Why doesn't Yorgos go and live with the son then?'

'Since Yorgos's wife died some years ago, his son he has tried to get Yorgos move to Vienna, or at least make a visit. But neither of them are willing to give up what they have.'

'So why does Yorgos keep working on the house?'

'He wants to sell it and then give the money to his son, not that the son needs what would be pretty small amount,' says Cali, adding, 'I think it is more symbol than anything – Yorgos passing on the place to the son just as he and his wife did intend.'

'It won't be easy to find someone to buy it, though,' Thanos points out.

'Near impossible around here, and he doesn't want to sell it to some rich jerk from Athens who wants to idle here for just a couple of weeks each year,' Elektra joins in.

Elektra looks at Miller and says, 'Would an Australian live in such a small simple house? I know an American wouldn't.' Melina explains that her friend spent a few years in the States.

'That's the thing,' Miller says. 'Here you don't need to live in your house like it's a box. I'd do my living in the garden, at the beach, in the square and the tavernas, and then happily sleep in a house big enough to fit just a bed.'

'Well maybe you could buy the house?' Elektra is the great matchmaker.

She has already winked at me enough times since Cali and I returned from our day on the mopeds to indicate she'd been as good as along with us.

'A few problems – no job, no chance of a permanent visa, no money, otherwise it's a deal,' Miller says cheerily.

I suddenly realise he might actually like to stay here, and it surprises the fuck out of me. The Miller I know has no home and no home town. And I'd stupidly assumed he liked it that way.

'I'll hide you in my place for as long as you like!' Elektra offers, and she's just sassy enough to mean it. She may not be quite Miller's normal demographic but he is certainly not without surprises himself.

Everybody laughs at the thought of Miller being kept by Elektra as some sort of toy boy, including Thanos, who seems unperturbed that his status as local hunk is being undermined by this newest of Greeks.

As the conversation weaves around stories of the island's traditions and people, long gone and still fresh, a name keeps coming up that I haven't heard any of them mention before.

'So, who is this Zeelan guy?' I ask.

'He went to college with me in Athens,' Thanos explains.

'Zeelan was my boyfriend,' Cali adds.

'Oh,' I say.

'What happened to him?' Miller asks, saving me.

'He and Cali, they were not very suited. Zeelan wants to run the world and Cali, she is just happy to live in it,' Elektra tells me directly, without even feigning this information is for anyone else.

'It did not work out,' Cali clarifies. 'We are still friends. He knows what is important to me and what is not.'

'Cali doesn't need his flashy life and wealth-chasing. She wants things to be ordinary and simple. Like you, Ash,' says Elektra, which has Miller laughing, Cali blushing, and Melina slapping Elektra with a loaf of bread.

'What did I say? Is it bad?' Elektra asks, surprised by the table's reaction to her labelling me as both Cali's love interest and ordinary and simple. Of course she meant it as a compliment and it actually makes me feel good. I'll take it to mean that Cali does not need to be dazzled, that she can see beyond hype and dressing. And this cannot be a bad thing for my cause.

Simon starts to clear away the plates but Melina tells him to leave them. 'You are not working yet. Now you are my guest.'

'I don't mind,' he says quietly, but Elektra refuses to pass up her plate to him and it's not because she's still hungry. Well, not entirely.

'Okay,' Simon says, defeated, and returns to his seat.

'What will we do without you, beautiful young man,' Elektra says fondly to Simon, as Melina, Cali and Elektra's eyes all instantaneously soften to glistening.

'What am I missing?' I ask. 'Where's Simon going?'

'To your homeland,' says Thanos. 'We're going to *Thelma and Louise* it together.'

'But who's going to help out here?' I say, looking at Melina and Elektra.

'How *is* your money holding out?' Elektra asks Miller and me knowingly.

'I don't know that I'd be much help,' I reply, aware that Miller can do just about anything whereas I'm sort of work-wired for very little beyond fucking about on the internet.

I look over at Cali and it's as if Miller has whacked me across the head.

'We'll do it!' I announce for both of us.

'So which of you wants to be the new Simon and do all the work, and who can take over from Thanos and smoke, swim and drink – often all at the same time,' Melina smiles, mocking her son.

'Let me clear this away,' Thanos says good-humouredly, and starts piling plates on the underside of his left forearm. 'If I can remember how, that is!'

And like magic, just as we set the tables and chairs back to their normal places, the first real diners for the night arrive.

Before it gets too busy I decide to check my emails on Thanos's computer and am surprised to find a message from Denise. I open it nervously, fearing bad news about Jake. She tells me matter-of-factly that Jake and she have separated, that Jake is now with Lucy, and that they've moved to Adelaide. Bizarrely, my initial reaction is happiness for Jake and real relief that he actually got out of Perth without crashing into something or being hit by an errant space object or bolt of lightning. I'd have felt sadder for Denise if I truly believed she was in fact sad herself.

Checking to see if Jake has emailed me this news himself, I find he hasn't. But there are a whole bunch of responses from my IDS workmates to my update from Athens. Before reading what they all made of me mistakenly sending them a link to a recipe for my old love – keftedes – in place of a link to a site about the Acropolis, I contemplate my response to Denise. Given she hasn't actually inquired as to how I'm going or when I'll be returning, or even where I am, I simply tell her I hope she's doing okay and that I'll give her a call soon. Maybe tomorrow. Maybe. And just in case Jake is unsure how to let me know that he's gone, I write to him saying that I hope he and Lucy are happy.

All up, five of my work friends have responded to my Acropolis update. Amelia says the place looks amazing, and Modern Bride says she wishes she was there. In a plate of keftedes I assume. The person I'd imagined would be least likely to bother clicking one step further than need be, Evan, informs me that I've attached the wrong link. He adds that the lamb meatballs sound quite cool but that he'd want to pick the cucumber out of the yoghurt sauce ☺ To be quite honest, Evan making a joke at his own expense, after showing some actual interest in what someone else is doing, is way more surprising than Jake leaving my sister for his physio.

Evan goes on to mention that his now hugely successful kid brother, Lewis, has just bought his girlfriend a ring worth more than the studio apartment Evan rents. Apparently it was his Lewis-proud parents who pointed out this disturbing fact to Evan. Of his own girlfriend, Zoe, Evan says nothing.

Downstairs the taverna has filled with people; inside and out they all seem to revel in the warm summer evening and the sound of the sleepy waves from the now-deserted beach. Unlike the tavernas in the main town, there's no recorded music playing here, just that which conducts itself.

Miller is already being shown the ropes by Simon, Melina smartly allocating the responsibility of role-model to the waiter who can actually wait. Thanos has not got past taking the order from the table with the Jennifer Aniston girl, who was here last night as well, and has instead sat down to describe the food to her in minute detail. I watch Cali, who seems to do it all – seating people, taking orders, preparing food, serving food, clearing away and fetching bills. But that's not everything. She also smiles, converses, laughs and charms.

Melina and Elektra claim they're not bothered that neither Miller nor me speak Greek, and say that once we officially stand in for Thanos and Simon they'll get some menus written.

The small car park – well, patch of grass actually – next to the taverna has some mopeds and only a couple of cars, belying the fact that this place is again full. Seems lots of customers just walk here, most coming from nearby homes, night after night. For these locals the presentation of a menu would seem ludicrous, as if your own mother ran you through a specials board as you sat down for dinner at home. Here, like with family, you get what you get. Thanos and Simon do infer you have a choice, but they masterfully direct you towards what Melina and Elektra do best. That said, I wouldn't recommend the place to any vegans.

The prospect of carrying stacks of plates, whether loaded with food or wiped clean, has me worried. My only previous experience in this industry was my long week at the pizza and gelato place in Amsterdam. Most of the plates and utensils there were made of plastic, so any real damage was limited to slipping in a puddle of melted ice confection.

Cali sees me watching her make it all look so easy, and takes a minute to reassure me I'll catch on fine. 'Anyway,' she tells me, 'smashing plates after a meal is Greek tradition.'

Watching Cali from my place at the base of the stairs, entering and leaving the kitchen more times than Elvis, I decide that as well as her humour and down-to-earth loveliness she has the most beautiful face I've ever seen. And yet this was not so when we first met. Then, she had anyone's attractive face. But I've come to discover she has what cannot be seen, what cannot be copied or faked, what cannot be easily captured or described – a way that is well clear of cliché and sameness. The smile, the eyes, the face are exceptional because they are Cali. And Cali is unique.

Occasionally, between long stints of Cali-watching, I glance outside to see Thanos and Miller working their way through charming the various single women, as if they're in some sort of competition, and Simon working just as hard with plate-ferrying and retsina-pouring. Miller will be able to take over both of these roles when Thanos and Simon head off, but I'm not so sure what I'm going to add to the mix.

By the end of the night I've only contributed slightly to helping with the taverna's workload, but plan to actually carry several plates at once tomorrow. Possibly. Elektra heads home, as does Simon. Thanos, I presume, is still becoming friends with Jennifer Aniston somewhere.

On the emptying terrace I outsit Miller and Melina and even Milou, who has finished cleaning the floor of scraps, and wait for Cali to finish in the kitchen and join me.

'Do you like it here?' Cali asks after she's finally done in the kitchen and finds me alone.

'I'm falling in love with the place,' I say.

She takes my hand and without a word we walk up the stairs, to her room.

'I think I just might be falling in love too,' Cali whispers as she pulls the curtains fully open so the moon can join us.

# 41

Waking up beside Cali, her head nestled into my shoulder, sure beats stirring to the sound of planes leaving you behind, or the sight of Miller being devoured before easing another chick out of his world. And it sure beats waking up without Cali.

Predictably, my mind starts considering the possibility that Cali will wake to find me here and quickly ease me out of her world. I'm sure she'd be heaps more subtle than Miller is with his succession of conquests, but my radar is pretty fucking sensitively set for worst-case scenarios.

'Are you awake?' I ask softly.

'Yes,' Cali replies, her voice muffled into my chest. How she could hear my question above the pounding of my heart is beyond me.

I wait a few more pounds, hoping she'll offer more, but nothing. 'Did you sleep well?' I enquire so as to elicit some sort of reaction to sharing the night with me.

'I think so – but I was asleep.'

Mostly Cali's English holds up as well as mine, but occasionally I'm reminded that it's the spin we place on how things are said and the clichéd customary patterns of conversation that differentiate the many versions of English you'll hear the further you venture. Unless, of course, she's joking with me.

Lying here awaiting some definitive sign, like an *Australian Idol* contestant enduring another ad break, I prepare myself for her polite dismissal of me from her bed, her home, her island, her world.

'I could stay here all day like this.'

It takes me a second to realise, jubilantly, that it's Cali who has made such a declaration out loud and not my inner voice. She's said what I'm thinking but am not brave enough to risk saying.

'Me too,' I say, and pull her even tighter into me.

'But I have chores,' she says regretfully.

'You have to start on lunch, I guess.'

'No. Elektra is doing that today. I've got things to collect in Paros.'

Pound. Pound. Pound.

At the third pound Cali finally follows with, 'You will come.'

I've no idea if that is an order or a question, but either way I say yes.

We lie there for a bit longer, the smell of the sea and Elektra's cooking competing for attention. Then Milou starts scratching at Cali's door.

'Once Milou decides I must be up then there is no argument,' says Cali, giving me my first kiss of the day and sliding out of bed. She gets dressed as I continue lying in the warmth of her sheets. When Milou is let in he looks genuinely dismayed to see a guy in Cali's bed, and that makes me even smugger, if that's at all possible.

'I don't think Milou is ready to share me,' says Cali laughing, before leaving the room, door wide open, me in her bed, and Milou at her heels.

I take this as my cue to get dressed, back into yesterday's clothes, and fairly skip down the corridor and down the stairs.

Miller is sitting with Thanos at an outside table and we can't really say anything with Thanos there, so I just look as happy as I feel.

Miller gives me a smile. 'I've been telling Thanos where he and Simon should go in Australia.'

'Better you than me,' I say.

'You don't want to go back there?' Thanos asks me, perplexed.

'No, I meant it's better Miller tells you what's worth seeing as I've never left the one spot.'

'Do you want to go back?' says Miller, loading Thanos's original question with way more spin.

'I'm going to have to at some point,' I say matter-of-factly, not yet ready to muse out loud with Miller the feeling that I should check in on Denise. Since reading my emails last night I've had no time to really think about Denise and Jake's separation. Still, the nagging thought that I should return to Perth is definitely buzzing around in the background. At the very least

I need to call Denise, and I'm scared this will be the beginning of a slippery slope to me having to go back. Thing is, it's inevitable at some point anyway. That's where Miller and I *really* differ – he is certain that nothing is certain.

Cali comes out of the kitchen with some warm bread and honey-flavoured yoghurt.

'What do you need in Paros?' Thanos asks his sister.

'Things you can't get here,' Cali replies somewhat evasively.

'Pretty well everything then,' Thanos declares, which is literally the first negative thing I've heard about this island.

'Maybe that's a good thing,' Miller says to Thanos. 'Keeps life simple.'

'And dull,' adds Thanos.

Suddenly I realise that, for him, tavernas, mopeds and waves are the equivalent of hamburger joints, noisy aircraft and suburbia for me. A few days back, when Thanos had referred to his trip as his visit to the New World, I'd laughed at the thought that the place I come from could be described so exotically. Seems we're not so different – both seeking a new world. It now seems laughable to stick with whatever is served up to you as your first course.

'Well, I'm off to Yorgos's,' says Miller, grabbing some bread to go. 'I'll see you all tonight.' He strides off after shooting me another small grin, looking happier than anyone you've ever seen headed for a day's work.

'Where's Mom?' Thanos asks Cali, using the same American pronunciation as Cali. It's nice that both Thanos and Cali invariably use English – with or without American inflections – when Miller and I are around.

'She's having a sleep-in, so try to keep your complaints quiet about how boring things are,' Cali responds fondly before going to give him a hug for no obvious reason.

'What's this for?' Thanos asks when Cali shows no sign of letting go of this twin who's ended up outgrowing her by nearly half again.

'I'm going to miss you,' Cali says, and I can see sadness in her dark eyes.

'It's just a trip. I'll be back,' says Thanos.

Looking at them both, I think about me and my sister and how different things can be on the other side of the world. And a bit the same as well. Will Denise and I get to the same place as Cali and Thanos seem to be? It occurs to me that taking on a younger brother after your parents have died would have been a whole lot tougher than growing up here. Maybe Denise would have headed off into the world herself, like me or Thanos, if she hadn't stuck by me, and been stuck with me, when I was the least likely to appreciate it. And then, just as I was capable of looking after myself, Jake wasn't.

# 42

'So what do you have to get here?' I ask Cali when the ferry docks in the small port of Paros after half an hour of bliss holding each other and dozing in the sunshine at the front of the boat.

'A farewell gift for Thanos. And for Simon too. Something to remind them of where home is, wherever they are.'

'Cool.'

'But since we are here, we hit a bar first.'

This is not what I expected at all. 'It's the middle of the day,' I say, like someone who hasn't just recently spent the best part of entire days sitting in Amsterdam hash-cafes and Berlin bars.

'Sounds like the perfect time to cool down to me,' says Cali and guides me by the hand, like the novice I am, up a winding alley to a small cheerful bar less overrun by tourists than the places we've dismissed on our way past.

'What sort of beer should we have?' she asks after we claim a table right in the window, so we can watch the passing parade of locals and visitors, donkeys and cats.

'A Greek one, I guess,' I reply, thinking that's what she's angling for.

'Forget that. Something different is always best, I think. Okay?'

'Sure.'

When the waiter saunters over, Cali has a long discussion with him in Greek and he finally heads off to explore the hidden recesses of the coolroom.

'So, where are our beers coming from exactly?'

'India!' Cali declares with a laugh.

'I'd never have thought of finding an Indian beer on a small Greek island,' I declare, to her obvious joy.

'This part of the world is not so dull as Thanos will tell you,' says Cali.

Two dusty bottles are placed in front of us, and the waiter nervously rips off the caps as if he's unsure what might burst out. We lift our bottles in unison and swig back the well-travelled beers, and for mine it tastes better than any I've had before.

'Not so bad, huh?' Cali says.

'You don't have to win me over,' I reply, getting a hint as to why we're here. Thing is, I'm already sold on this part of the world and need no more convincing. Not even with Mumbai beer.

'Well, Indian beer is the last thing you expect to get here,' Cali tells me, adding, 'And anyway I am sick of being told to buy Greek all the time by the television.'

I laugh and tell her that in Australia we're also

encouraged to buy local to keep all Australians in a job. It seems it's the same here.

'Does a Greek deserve a job more than an Indian? I do not think so!' Cali says, and it reminds me of how, when I first met her in Amsterdam, she decried the focus on saving dolphins from tuna nets, with nary a thought for the tuna. Like one was more deserving than the other.

'Here's to the underdog!' I declare. After I've explained to Cali what exactly underdog means, she joins in the toast.

After the Indian beers the waiter is dispatched to find some beers from Malaysia, and I decide it's as good a time as any to find out a bit more about Cali's old boyfriend, Zeelan. Specifically, why he's no longer about and how I might avoid the same fate.

'Oh, he wanted to live in Los Angeles and so now he does,' Cali replies to my question in this direction.

'You wouldn't move so far away?'

'Not for anyone.'

'Not for anyone?' I repeat back.

'How do you say it? Not just for anyone. Not for *just* anyone. That is it.'

Phew. I'm still in with a chance.

'It was not the place he wanted to be in that worried me. It is what he wanted to be there for,' Cali explains. 'More money than you can spend and a big job – things I never want to chase.'

We speak easily and it seems at times that I'm falling in love with a communist. But then she's an anarchist, a radical environmentalist and, by the end of our second beer, someone complicated enough to keep you wanting more.

After a taste of India and Malaysia we head into the chora of Paros. I linger outside the tiny bookstore in the main square after Cali squeezes inside to get what we're here for. I think about how to tell Cali that I'm seriously considering calling my sister and this may well result in me heading back to Perth sooner rather than later to sort out things that I can barely sort in my head.

Nothing is really stated between me and Cali, and I'm reminding myself not to assume too much. I want to phrase things in such a way so that whatever she feels cannot be hidden within a hard-to-decipher reaction. Knowing where you are is as important as knowing where you belong.

A strong, carefree Aussie accent catches my ear and I'm surprised to feel a happy sense of familiarity, rather than the normal cringe. I turn to check out the tourists with the brash Australian voices. It's a group of twenty-somethings – all Vietnamese-looking – wearing boardshorts and AFL singlets; one even carries a cricket bat. The loudest of them nods at me with a broad smile and asks where I'm from.

'Perth,' I reply, acknowledging he'd guessed me immediately.

'Knew you were one of us, mate,' the guy says, introducing himself as Ky.

'Tien is from Perth,' Ky says, indicating one of his friends. 'Fucking long way, hey?'

'Sure is,' I reply.

'Bet you miss it,' Ky says as his mates leave him lagging behind.

'I do a bit,' I say.

I farewell Ky as Cali joins me, bag in one hand. Taking my hand in her free one, we head back to the port pretty much in silence.

'So what did you get the guys?' I ask her as we board the boat and head straight towards our spot at the front.

She pulls out two leather-bound mini-atlases of the world – each with a different-coloured binding.

'Red for Thanos, blue for Simon,' Cali says.

The ferry reverses out of its bay and then crunches into forward gear and rounds towards the direction of the smaller island.

Cali's hair waves against the breeze and she closes her eyes into the wind. She grips my hand and dares me to hold on as long as she can. I contemplate calling out like Leonardo in *Titanic* that I'm king of the world, but as good as I feel, just now I might only be king for a day.

# 43

With the relaxed chaos of the dinner service in full swing I head to Thanos's room to check my emails, and there's one from Jake. His note is cheery, and I think he's relieved I already know about him having left with Lucy. He writes fondly of Denise and how calmly she took his final decision to leave. It seems serendipitous that he should be reminding me how much my sister, his wife, has done for us both. Even though I've had little communication from Denise (I guess she's had other stuff on her mind of late), Jake reckons she never stops talking about me and how I might be doing.

He encourages me to keep using the frequent flyer points, as many as I need to, which I take as a thinly veiled suggestion to come back and check in on Denise. And maybe, I hope, he won't mind seeing me either. On a lighter note, he tells me that Lucy loves Adelaide – big surprise – and she's perfected a pizza that combines asparagus with nectarines.

Inspired by Jake's email, I call Denise. She sounds tired but pleased to hear from me nonetheless. She says she's been thinking we should sell our house but had wanted to talk to me, rather than use email, to ensure I was okay about severing this major link with our parents, disposing of the only real home I'd lived in. Suddenly it makes all kinds of sense to offer to fly home and help with the whole ordeal. Having seen the way Cali is with Thanos (who, like me, undoubtedly has his own collection of frustrating traits), I'm coming to appreciate the sacrifices Denise has made in her life since our parents died, and coming to realise Denise may have lost a whole lot more than me.

The decision made, I lie on my bed a while so that I might enjoy listening to the music generated by waves and happy voices.

I head downstairs to find Miller and at least pretend to help with the tidying up now that the final diners have drifted off into the darkness. I tell him of my plans to return to Perth for a while. A part of me wants him to offer to leave with me, but the better part of me plans to refuse him if he does. He does offer and I do refuse. We both try to play down the significance of us separating at this point – for my part I'm convinced it has to be just temporary.

Cali, hovering nearby, senses something is up but I wait till we're alone again to explain to her that I have to head back to Australia. After just a few weeks with her I can't expect her to do anything other than let me go, and then see if I'll migrate back before summer ends.

'Let me take you to the ferry in Paros tomorrow and we can make it a long goodbye day,' she says, and though it sounds a bit weird it is just about the best farewell I could ask for.

In the morning Miller gets ready to head over to Yorgos's place. Before going, he bear-hugs me long enough so there can be no way I cannot return. Or maybe it's him farewelling me forever.

'You know I love you, right?' he says once our hug ends.

Even if I had known this, I sure hadn't known he could say it. Not to anyone.

'I'll be back before you know it,' I say, wishing I felt so certain of it. I'd never returned to Perth in my life, not from anywhere, least of all another world. It was another first, and you never knew where they'd get you.

Melina and Elektra, Thanos and Simon, all fully expect my trip to be exactly what I'd said it was, and so they wave me off confident that I'll be dropping more plates back at the taverna in no time. In fact, Thanos actually suggests him and Simon starting their trip to Australia by coming along with me to Perth, but I warn against such a level of disappointment so early in their adventure.

As we wait for the boat to Paros, Cali tells me that Milou is refusing to speak to me – he's that upset. He'd looked fine to me, though.

Once we again reclaim our favourite position at the front of the boat, Cali suggests that Miller is staying on the island to ensure I'll return. She then says she'll do the same – wait for me to return, that is. We say little else to each other on the short voyage – the first leg of the longest trip I'd ever set out on.

'What do you want for your last meal?' Cali asks, and it sounds so ominous that I reply I'm not hungry.

'We still have an hour or so – let's take a walk around to the beach,' she suggests, pointing out a small cove that's well away from the tourist throng.

'Okay,' I say, and we set off.

'Other than me, what you most going to miss?' says Cali with a smile.

'Just about everything,' I reply, then add, 'maybe not carrying stacks of plates or helping Elektra bone the fish. Who am I kidding? I reckon I'll miss even those things as well.'

At that, Cali grips my hand tighter and says, 'When you come back I make sure that all the fish is off the bone – I get Milou to help me.'

I laugh and Cali laughs along. Out of her bag she takes the blue leather-bound atlas. 'This is for you.'

'I thought it was for Simon.'

'I will get him another one. I need you to have this so you do not forget us.'

'Do you want me to bring back anything?'

'Just you,' Cali says, as I'd hoped she would. 'Oh, maybe one of those Australian Rules footballers too.'

We sit down on the low white-washed stonewall that overlooks the thin slash of sand rising out of the waveless water and kiss until the clock makes us stop.

Back at the jetty, Cali holds my hand and nuzzles into my shoulder until the patient ferry-master refuses to wait any longer. I say I'll let her know exactly when I'll be coming back as soon as I know myself.

'Look after Miller for me,' I say before boarding. 'And look after you as well.'

'So long as you look after us,' she replies and starts off for the boat to Antiparos before my ferry has even blasted its final intentions.

# PART 4
## HOME

# 44

After being cleared of carrying weapons or deodorants for the third time, I join the rest of the plane's human cargo in the final waiting area. Taking my first flight without Miller has inspired me to buy a book, something I only do once every decade or so, whether I need to or not.

My fellow passengers are watching a ten-year-old kid embarrass his parents by rewarding their indulgences with the sort of wild behaviour usually attributed to crystal meth. His folks, who've clearly already decided it's too late to take a stab at parenting, stick with trying to be their child's coolest friends, while everyone else considers upgrading to business to avoid getting stuck anywhere near this modern family. Reports that forty is the new thirty seem more believable as this wailing brat proves ten is the new zero.

As soon as I'm seated, a window on one side and a moderately sized woman on the other, I start with the book. However, it's a stop-start affair as my thoughts keep reverting to Cali in a way that makes me smile.

Once I've wallowed in memories of Cali, I stare out the window and think about the last week or so. And then back through the last month and some. I resolve, as the air-conditioning freezes me awake, that this is not going to be my last flight and that it can't be the end of anything. Not Cali. Not Miller. The woman next to me asks after my book, though I've only turned a few pages.

'Mustn't be very good,' she says kindly, noting that I've held it in front of my face for the best part of two hours.

'I'm not much of a reader,' I admit.

'Stick with your own dreams,' says the mind-reader, and I nod agreement, put the book down, and close my eyes so I can better see my future.

Once I ditch the pretence of doing anything other than daydream the flight away, my mind falls easily into thoughts of Cali and Miller, Amsterdam, Berlin and Greece. For mine, the glowing endorsements on the book's jacket should be replaced with the shout line, 'A joy to put down' – Ash Lynch, *The West Australian*.

I wake, book on the floor, head in the clouds, just as the onscreen flight-route map indicates that the Northern Territory is directly beneath us, and look out the window as the plane cuts through the dark that has set over Australia. Even from up here there's little to see as we head towards Sydney. I didn't tell Miller about this detour to Sydney to sort what remains of his family before I do the same with my own.

My night in the cheapest of the airport hotels is made bearable by my reconnection to Cable. We parted company nearly two months ago, with just a brief reunion in Jarmo's apartment, but it's immediately like we've never separated. Nothing has changed.

Having slept away a bunch of the latter part of the flight, I take the opportunity to recharge my Australian batteries by feasting on the variety of channels and the ease of the language through much of the remainder of the darkness.

Drina Balcescu's address means nothing to me but certainly makes the cabbie happy. The taxi ride costs me more than my entire time in Antiparos and is way less pretty. Mr Smith, the music impresario, is well dead, so I'm simply going to be the friend of her son who called from Greece in the middle of the night, and then just let what happens next happen. If I die here, no-one will ever know.

Drina's apartment looks government-issue and the elevator appears riskier than Aeroflot, so I struggle up several flights and knock on her door, which rattles back. Initially I can't make out any sounds from within, but something tells me to wait and I'm eventually rewarded by the appearance of the sort of caricature we're told cannot exist. Drina is built like something you stir a cocktail with, and her face shows the effects of years of pub damage. Miller may get his dark looks from his mum but the good looks are more likely his dad's, a man Miller has already clued me in as just one of many possible long-gone paramours.

'Who are you?' Drina Balcescu barks at me from behind her torn flyscreen door.

'Hello, I'm Ash Lynch. I spoke to you a month back. From Greece. The country, that is,' I say, trying to look perky but not too Mormon.

'I don't remember,' she says, and I believe her. She probably barely remembers her last decent meal. Or her son.

'I'm a friend of Jet. He asked me to check in on you,' I lie.

Drina thinks about this a while and then looks at me, as if she's scrutinising me for scams, like I'd done with Georgina in Athens.

'What does he want?' she finally asks me.

'He wants nothing but to know you're okay.'

She has not seen him since he was five so will hardly know that this is so unlikely it hurts.

'Can I come in?' I ask, more to get out of the cold than out of any remaining curiosity.

'Not for long,' she replies.

'Not a problem,' I say honestly, immediately hoping that didn't sound sarcastic. Though I suppose identifying nuances is probably not one of this lady's strengths.

The flat is larger inside than you'd guess and is full of decent enough furniture and loads of the sort of objet d'arts you can purchase from a tobacconist's. She doesn't offer me a drink but quickly locates her own pre-poured one.

'So how is Jet doing?' Drina asks, again somewhat greedily, and I'm reminded that maybe he'll only earn her interest if he himself is earning some interest.

Now that I'm here and have met her there's no need to string her along, so I decide to tell it as it is, that Miller and me are living simple. Her attention immediately wanes and most likely I'll only be allowed a couple more questions before she discards me as well. As she refills her drink (no offer made of one for me), I try to think of a diplomatic way to ask after Miller's father.

When Drina asks me straight out if Jet has any cash to tide her over, I feign naivety and ask, 'What about Jet's father – doesn't he help you some?'

'We only met once,' Drina replies, trying to shock me, and giving a smoky laugh as her cigarette clings tight to her lower lip. It's almost as if she's an actress reading for the part of Cinderella's evil modern stepmother.

'Do you have any other family?' I ask.

'No, they're all back home and I never hear from them,' Drina says, assuming I'd know where she means.

She continues to answer my interrogation so I guess she still hopes she's a chance for some money.

'Where's back home?'

'Romania. We've gypsy in us, me and him. Can't sit still,' says Drina proudly, sitting still on her well-worn sofa. Maybe that's the excuse she uses to herself for moving on from Miller.

'You were born there?'

'Sure.'

A lightbulb goes on in my head. Or is it above? Either way, Drina is now over it and probably realises I'm not going to be of any use to her financial situation and is moving to wind up the conversation. I let her wind away, and it's not long before she opens the flimsy door and fairly shoos me out like I'm some stupid bird that accidentally got stuck indoors.

'See you,' I lie.

'Whatever,' she replies.

# 45

I hadn't actually told Denise exactly when I'd be arriving back home, so I decide to stay another night in Sydney because I can. This is very unlike Australian Ash.

Before jetlag descends, as I reckon it surely will, I take the opportunity to see something of Australia's largest city, other than a creepy gypsy lady languishing in the suburbs. It's pretty cold, summer having remained behind in Europe, but I get the taxi to drop me off right in the centre of town, among the throng – and I have a suspicion that this was likely the only place the cabbie knew the way to anyways as he'd tossed me the UBD as soon as I'd convinced him to stop just outside Drina's place.

For a laugh I see if I can find my way to the editorial offices of *InStyle* and some of the other magazines that IDS distributes for. They'd mentioned that the office block they were in was one of the tallest buildings in the city and that at the very top there is a viewing tower that offered amazing views over the harbour. The address is burned into my memory from years of seeing it on the packages that contained my very own gratis copy of *InStyle* each month, which I immediately passed on to Amelia in exchange for her copy of *Inside Sport*, which also remained unread by me but seemed to make Jake happy.

I find the tower and it certainly is the tallest in the crowd – it's the Miller of office buildings. Previous Ash would never have come here for fear of running into any of the folk who occasionally visited us at IDS to see what the fuck we were doing. Now, however, I'm sort of hoping I'll run into someone I know so I can crow about what I've been up to after I left IDS. New Ash ain't entirely without his vanities. But actually calling in at my old colleagues' level is not going to happen – I haven't changed that much.

The viewing tower is open to the public, so the only button I can illuminate, without a pass, is 76. Just as the doors are about to close I see a young suit making a lunge to get into my lift. I press the 'open' button just in time and the confident, young go-getter with the show-pony hair nods me thanks as he gets into the lift. Just as the lift is again about to close its doors, I see an older man also determined to climb aboard this particular ascent, lest he has to wait a half a minute. The young guy I let in reaches over to the buttons and presses 'close'. 'I'm sort of in a rush,' he says.

'Welcome to Sydney', I think to myself and I keenly watch the numbers until we drop 'the important one' off at 39 and then I watch myself in the mirrored wall panels.

At level 39 I join the American and Japanese tourists who've no doubt been higher but never with this view to look at. It is truly beautiful, and this is from someone who has finally seen what beauty can look like. I walk the entire way around the building looking out north, over the water to the affluent suburbs, east to the very affluent suburbs, south to more suburbs, and west to Perth. Okay, I don't see Perth but I'm squinting real hard and I can feel it out there. Waiting.

Back on the ground and I'm already forcing my eyelids to stick with the plan and stay open a bit longer. I decide to find a tacky tourist shop, which takes all of three seconds, and buy dumb items to take back for Cali, Miller, Melina, Elektra, Thanos and Simon. It would make sense to buy a big boomerang and strap it to my back so I might get back to where I belong, but as they're all made in Taiwan I don't want the thing to take me back where *it* came from.

I spend up on a bag of kitsch, the bad taste barometer maxing out with Thanos's gift, a crocodile-shaped ashtray, and head off to find the shuttle bus to drop me at my airport hotel. As I wait for the bus I watch the people of Sydney, most looking like refugees from a high-powered motivation seminar or the Big Brother house, dashing about with the certainty that they truly are starring in the world's greatest city. Mostly the stiff ones all wear suits entirely the same colour and cut, and the cool ones mix it up with T-shirts featuring tired pop culture references to The Ramones, AC/DC, The Hoff and fucking Che Guevara. Same, same, same.

The bus rocks up, and it occurs to me that this will be about my five-thousandth trip on an airport shuttle bus but the first as a legitimate tourist.

Back at my hotel I hog the computer in the foyer and send a load of emails: to Miller, without mentioning my visit to his white-trash mum; to Cali, again failing to risk telling her I love her; and to Evan, asking if he'll collect me tomorrow morning from the airport. Next I revert to type and collect some Burger King from the familiar-looking joint just down the street and hook into Cable back in my room. It's still not as good as I remember, and soon I'm knocked into sleep by the Whopper and another shot of jetlag. And dream of Drina the gypsy and her empty crystal ball.

'Hey,' I say as Evan pulls up in his olds' car to collect me.

'Hey,' Evan replies, looking at me as if I've changed, which I haven't.

'Thanks for picking me up. How's it going?'

'The same,' he responds dryly, then proceeds to reinforce the point by squeezing updates on IDS, his family, and last of all Zoe, into the short time it takes to drive to my place. Apparently he and Zoe are no longer, and he doesn't give a fuck, it seems. Neither do I. Once that would've coloured me delighted, but now I care as much as the last Liberal government did for the environment.

Evan stops in the middle of my street as there's already a line of cars parked outside my home. He invites me to come by his parents' place tonight for their regular first-Saturday-of-the-month barbecue. Normally I'd automatically say no – I mean there'd be Jake to hang with and all – but now there's no such excuse.

'Sure. Thanks,' I say and wave him off.

Loads of people, couples mostly, are walking around our front yard and into the house, and I probably appear to be just another weekend real-estate browser. Our huge gum tree is making more bird noise than it's ever done before, though as I walk towards it I fail to see a single bird. Up close I see someone has recently nailed a twee birdhouse to one of the gum's ladder-reachable limbs.

The 'For Sale' sign that's been erected near the front path describes a place I barely recognise, failing to mention a single reason the place was once so valuable to me.

Walking inside, I'm hit by the wafting smell of fresh bread. In the front room there are huge vases of colourful flowers. But no Jake. Denise is busy in the kitchen attending to her first ever attempt at baking bread while answering questions from various prospective buyers about termite infestations and plumbing peculiarities.

Upon seeing me, Denise excuses herself for a moment and wraps her oven-mitted arms around me, just long enough to make me feel warm.

'When did you arrive?' she asks.

'Now,' I reply.

'Are you happy to be home?' she says then stands

back, looking at me as if I've changed in this short time away. Which I haven't.

'But it's no longer our home, is it? Well, not for much longer.'

'Well, Perth is,' she says, removing four fat loaves from the overworked oven.

The chatter of the birds, the bright flowers and the steaming, fresh bread reminds me of that first morning in Antiparos. That is, until the open house session ends and the last interested buyer has taken the last sales flyer and left, and Denise unceremoniously dumps the uncut loaves directly into the rubbish.

'So do you think you've found a buyer?' I ask Denise as we sit down on Jake's sofa and switch on the television to kill any silent moments.

'It's as good as sold. Just the final price to work out as the two couples who really want it try and outbid each other!' she says.

'Well, I guess you didn't really need me to come back and help after all,' I say.

'I didn't realise it would sell so quickly,' Denise replies, adding, 'anyways, you can't be away forever.'

There is in fact a lot to catch up on, and it appears Jake leaving with Lucy was indeed amicable enough. Denise is now happy to talk openly about her new old boyfriend. His name is Gustavo, originally from Argentina, and most importantly he loves her. It took just one of Jake or Denise to have the courage to leave, it seems.

Denise surprises me by showing genuine interest in my news about Greece and Cali, and Miller as well, but then subtly reminds me my visa to that other world has an expiry date.

Before setting out on my long walk to Evan's parents' house, I catch Denise refreshing the flowers in the front room with a spray of scent from a can. Seems the flowers are plastic and the vases as dry as Miller's mother needs to be. Denise walks out with me to the front yard, where she asks me to climb the ladder and turn off the tape of bird noises that's running from inside the bird house.

'What happened to the actual, real live birds that used to sing here?' I ask.

'They must have gone east, with Jake,' Denise says flatly.

# 46

'This is our son Lewis and this is Evan.'

Evan's parents are introducing some barbecue first-timers around. The group loiters about the pool surrounds like so many antelope around a watering hole. Antelope with canapés, that is.

Lewis and his girlfriend, who's sporting a ring that Elizabeth Taylor would fear too ostentatious, are clearly the centre of not just tonight but Evan's parents' entire world. Moreover, now that Lewis has finished university, immediately finding a position paying well above what seems decent, this focus on Lewis at the expense of Evan is only going to become even more obvious. And, as they would have it, then there is Evan.

From what I've occasionally observed over the years, Evan mostly allows the slights and indifference of his parents to wash over him. But occasionally he can be encouraged to rage against his olds. The irony is that Lewis, cocaine habit aside, is a nice enough guy and sometimes seems as embarrassed by his parents' affliction as the rest of us.

I realise I hadn't paid enough attention in the past to what Evan has to endure here. In fact I'd always wondered why all the family money and comforts hadn't shaped Evan into a more generous spirit. Thing is, it now seems to me to be some sort of miracle he's not an even bigger jerk.

While Evan busies himself removing the mushrooms from his skewers, I listen in as Evan's dad regales a business associate with an update on Lewis's life for near-on ten minutes, after the associate politely inquired, 'And how are your children doing?'

After the Lewis-revering finally finishes, the associate then follows up with, 'And Evan?'

'Oh, he's fine,' Evan's dad replies.

Suddenly I feel real bad about having often thought so poorly of Evan in the past, especially when presuming to compare all the benefits he had growing up with the lack of opportunities Miller's family had afforded him.

I suggest to Evan, after he's de-mushroomed his dinner and sifted through the salad, that we eat inside in the safety and company of television, thinking, though not saying, that he shouldn't have to listen to any more of this fucked-up shit from his olds.

'You should come and visit everybody at IDS,' Evan suggests as we sit down in front of one of the house's five large-screen plasmas.

'Yeah, maybe on Monday,' I reply, not entirely convinced.

'I'm actually thinking of leaving some time this year,' Evan announces, attempting to gauge my reaction for the first time I can ever recall.

'Sounds like a plan, dude,' I say, impressed by this new-version Evan who, while it may never come to pass, has at least considered a change. Like I should have done years back.

'What would you do?' I ask.

'Not sure,' he replies – an answer I completely understand.

'I reckon you should just do it!' I say, as upbeat as I can.

'Do what?' Evan looks at *me* for advice. Another first.

'I reckon it's time to put some distance between you and this lot,' I reply, realising that maybe I shouldn't so openly diss his family.

'Yeah, maybe.' Evan is now deep in thought and hopefully it's on topic and not back to him dreaming about ways to sabotage Shaun's meteoric rise at IDS.

It occurs to me that suddenly in Perth there's a whole lot of leaving going on, whereas the last time I'd checked the entire population had seemed stuck fast. Jake has left not only Denise but this town, Lucy likewise, and Denise is leaving her home. Even Evan has itchy feet.

Lewis comes down some stairs and walks into the room, looking wired, then shakes my hand for no apparent reason before launching himself back on to his pedestal by the pool.

'Don't you think it's bizarre that your parents think Lewis is perfect and favour him so much while you're the one *not* fucked up by drugs?' I say to Evan.

'It's all relative,' he says. 'They're totally clueless about Lewis's love of blow. I remember a few years back he was heading out for the night and my mum warned him off drinking and he was all 'I don't drink' and then asked to borrow $275. Exactly $275!'

'Did they give it to him?' I ask, incredulous.

'Of course, and Lewis got to cram another gram up his nostrils.'

We both laugh, imagining his parents financing the illegal narcotics trade that has always struggled to get a strong foothold in this town.

As Evan and me run out of things to talk about and television makes our silence numbingly comfortable, my thoughts become peppered with imaginings of what Cali and Miller are doing. I hope they're missing me like I miss them. Thoughts of Evan stuck in this place remind me that not so long ago I *was* Evan. I hope there's no reverse gear on this ride.

# 47

'Ash, phone!' Denise calls out into the backyard as I'm sitting alone trying to recall what had held me in this town for so long. It'd be easy enough to explain it away as Jake or Denise, but it was just down to me I reckon. Fact is, I wish I could completely dismiss this world but a nagging feeling that I now have two places to be, both with good and bad points, is making it less easy to feel so sure about things.

Maybe it's as simple as now it feels like the next time I leave it'll be for good, and that makes for more doubts, though I'd be hard pressed to justify staying on this side of the world when most everything I've ever wanted is on the other side.

I shrug on my jacket and head back into the slowly emptying house that will shortly be no longer ours to drift about in.

'Hey, it's me,' Evan says too brightly for someone stuck in a Monday office. 'We've decided to have some impromptu drinks tonight. You up for it?'

'Sure, I guess,' I reply unconvincingly.

'What else you going to do?' Evan says, reading my mind.

'Sure,' I say, with more certainty this time. 'The birthday bar?'

'Nah, there's a new place that opened recently that we go to now,' he says, surprising me somewhat – some things have changed while I wasn't watching.

'It's even closer to the office. Right next door,' he adds, diluting the surprise a whole bunch. 'It's called Keith's Bar. We'll be there at six.'

I forget to ask who else is going but suspect there'll be few surprises. Used to be I took comfort in things being the same and new faces staying well away, but the longer I'm back in Perth the more I'm realising the old Ash is long gone.

'You going out tonight?' Denise asks as soon as I'm done talking with Evan.

'Just some drinks with the IDS guys,' I say and Denise is fine with that. Or maybe she's resigned to change now and making the best of it. Either way, she doesn't guilt me into hanging with her in this Jake-less house.

The long walk into the city seems a little foreign now, and I'm glad of it. Fighting off feeling comfortable has been getting harder the longer I'm here. Passing by the birthday bar, I stop to look in and wonder if seeing Miller behind the counter would make me happy or sad. Keith's Bar, like its name, is completely unoriginal and contains pretty much the same fittings, furniture and people that Miller left behind. It also contains Zoe.

Much like the first time I saw her, she again stands out from the familiar faces of Evan, Amelia, Modern Bride and even my old boss, Cynthia. Back then she'd seemed as elusive as trying to watch yourself blink, but now she's the first, in fact the only one, to get to her feet. She offers me a single kiss on the cheek, a third of what Cali would.

We chat a while before I make for the bar, and Keith, I suppose him to be called, takes my order for beers. He's tall, slim, good-looking and dark-haired, same as Miller, but nothing like him.

Returning to the table I sit next to Zoe, something that a few months ago would have taken well more than I had. Listening in as the IDS colleagues prattle on, I start to realise the only thing that's changed with them is the magazines they look after. Their names are all going to be screwy now and their identities gone. Evan tells me that Fortune ran into some of his own and snared *InStyle* after I left. Those behind him in the pecking order then got to shift up one and there's a new, desperate recruit stuck with that saddest mag of all – *Pet Problems*.

Fortune and Practical Parenting cuddle their way into the place and over to our table, barely acknowledging any surprise that I'm sitting at it. Evan reminds them that I've been away, and they immediately segue into a long diatribe about the trip they're planning. Seems they're going to Hawaii, if their plane is happy to take them.

'I'm a bride!' Practical Parenting shrieks at me when she realises my confusion over who is exactly who, and for the briefest of moments I think that she's gone and married Fortune, or InStyle as he's now called, and the Hawaii trip is their honeymoon. But she's actually announcing she's now Modern Bride. My brain starts to hurt and I wish I'd bothered to learn their real names. I'm so relieved that Amelia always barred anyone referring to her as Inside Sport, and I'm sure she's no more likely to want to be called Fortune now – people might think it's her who's dating Practical Parenting, I mean Modern Bride. Fuck!

Amelia and Modern Bride (I decide to keep calling them by the names I knew them as – they certainly don't deserve this level of attention to detail, I reckon) want to know if I've met any celebrities in my travels, and the best I can come up with is the girl who looks somewhat like Jennifer Aniston. I neglect to mention Axl's doppelganger. The Bride is quick to reassure me that someone as important as Jennifer Aniston is unlikely to be found in such a small and remote place. How wrong can someone be?

I decide to spend the rest of my drink talking with Zoe and finding out more about who she is in reality, beyond the fantasy I constructed.

'So what have you been doing for the last few months?' I ask.

'Oh, nothing as exciting as you. I haven't dated anyone since Evan,' she says.

'Are you happy being single?' My question seems a little personal once it's out there.

'No.'

She is as beautiful as ever. In fact more beautiful than Reese Witherspoon. And unhappily single. Evan mentioned yesterday that he thought Zoe and I might actually make a good couple, and yet I slept last night with as few tosses and turns as Jake could manage after his accident.

The night struggles to a close after Cynthia cryptically suggests, before leaving, that I call into the office for a chat during the week. Soon Zoe and I are left by ourselves, Evan having winked me goodnight. We have a game of pool before Keith sets about closing up. Silence ensues so we walk out together, and the thought of slipping her hand into mine appears from nowhere but just as quickly retreats. I think about the promise I made to myself when I last saw Zoe, the day Miller and me flew out. *Never let an unattached, and possibly interested, Zoe escape again.*

The taxi rank is empty of people and cabs so we wait, though it's not exactly clear for how many cabs we shuffle our feet.

'So are you back for good?' Zoe asks me as we stand with our hands centimetres from clasped.

'Not sure,' I say, and then, just as quickly, 'No.'

'So why did you return?'

Good question. 'To help my sister out,' I reply, suddenly unsure why I'm here at all.

'Have you done with helping yet?'

'Pretty much,' I say, and wave at a cab that's already seen us.

'How's the photography going?' I finally ask, wishing I'd thought to enquire earlier.

'I love it. I'm seriously thinking of shooting some real wildlife in Kenya,' she replies, then laughs and adds, 'With a camera I mean!'

The cab driver takes the opportunity, with us standing on the precipice, to enjoy his cigarette in peace.

'That's great – you should really do it!' I say, spruiking the same encouragement I'd thrown at Evan.

'I *really* think I will,' says Zoe, gently ribbing my overly enthusiastic tone.

'You know, I never got the message,' I say, out of the blue.

'What message?' Zoe asks, seemingly clueless about what I'm referring to.

'Just after we first met, before you were with Evan, you came by my place and left a note. My sister forgot to tell me until it was too late,' I say.

'Oh. That seems so long ago now,' Zoe says, and I can't tell now if the ignored Post-it concerned her like it did me.

I stand there, as the cabbie taps his yellow-stained and now empty fingers on his window sill, unsure as to why I've even bothered to tell Zoe this now. Part of me wants her to know that she was not dismissed by me, and the other part I can't decide.

'Should we share this one?' Zoe asks, looking directly into my eyes with the courage of the beautiful.

'Nah, I need the walk,' I say, kissing her goodbye and starting on my long journey home.

# 48

Drinks with Zoe and the others has unsettled me. Visiting the IDS office is less revelatory; nothing seems to have changed and it's all I can do not to sit down at my old desk beside Evan and carry on the exact conversations we'd had when I'd last slacked off there. The only change is the shuffling of magazines. Fortune now swings in my unfaithful chair, ensuring *InStyle*'s circulation figures will never surprise anybody.

If I'd been sitting in a chair, my old boss Cynthia's suggestion of me returning to the company would have knocked me out of it. My performance over the years at IDS can only be rated mediocre, but that's nearly the corporate slogan, I guess. The untimely retirement of the account manager for *Needlework Update*, at just sixty-seven years young, has created one of the few openings in this place since I'd quit.

Waking in my old bedroom to the sound of the same planes I'd abandoned, I think of Cali. And Miller. Miller who hasn't replied to either of my emails since

I've come home – even though I'd set him up with a hotmail account the night before I left. Leaving this place once and for all is, in the end, not a hard decision to make. But there's someone I must see for one last time before I go.

'Do you miss Jake?' I ask Denise as she sits on the step of our empty home, preparing for the last fixture, me, to be removed once and for all.

'Of course,' she replies softly. 'He will always have been my husband. We just drifted apart, well before you'd have guessed it, and neither of us knew how to deal with it.'

'Are you happy now?'

'I think so. I've never been a big fan of change – but it seems that I'm catching on to its merits,' Denise replies, and it makes me feel a whole load better that she isn't going to try and hold onto something that's gone.

'You can't stop progress,' I say, mimicking the Dad character from *Muriel's Wedding*, and she laughs without any hesitation.

'If I'd made Miller more welcome, then maybe less would have changed and you'd not be the happy Ash you are now,' Denise tells me just as I go to hug her – not just because she's family but because I love her. Returning has been worthwhile just for this.

As Evan waits outside in a car his parents would consider too dangerous for Lewis to risk his life in, I stand up and make to leave.

'Gustavo seems real nice,' I say, in case my opinion might matter, and it seems it does.

'I'm glad you got to meet him.' Denise tells me, walking me to the street.

'His house, *your* house, is cool as well,' I say.

'Do you think it would be a nice place to raise a family?' Denise asks, giving me a jolt.

'Are you trying to tell me something?' I say, grinning suddenly.

'Not yet, but who knows?' Denise smiles and I realise I've never heard her mention wanting to have children before. I expect that's because it would've only made Jake feel worse.

'You seem happy,' Evan notes as I get into his dodgy car.

I continue to hang my face out the window well beyond losing sight of my sister's wave.

'Farewell Porpoise Spit,' I call out of the window of Evan's car as we approach the airport, but he doesn't get it.

Evan is surprised when I announce towards the end of our short trip to the airport that he should drop me off at the domestic terminal. I'd decided to make a slight detour before heading back to my new home, and Denise had even reckoned it was a top idea.

'Thanks for the ride,' I say to Evan and then leap out of his car with more spring in my step than the bounciest of contestants from *So You Think You Can Dance*. Never before has an airport felt so warm and inviting.

There's just enough time on this leg to watch the episode of *Friends* I'd seen on my last flight, stab some plastic cutlery into an overcooked disc of meat made slightly less dry by a thin sauce, and prepare to see my old buddy Jake.

When I called Lucy last night to fly the idea of me visiting her and Jake in Adelaide she was as excited as I'd ever heard her – and that's really saying something. She was more hyped than the release of a new version of Windows. Of course, we both thought it would be even cooler to surprise Jake, and Lucy declared she'd make sure he didn't disappear and spoil the moment. Jake would have laughed at that so I did.

I get the cab to drop me at the top of the street as I want to be discreet on arrival so as to keep up the element of surprise. The suburb Jake and Lucy live in is really close to the centre of town, close to the university, but all the same the street could just as well be in the outer suburbs of Perth. While Perth is a smidgen bigger than Adelaide in population, they seem quite different cities so far as my initial impression goes.

The houses are a mixture of older-style bungalows and terraces, some attached and some detached – like the crowd at any dark nightclub. A lot of the places look like they might be shared by uni students at best, or squatters at worst. As I get closer to the number Lucy gave me last night I see a terrace with a large tree out front. All the leaves are off the tree but there's a tight collection of branches and twigs and there are what appear to be some items hanging from a bunch of the higher branches. Some are colourful, like deflated balloons or jaded Christmas ornaments that have been snagged. I look a little closer and I realise that they are in fact spent condoms, which I'm guessing have been discarded through the open doors that lead out onto the upstairs balcony.

Next door is a bungalow which is more neatly presented. A handsome Maori-looking guy is sitting out front and winks at me as if he's expecting me. I nod back as I'm aware the rule seems to be the smaller the town the more familiar the greetings.

Jake and Lucy's place is just like their friendly next-door neighbour's, and I step lightly up the couple of steps and onto the porch. Lucy opens the door before I get a chance to knock and raises a finger to her lips, all the while putting her arm around me and her kiss on my cheek. She looks just as sweet as she always did and is dressed as if she were waving the final lap flag at a grand prix. She leads me by the hand through the house and we stop at the back door. I can see Jake sitting beside a huge brick barbecue, and he's midway through turning and burning a bunch of sausages with his good arm. Lucy stays inside as I head out towards Jake, who turns just as I'm a few metres away.

'Fuck me!' Jake yells and flips his tongs into the air, and before they've landed I'm hugging him real strong – partly because I can and partly because you can't break him.

'Where've you come from?' he asks shakily, his strong face quivering and his eyes misting faster than he can wipe them clear with just one hand.

'Perth. Greece,' I reply, grinning like a fool.

Soon Lucy has joined us, filling Jake in on every step in our great surprise. She's so delighted to see him so delighted that I realise how perfect things are for him now. As perfect as they can be.

'I was wondering why there were so many sausages, but then I thought Keir eats as much as you serve him,' says Jake

'Who's Keir?' I ask.

'Our next-door neighbour,' Lucy explains just as the Maori guy comes through the back door and introduces himself.

'I'm Keir,' he says, shaking my hand and smiling broadly. He's about Jake's age, I guess, and has a small march of green dots tattooed across one cheek, over the middle of his nose and across the other cheek. It's a very decorative street, what with the condom tree and all.

Keir looks like he could lift us all up with one hand and mow the lawn with the other, and he pretty well proves it by easily carrying Jake over to the outdoor setting as Lucy rolls the snags off the hotplate and onto a cold plate, the tongs having disappeared.

Under instruction from Lucy I go inside to grab some beers from the kitchen, and when I return there it is. A chicken. With feathers and a heartbeat – no bun, no lettuce, no mayo. The thing is pecking around my feet and it seems so out of place in a regular house just minutes from the city centre.

'Don't you like chickens?' asks Lucy.

'I like chicken,' I reply, and Jake laughs.

'Well you can't eat this one,' says Jake.

'What's his name?' I say, warming to the thing now that Jake is obviously attached to it.

'Chicken,' replies Lucy, smiling.

'Easy to remember,' I say, and join the others for the snags after stepping over Chicken.

Hours pass as I run Jake, Lucy and Keir through all the bits I reckon are worth mentioning – from Amsterdam to Berlin to Greece. From Miller to Lars to Cali. And then Drina and Sydney, Evan and Denise and Perth. Jake and Lucy are fascinated and Keir does his best. After I shut up, Jake tells me about his parents' farm that is just half an hour away, and Lucy fills me in on her job at a local nursing home.

After Keir, who has been brilliant in his role as the strong, silent type, carries Jake back inside, we settle into the living room in what seems a very familiar setting. I don't want to check out the town or track down any sights; I just want to enjoy the warmth that comes from this home.

Keir and Jake seem real tight, going to Jake's folks' place in Keir's car and generally hanging out while Lucy works. I've realised that when I lived in Perth I was just about as incapacitated as Jake, but Miller, and now Cali, have given me wings just as Lucy and Keir have given Jake his.

'How long do we have you for?' asks Jake.

'Just the night – my flight is mid-morning.'

There's somewhere I need to be, I think to myself.

'I can give you a ride to the airport tomorrow if you want,' says Keir.

'Cool. Thanks.'

Keir wanders off to leave us to more catching up, and tells us he'll come by tomorrow morning.

Lucy also disappears, saying something about preparing a 'special' dinner – fortunately I'm still full from lunch. Jake gives me a knowing smile and I ask him if he needs me to send him food packages from Antiparos.

'Her cooking's getting better, I reckon, and I'm certainly not complaining,' Jake says, and I think to myself that he never does.

Speaking of sending him care packages, I take this opportunity to mention the BankWest account I set up for him before I left.

'Have you used any of the money, dude?' I ask, full well knowing he hadn't been comfortable with me giving it to him.

'I really appreciate it but we haven't needed it,' says Jake, adding, 'Besides, it would have felt weird to use it to finance me breaking up with your sister.'

'Fair enough. It's there and I reckon it should be for something special – like you and Lucy coming to the Greek Islands.'

'You'd want us to come see you?' Jake says, making me feel sad that he'd even have to ask.

'I demand it!' I say, and remind myself to whack some of the money from the house sale into the account just as soon as it comes through.

'And don't forget,' I add, 'there's still a bunch of frequent flyer points with your name on them.'

'You might need them yourself, Ash, to come back to Australia or go somewhere else,' Jake says.

'Nope – next time I'm going to see you is in Greece, buddy,' I say, and Jake looks well pleased with that notion.

'The soup won't defrost so we have my famous gourmet pizza!' Lucy announces as she joins us in the living room, and I swear it feels just like it did six months ago.

'Ash, I think I've mentioned the asparagus and nectarine combo in an email,' says Jake, straight-faced.

'You sure did,' I say. 'One of the smaller slices to start, thanks Lucy.'

'Don't be too slow – Jake will hog it otherwise,' she warns.

After the pizza goes down slowly we slump further into the sofas and Lucy selects a foreign movie on Cable, but I'm too tired to read the subtitles so keep chatting to Jake, who's ploughing through a dessert concoction that's groaning with sugar.

'It sort of feels weird watching Keir help you with stuff rather than me,' I say, out of the blue.

'Stuff changes, buddy. That's good,' Jake tells me, 'You have to find your place.' And I smile because I reckon I finally get it.

# 49

The short boat trip from Paros to Antiparos, awash with my excited anticipation of surprising Miller and Cali, reminds me that I don't want this to be just a vacation. I want this to be it. I'd feared that I might only desire this different life because it couldn't last, but now I think about Cali, how it is her normal life, her permanent life, and how happy she seems to be.

Miller has shown me how to refresh my world like a computer screen, and somehow I've got to find a way to avoid having to return to my old screensavers of sterile spaces, distant connections and compromise routines.

Yorgos isn't pounding octopi on the rocks when I disembark, so my surprise is safe till its end, just like with Jake, and I enjoy every ray of the mid-afternoon sun that warms this triumphant march towards this family I adore. Jetlag be damned.

Lunch will be over so I should get Cali all to myself and then, presuming Miller is at Yorgos's place, I'll walk over and shake his day some as well.

As I turn the final bend, the taverna comes into

sight and I immediately spot Cali alone on the terrace, feet up on one of the chairs, looking towards the water, which is rippling softly around the few tourists who've discovered this place. Then Miller appears, as if coming from the direction of Yorgos's houses. He's carrying a large bunch of store-wrapped flowers and walks up behind Cali. Miller gives the flowers to Cali, who reads the card and hugs Miller fondly, kissing him on both cheeks before wiping tears off her own. Before even deciding to, my entire being burning, I turn and walk away from the taverna.

There's not enough space in my brain to process everything so quickly and it feels like my head will simply explode. I taunt myself that I should have seen this coming. I shiver uncontrollably and curse both Miller and Cali.

Before I know it I'm back at the jetty and it seems an appropriate place to weigh up what I have and what I've lost. I don't need to look around to realise that I'm alone here.

I try to find some sort of explanation that won't destroy me, but each thread of thought brings me back to the same bleak conclusion. I know it's not Cali's birthday – she's a Scorpio like Miller. Moreover I had initially taken Miller's unresponsiveness to my emails as his way of protecting himself from disappointment rather than what it has proven to be – his preparation for the death of our friendship. Naively thinking he'd stayed so that I would more likely return has me so covered in egg I could puke.

The wait for the early evening ferry back to Paros provides enough time for me to pity myself something rotten. I bemoan the fact that I'd steered clear of Zoe when she was with Evan even though he seemed like he could hardly care less and probably wouldn't have done the same if our roles had been reversed. The reality is that I'd do things the same, and though it's now of no consequence it still fucks me up. But what really pisses me off is contemplating the possibility that as I was tracking down Miller's mother he was tracking down Cali.

I'm also fucking devastated that I'd got Cali so wrong. She was meant to be the non-cliché I'd dreamed of, and now it seems she *was* just a dream. The fear with any dream – that it must be too good to be true – had made me wary of being certain I was going to return here, to what I thought I had. As I ruminate for hours, the anger about Miller slowly switches to sadness. The sadness you feel when your hero becomes human.

Unsure whether I should leave Greece without a single word spoken, I choose instead to straddle the barb-wired fence and stop in Paros while my thoughts continue their battle. The trip across the short strait that separates the islands seems even quicker now that my mind is racing Formula One fast. Paros's beauty holds no interest, and I barely acknowledge its welcome as I accept the first tout's offer of a nearby room for way more euros than I can be bothered negotiating over.

The prospect of getting some sleep tonight is akin to the chance I'll ever again feel as happy as I had on my way back to Greece. Once I'm shown to my simple room, in a small hotel resting behind a donkey parking station, I strip off and get onto the sheetless bed, allowing my thoughts to cover me until the morning asks for my next move.

# 50

As I lie awake through the warm night, wide-open eyes contemplating whether to return to Antiparos and seek resolution, I instead call upon those more frequented islands of Chaos and Pathos. My mind also re-tours the places I'd been introduced to in such a short time and in such rapid succession: Miller's world, Lars's world and Cali's world. It had felt like my life had only just begun and I still had plenty of ground to make up.

Until this trip I'd only ever been sure of what I didn't want. And just as all this world has to offer had started to become visible, it had moved away again. Surely the fact that I'd seen what I wanted, even if it had proved as fleeting as Sasquatch, had to be for something. So, I decide, even if I can't have Cali, and Miller, this has all been worth something, and wherever I go next it can't be Perth.

Just knowing this is vacation enough.

Waiting for my ship to come in, I contemplate the small waves that not so much pound the jetty as nudge it. After seeing Cali and Miller now, I feel totally prepared to handle however it may unfold. And maybe that's what this whole trip has been about – even a fucked-up result is better than never participating in the game at all.

Again the boat trip to Antiparos is butterfly-inducing, but this morning it's for entirely different reasons to yesterday's joyous return. I haven't prepared what I plan to say to Cali and Miller, and fear that I might just freak out. Dignity, poise, pride. And repeat.

My stomach churns as if I've eaten some old prawn that even Milou had considered too suspect, but is slightly remedied when I find the taverna still asleep. Of course the place won't be locked, so I walk across the terrace and into the inside dining area. Staring me out is the exact same bunch of flowers Miller gave Cali yesterday, sucking up some water in a vase while still swathed in the wrapping so lovingly picked out by my best friend. I glimpse the card and read the message that had Cali's eyes give way immediately.

The message is from me.

Miller has organised flowers to Cali for something called her name day, which I now vaguely remember reading somewhere is a bigger celebration in this part of Europe than one's birthday. He's written that I wish I were with her for her name day but that I will see her soon. The card is signed 'Ash'.

The tears I've held onto for near on a lifetime are now streaming down my cheeks, thankful to be released finally, as I vow never to be such a fuckwad again. Two steps at a time I clamber up the stairs and knock gently on Cali's door. She says 'yes' in Greek and I enter the room to find her face a match for my own. We hold each other silently on her bed and kiss for not long enough.

'Did you just get back?' she asks.

I nod, cursing myself for wasting a day that I could have been here.

'Thanks for my flowers.'

'Miller helped.' I owe him a bunch.

'He has missed you too,' Cali says, rolling her fingers through my hair as we lie on the bed facing each other. 'I think you have changed his world just like he has changed your world.'

'I didn't hear from him once,' I say.

'Maybe it is safer for him that way. In case you are gone for good.'

Miller is human and the more heroic for it.

'You should surprise him,' Cali suggests. Not another fucking surprise, I think to myself, and snuggle into the warmest Cali embrace I've had so far.

Later, I make to head for our room to find my best mate, but Cali tells me he now goes to Yorgos's early to work on the house, before the sun pushes him off the roof and he heads back for his stint at the taverna.

Miller sees me coming from his vantage point and is on the ground before I've had a chance to really hit it myself.

'Fuck I'm glad you're back!' he announces, hugging me fast.

'Me too,' I say and thank him for sending Cali flowers on my behalf.

'Not a problem,' he replies. If only you knew, I think.

'So how's the place coming along?' I ask.

'Nearly finished,' he says. 'I'd better get the tools down. It's just about time for my shift at the taverna.'

'Where's Yorgos?' I ask.

'In his place, I think. It's still too early to beat up on some squid,' Miller replies before he returns to the roof.

I knock on Yorgos's door and he calls out something in Greek. I find him sitting out the back and enquire after his health.

'So, how is the house coming along?' I ask, after we've chatted a while.

'Which one?' Yorgos replies.

'The one for your son.'

'It is very nice. Miller, he takes such care. Hopefully one day someone lives there that loves this island like me,' Yorgos says with a hint of sadness.

Before Miller has a chance to join us, I ask Yorgos if he would be happy if Miller bought the place next door.

'How can he do this? Only Europeans can stay here for so long,' Yorgos replies, looking disappointed.

'What if he could? Would you be happy to sell to him?' I ask.

'Of course, other than my son he would be the best neighbour for me,' Yorgos tells me.

'I haven't told Miller this yet but it seems his mother was born in Romania, which means he can get a European Union passport.'

'But what of the money I need to send to my son? This is what my wife would want,' Yorgos says.

'My sister in Australia will soon be sending me my half of the money from the sale of our house. I want to use part of it to buy next door for Miller. He needs a home.'

The fact is that the small house, so basic yet so welcoming and warm, will cost just a fraction of what Denise and I got for our family home.

The deal is done with a strong handshake and Yorgos looks as delighted as I know Miller will be.

I tell Yorgos that this will be my present to Miller on his own name day, which, given that Jet is unlikely to be on the calendar, I plan to establish for some day real soon.

Once Miller is down off the roof we start the walk back to the taverna, and it's as good a time as any to tell him that I met his mother.

'What's she like?' he asks coolly.

'Buddy, you're a son of a bitch. Literally,' I reply, and slap him on the shoulder, adding. 'And I don't think you should give her a chance to have you back.'

Since our fight there's been a silent understanding that I can continue to tug at this raw nerve only so long as Miller is my only reason for doing so. I decide I'll tell this gypsy about the whole Romanian thing on his name day, and hopefully then he'll no longer need to move on anymore.

For the rest of the short amble I talk about my feelings for Cali. Miller encourages me to tell her once and for all that I love her, and suggests I reacquaint myself with retsina tonight to help me along.

'Thanks, dude,' Miller tells me when we arrive back at the taverna. He means for saving him from ever having to risk a second discarding by his mother. And maybe he also means for returning.

'I just feel bad you scored such a crap family,' I say.

'You're my family now,' he replies matter-of-factly as we arrive back at the taverna, and then before I have a chance to brace myself I'm smothered in a Melina and Elektra embrace.

After escaping their longwinded interrogation, I seek Cali out in the kitchen and tell her about my discussion with Yorgos. Cali thinks it's a great idea – the house and the name day for Miller – and wonders out loud how I might also get to stay here in Greece.

'Maybe I'll discover that I was adopted and am actually the son of some Bulgarian beet farmer,' I reply lightly, though the thought of ever leaving now weighs heavily.

'There's always the marriage way of staying,' Cali says with a smile.

Just as I embrace her she adds, 'Elektra can get quite lonely,' then laughs herself into tears.

Leaving Cali in the kitchen, after getting just enough comfort to make me feel she's not going to let me go, at least for the moment, I rejoin Miller and the ladies, who are fussing the tables back into place on the already steaming terrace.

Seeing me, Elektra passes me Simon's bottle opener and says, 'Thanos and Simon have taken your place and you and Miller are taking theirs. A neat swap.'

Suddenly I realise that my vacation is indeed over and I've found my way home.